Trouble at High Tide

A *Murder, She Wrote* Mystery

Trouble at High Tide

A *Murder, She Wrote* Mystery

A NOVEL BY
JESSICA FLETCHER & DONALD BAIN

Based on the Universal Television series created by
Peter S. Fischer, Richard Levinson & William Link

AN OBSIDIAN MYSTERY

OBSIDIAN
Published by New American Library, a division of
Penguin Group (USA) Inc., 375 Hudson Street,
New York, New York 10014, USA
Penguin Group (Canada), 90 Eglinton Avenue East, Suite 700, Toronto,
Ontario M4P 2Y3, Canada (a division of Pearson Penguin Canada Inc.)
Penguin Books Ltd., 80 Strand, London WC2R 0RL, England
Penguin Ireland, 25 St. Stephen's Green, Dublin 2,
Ireland (a division of Penguin Books Ltd.)
Penguin Group (Australia), 250 Camberwell Road, Camberwell, Victoria 3124,
Australia (a division of Pearson Australia Group Pty. Ltd.)
Penguin Books India Pvt. Ltd., 11 Community Centre, Panchsheel Park,
New Delhi - 110 017, India
Penguin Group (NZ), 67 Apollo Drive, Rosedale, Auckland 0632,
New Zealand (a division of Pearson New Zealand Ltd.)
Penguin Books (South Africa) (Pty.) Ltd., 24 Sturdee Avenue,
Rosebank, Johannesburg 2196, South Africa

Penguin Books Ltd., Registered Offices:
80 Strand, London WC2R 0RL, England

First published by Obsidian, an imprint of New American Library,
a division of Penguin Group (USA) Inc.

First Printing, April 2012
10 9 8 7 6 5 4 3 2 1

Copyright © 2011 Universal City Studios Productions LLLP. *Murder, She Wrote* is a trademark
and copyright of Universal Studios.
All rights reserved.

OBSIDIAN and logo are trademarks of Penguin Group (USA) Inc.

LIBRARY OF CONGRESS CATALOGING-IN-PUBLICATION DATA:

Fletcher, Jessica.
Trouble at high tide: a Murder, she wrote mystery: a novel/by Jessica Fletcher & Donald Bain.
pages cm.—Murder she wrote; 37)
ISBN 978-0-451-23632-6
1. Fletcher, Jessica (Fictitious character)—Fiction. 2. Murder—Bermuda Islands—Fiction.
I. Bain, Donald, 1935– II. Title.
PS3552.A376T76 2012
813'.54—dc23   2011045099

Set in Minion
Designed by Ginger Legato

Printed in the United States of America

Without limiting the rights under copyright reserved above, no part of this publication may be
reproduced, stored in or introduced into a retrieval system, or transmitted, in any form, or by any
means (electronic, mechanical, photocopying, recording, or otherwise), without the prior written
permission of both the copyright owner and the above publisher of this book.

PUBLISHER'S NOTE

This is a work of fiction. Names, characters, places, and incidents either are the product of the
author's imagination or are used fictitiously, and any resemblance to actual persons, living or dead,
business establishments, events, or locales is entirely coincidental.

The publisher does not have any control over and does not assume any responsibility for author
or third-party Web sites or their content.

The scanning, uploading, and distribution of this book via the Internet or via any other means
without the permission of the publisher is illegal and punishable by law. Please purchase only au-
thorized electronic editions, and do not participate in or encourage electronic piracy of copy-
righted materials. Your support of the author's rights is appreciated.

In memory of Craig Thomas, whose untimely death took from us a dear friend, and deprives the book world of a skilled, insightful writer. Craig's eighteen thrillers, including Firefox, *whose film version was directed by and starred Clint Eastwood, set the stage for all techno-thrillers to follow.*

And for Jill Thomas, Craig's wife and astute editor, who shared his remarkable ride through life with a smile capable of creating global warming.

Their friendship will always be treasured.

ACKNOWLEDGMENTS

Writers working today have the benefit of a full library at their fingertips in the myriad online resources available to consult and explore. While we are ardent fans of Bermuda and have spent many happy hours enjoying the island, its people, and all the wonderful amenities it has to offer, we admit to using the Internet to jog our memories on some of the details.

In doing research for *Trouble at High Tide*, we owe a debt of gratitude to numerous online resources, three in particular: Wikipedia (wikipedia.org); Casebook: Jack the Ripper (www.casebook.org), Stephen P. Ryder, editor; and Bermuda Online (www.bermuda-online.org), written and published by Keith Archibald Forbes.

We also thank Suzanne Wenz, regional director of public relations, and Lori Holland, executive director, Fairmont Hotels & Resorts; Alicia Hunt at Benchmade (knives); and former police investigator and current police consultant—and mystery writer's best friend—Lee Lofland, author of *Police Procedure & Investigation*, and blogger on The Graveyard Shift (www.leelofland.com/wordpress/).

Thanks to them all. Any errors are, of course, ours.

Trouble at High Tide

A *Murder, She Wrote* Mystery

Chapter One

He was ahead of me in line. A stocky man with thin red hair parted on the side and muttonchop sideburns that reached up his cheek to connect to a bushy mustache. He wore a heavy brown tweed suit, carried a book under one arm, and toted an old leather valise held closed by straps across the top. He was the image of a late-nineteenth-century traveler—and a strange sight to see as we inched our way forward toward the twenty-first-century customs agent in Bermuda.

"Have your passport and other papers out and ready, please," an officer called to the crowd. The man in front of me set down his suitcase and groped around in his jacket for his papers, dropping his book in the process. I scooped it up and, startled, looked into the bleary eyes of the book's owner. Part of the title was spelled out in large red letters dripping with blood: *Jack the Ripper*. The man mumbled his thanks, and quickly turned his back to me.

"Next! Step lively, sir. We don't want to keep all these people waiting."

"Odd-looking chap," a man behind me murmured to his wife as the redheaded man moved forward to the podium where the customs agent waited.

"He must be an actor, doncha think?" she responded. "Who else would dress that way?"

Fifteen minutes later, I was riding in the rear of a limousine making its way from L.C. Wade International Airport through St. George's Parish. I pulled a copy of the local newspaper out of the seat-back pocket in front of me. The headlines trumpeted the appointment of a new deputy chairman of the United Bermuda Party; the health minister's call for blood donors to meet the dire need; and an extension of the school lunch program to include breakfast for children whose nutritional needs were not being met in their home lives. In a box at the bottom of the front page, an article bemoaned the lack of progress made in finding and arresting a serial killer. The body of a woman from the Dominican Republic had been discovered only a week ago in an alley behind the Hotel Rampling in Hamilton. Her throat had been slit. It was the third such death in two months, sending shock waves through the population. While Bermuda's rising crime rate was of grave concern to the island's sixty-five thousand residents, in the past, killings had been either drug- or gang-related. The current victims—all recent immigrants—seemed to lack those connections, although their murders were characterized by other, more disturbing similarities.

All three bore striking parallels to the infamous "Jack the Ripper" killings in London's impoverished Whitechapel district in the 1880s and '90s. As with the Ripper cases, all three women had been prostitutes. All had had their throats slashed, and the bodies of the three victims had been mutilated.

I'd heard about the Bermuda crimes at home, of course. Anything sensational gets immediate coverage on the Internet, and disappears just as quickly. Big-city newspapers had taken note of the killings, and television networks made brief mention of them, though I doubted they'd sent a team of reporters to the scene. Had the victims been American tourists, it would have been an altogether different situation. In any case, that was not why I was in Bermuda.

In the article, police dismissed the Ripper analogies, assured the public that the streets were safe, and speculated that this latest victim may have been killed by a client. However, when the article jumped to the back page, additional complications were revealed. The police commissioner was quoted complaining that "international coverage of the crimes has sparked some unfortunate tourism." It seems ghoulish visitors captivated by the macabre murders— "ripperologists" they called themselves—had arrived on the island and were conducting ad-hoc investigations, which were hampering official police activities. My mind immediately flashed to the man at the airport. Was he another one of these ghoulish visitors, a Jack the Ripper "fan" so to speak, hastening to the scene of similar crimes?

The article also disclosed that police were contending with a raft of false leads. As had occurred in London at the time of the original Jack the Ripper killings, public fascination with the crimes had inspired a number of fabricated "tips" that authorities were nevertheless obligated to track down. The commissioner promised swift convictions of anyone found to impede police business.

"Here on vacation?" my driver asked as I put down the newspaper.

My eyes met his in the rearview mirror. "Yes," I said, taking a deep breath. "I'm planning just to sit on the beach, watch the breakers come rolling in, and catch up with my reading."

"You'll be a bit busier than that, if the judge has anything to do with it."

"Oh? I hadn't known he'd be here."

My host, Thomas Betterton, was a federal judge from New Jersey who had written a controversial book on reforming the federal court system. I had been introduced to him by my publisher, Vaughan Buckley, and we had met again when we'd sat together on several book-and-author panels over the past year.

"If you're ever in need of some R-and-R, come down and stay at my place in Bermuda," he'd said the last time I'd seen him. "I've got a boat, a couple of cottages right on the beach. You can have one all to yourself—even if I'm not there. And if I am there, you don't have to feel obligated to spend time with me in the main house. You can come and go as you please."

"That's a very generous offer," I'd said. "Be careful or I might take you up on it."

"I want you to. They're just sitting there gathering dust.

But I'll have my man, Adam, clean one up for you. How's next month?"

He must have caught me at a particularly vulnerable time. I was weary from traveling across the country on a book tour, and the prospect of staying in a private cottage on a beautiful sunny island was appealing. I'd been to Bermuda before and fallen in love with its pastel homes, pristine pink beaches, turquoise waters, and the genteel manners of the people. I don't remember agreeing to go, but the following week a package arrived. I took it to my desk, slit open the padded envelope, and drew out a pink cap with "Tucker's Town" embroidered in script above the brim. I held up the hat and a set of keys fell into my lap. A note attached to the keys read: "Jessica, it's yours for the whole week. Just call this number and let Adam Wyse know when your flight comes in. Catch you another time. Busy season for me. Have fun! Tom B."

I'd looked out my window at the gray skies and pouring rain that had engulfed Cabot Cove and picked up the phone.

I pressed the button to roll down the window and leaned over to feel the warm Bermuda breeze on my face. We were on the road between Harrington Sound and Castle Harbour, the deep blue of one a contrast to the more turquoise waters of the other. Just breathing the salt-tinged air filled me with contentment.

"Yup, he likes to entertain, the judge does. Tonight, he's hosting another one of his 'intimate soirees.' That's what he calls them," Adam, the driver, said as he maneuvered the town car past a jitney filled with tourists taking pictures of the view. "I think the party's in your honor. He invited all the biggies, and I overheard him brag about you coming to stay."

Well, it's only for one night, I thought. *I can be a gracious guest for one night and meet the judge's friends. Then I'll make my excuses and hide away in the cottage.*

"He's got a couple staying at the other beach house, the one next to yours, and the guest rooms in the main house are full. I've been hauling cases of wine around all week, and Norlene, that's the cook, had to hire an extra assistant to help prepare the meals."

Oh dear, I thought. I could see my peaceful island escape slipping away. "I don't think I packed appropriately for this," I said aloud, mentally calculating what I'd brought that could serve as party clothes.

"Yup, the judge likes lots of action."

"Have you worked for Judge Betterton for very long?" I asked.

"Only about six months. I was between jobs and my cousin knew his cousin and recommended me. I'm his first PA—that's a personal assistant. He never had one before, so I don't know how long I'll be working for him. But I only sign on for a short period of time anyway, no more than a year. I like to keep my options open."

"I haven't met many personal assistants," I said. "What keeps you most busy?"

"You basically do whatever your boss needs you to do. I go where he goes. Sometimes I drive, like today, escort people around. Other times I'm running into town to pick up something at a store for him or one of the family. In Bermuda, residents are only allowed one car per household, so a lot of what I do is chauffeuring. But I also answer the phone, pick up the mail, take the guests out fishing on the judge's boat. It varies, but I like to travel. I get to meet some interesting people and see different parts of the world."

"It sounds exciting, but I imagine it can be very difficult, too. How many people have you been a personal assistant for?" I asked.

"The judge is my fifth. And it's true, sometimes you get people who take advantage or don't treat you nicely. They're really looking for a slave, not a PA. I worked for one rich guy who kept snapping his fingers at me. 'Adam, get me a bottle of water.' 'Adam, I left my pipe upstairs.'" He snapped his fingers to illustrate. "'Adam, the dog made a mess on the carpet.'"

"Doesn't sound like a pleasant job or a pleasant person to work for."

"Don't get me wrong. I don't mind any reasonable request. That's what I'm there for. But this guy, he never learned the words 'please' or 'thank you.' Just—" He snapped his fingers again. "I was out of there in a month."

"I don't blame you," I said.

"Now, the judge, because he never had a PA before, he's not always sure what to do with me. I'm kind of teaching him as I go along."

I laughed. "Why would he need a PA?" I asked.

"Actually, he had this law clerk, Barry Lovick, working for him before, but he told me he likes to do his own research and I figured out he likes to keep his papers private.

Apparently this guy Lovick was copying files and taking them home. At least that's what I hear."

"I wonder why," I said.

"Beats me. I never did get all that legal mumbo jumbo. I even had trouble understanding the lease when I had an apartment in New York. All that party-of-the-first-part stuff leaves me cold."

As Adam drove inland, the landscape changed to expanses of green lawns and trees and occasional glimpses of lush gardens through gates. We passed several communities where the homes were clustered together, and Adam wove in and out of small roads before the water came into view again and he turned onto Tucker's Town Road. He made a right at the crest of a hill into the brick driveway of an elegant yellow stucco house and pulled up to the entrance under a porte cochere supported by white columns carved to resemble palm trees. He hopped out and came around to assist me as I exited the car. Large pots of frangipani on either side of the Palladian door perfumed the air.

The house was situated on a bluff that overlooked the harbor across the road, and the ocean in the back. Adam opened the door into the breezeway and deposited my rolling bag on the tile floor. I could see through to the rear of the house and beyond it to an expanse of blue water.

"The cottage is around to the back and down a path to the beach," Adam said. "I'll bring your luggage there in a while, but the judge wanted you to join the family for lunch before you settle in. Okay?"

"Certainly," I said. "I'd like to thank him for the opportunity to stay in such a lovely place."

"The beach houses don't hold a candle to the guest rooms up here, but they're comfortable and pretty private. I stayed in one until I got booted out to make room for the couple who arrived yesterday. Now I'm in a room off the kitchen. But I'm flexible. You have to be if you're a PA."

He led me through a large living room furnished almost entirely in white, including an ivory grand piano in one corner and a fireplace in another. Groupings of plush sofas in bleached canvas and bone-colored upholstered chairs, punctuated by a few bright pillows, created an inviting environment. The pale palette called attention to the spectacular view of the deep blue ocean with waves spilling onto a sparkling beach. A young woman with a book, her face obscured by her long blond hair, was curled up in a tan-and-white checked armchair by a broad window. Next to her was a telescope aimed at the pink sand. She didn't look up from her reading as we crossed the room, nor did Adam acknowledge her, which I thought was strange. Perhaps he didn't notice her, I silently rationalized.

"Well, well, our star has finally arrived," Tom Betterton boomed out from his place at the head of the table when Adam escorted me into the dining room. Two others were already seated with my host. They looked to be in their late twenties.

"Please don't get up," I said. "I'm sorry I'm interrupting your meal."

"Nonsense," Tom said, hauling himself up from his chair. "We've been eagerly awaiting you. Norlene has your plate in the warmer." He paused on his way to greet me, plucked a bell from the sideboard, and gave it an energetic ring. "Good to see you again," he said, enveloping me in a bear hug before I could step back. "Here, here, sit down." He held out the seat opposite his at the end of the table. "I was just telling these children about the last time I was in Washington visiting the White House. Every American should see that magnificent building."

"Did you get to sleep in the Lincoln bedroom?" the younger man asked archly. He winked at the woman across the table from him.

Tom ignored the comment. "I imagine you've been to the White House many times, haven't you, Jessica?" he said to me as he pushed in my chair.

"Well, I've taken the visitors' tour," I said, looking up.

"Spectacular place, isn't it?" He returned to his seat, pausing only to ring the bell on the sideboard again. He sat heavily and raised his eyebrows at me. "Hope you like fish chowder."

"Love it," I said.

"Adam caught some of the fish our cook used," Tom said. "A real jack-of-all-trades." He picked up his napkin and waved it at the young woman to his left. "My daughter, Madeline Betterton."

"Stepdaughter," the young man corrected as Madeline leaned over to offer me her hand.

"Adopted daughter," Madeline said. "My mother was wife number one."

"Her sarcastic brother, Stephen," Tom said, cocking his head at the fellow in question.

Stephen rose slightly from his seat and gave a short bow in my direction. "A pleasure, Mrs. Fletcher. We're desperately hoping you can enliven the conversation. We've had this verbal tour of the U.S. capital one too many times."

"And no talk about Sagamore Hill either," Madeline said with a fake shudder. "We've heard enough about Teddy Roosevelt's home to last a lifetime."

It was no surprise to me that Judge Thomas Betterton spent considerable time in the nation's capital and enjoyed discussing his visits there. Although he sat on the bench in New Jersey, he had numerous connections in Washington, the most noteworthy of them the president of the United States, who'd been Betterton's law school classmate years earlier.

"Where's Alicia?" the judge asked as Adam pulled out a chair next to me, preparing to take his place at the table.

"I believe I saw her in the living room reading, your honor," Adam replied.

"Always has her head in a book, that one," Tom said, smiling at me. "Well, go get her," he instructed Adam. "She'll want to meet our honored guest. Besides, she hasn't eaten yet."

Adam did as directed and returned shortly with the very pretty girl with long, wavy blond hair who'd been reading when I arrived. I estimated her to be in her late teens to early twenties. He pulled out a chair for her next to Stephen, who continued eating without acknowledging her presence.

"Alicia has been so excited about you coming here," Tom said to me. "She's a writer, too. Say hello to Mrs. Fletcher, Allie. She's the famous author I was telling you about. Alicia is my niece, Jessica."

"Yes. The favorite child," Madeline said.

Alicia batted her eyelashes at me and smiled prettily. "So glad you could come," she said.

"It was very kind of your uncle to invite me."

Our introduction was interrupted by the entrance of the cook carrying a huge silver tray.

"Ah," the judge said, grinning. "You're in for a treat now. Norlene is the finest cook on the island."

Adam raced to Norlene's side, relieved her of her burden, and set the tray down on a built-in sideboard under a stucco arch. The cook wiped her hands on her apron and picked up two bowls, setting one in front of me and the other at Alicia's place. Adam took a third bowl for himself.

"It's fish chowder," Norlene announced. "Should still be good. I've been holding it a while." She slipped a basket of rolls between my place and Alicia's.

"I'm sure it will be wonderful," I said, picking up my spoon and tasting the spicy stew of mixed fish and vegetables in what looked like a tomato-beef broth.

Without being asked, Stephen set a bottle with a black label next to Alicia. "Hot sauce for the hotshot?" he said.

"I thought you were supposed to be on your best behavior today," Alicia said, taking off the bottle cap and shaking several drops into her bowl.

"No. That's your department."

"I'll have some of that," Adam said, reaching for the bottle. "Mrs. Fletcher? Would you like to try it? It's an island specialty."

"No, thanks. This is hot enough for me," I said. "It certainly has an unusual flavor."

"That's probably the rum," Adam said. "Takes a bit of getting used to."

"Oh," I said, helping myself to a roll. I hoped that Norlene had cooked some of the alcohol out of her stew, but if she hadn't, I wanted some bread to soften the blow.

While the three of us ate, Tom, Madeline, and Stephen discussed the guest list for the party. A number of notables were expected, including a local judge, the commissioner of police, and the owner of an art gallery in St. George's. The menu was also analyzed. When the conversation drifted to the relative merits of Bermudian versus Jamaican rums, I leaned over to Alicia, who had been silently concentrating on her soup.

"Your uncle said you like to write. What kind of writing do you do?"

She shrugged. "All kinds, I guess. I had to do a lot of writing for school."

"You don't have a favorite genre? Poetry? Stories? Essays?"

She shrugged again.

So much for her excitement at my arrival. I tried a different tack. "I noticed you were reading when I came in," I said. "What kinds of books do you like?"

She gave me a strange smile. "Mysteries mostly. True crime, the more bloodthirsty the better."

"And what are you reading now?"

She reached into the pocket of her sweater, slipped a book on the table, and withdrew it just as quickly, but not before I'd had time to read the title: *The Crimes of Jack the Ripper.*

Chapter Two

"Pretty little chit, isn't she?" Godfrey Reynolds said, his eyes following Alicia as she wound her way around clusters of guests while sipping from a martini glass. "Betterton needs to keep a leash on that one."

Alicia's long hair was caught up in a loose ponytail with soft curls dangling next to her cheeks. She was wearing what appeared to be a modest white sundress with a high ruffled neckline in front but which, when she turned around, plunged to below her waist at the back.

Godfrey's wife, Daisy, rolled her eyes. "She has a boyfriend, darling." Daisy turned to me. "My husband always has an eye for the sweet young things."

"You were once a sweet young thing, too, my love." Godfrey raised his glass to his wife and smirked.

"Yes, but no more. I understand you very well," she replied, pressing his wrist to lower his arm. "Try to keep it down to three or four tonight, will you? You're so much more charming when you're sober."

The "intimate soiree" Adam had forecast was underway. Forty people crowded into the white living room and spilled onto the broad terrace overlooking the ocean. As a pianist played popular tunes on the piano, white-coated waiters passed trays of hors d'oeuvres and delivered drinks to the guests who gathered in small groups. Most of the men wore dinner jackets over dark Bermuda shorts and high socks. The women were arrayed in a palette of hues to rival the shades of the island's famous pastel buildings. I had paired a crisp white shirt and dangling necklace with a long print skirt I'd actually brought to cover my bathing suit. That it could do double duty as party attire was a relief. And as long as I didn't meet any of these people on the beach later in the week, no one would be the wiser.

Earlier in the evening, Betterton had guided me around the room, introducing me to his guests, a multiracial group reflective of Bermuda's mixed population of blacks, whites, and Asians. He had extended an invitation to several of his neighbors on Tucker's Town Road. Unfortunately, New York City's mayor had another engagement, and the Italian prime minister was not in residence, but my host had pointed out a couple who lived next door, Daniel and Lillian Jamison, he, a Wall Street survivor of the bailouts and consolidations, she, a Manhattan real estate agent. Tom confided in me that the Jamisons had brought a suit against him over his plans to erect another building on his property that they claimed would spoil their ocean view.

"Maybe after they've taken advantage of my hospitality, I can soften them up a bit, get them to drop the action," he whispered to me. "I'm sure I can talk them into it given enough time. Worse comes to worst, I can send Alicia over to work on them. She knows how to wrap people around her little finger, that minx."

Since I had not yet been exposed to Alicia's charm, I didn't comment on the judge's plans.

Godfrey and Daisy Reynolds were the last couple Tom introduced me to before he was called away to consult with Adam over the need to bring in more champagne.

Godfrey was the British publisher of Tom's book on rooting out corruption in the federal judicial system. I was surprised that there would be overseas interest in this topic, but was intrigued by the idea.

"I didn't realize there was a British market for books on American judicial reform," I said.

"There's always professional curiosity about how one goes about reforming any legal system," Godfrey replied. "Oxford put out a volume some years back on comparative perspectives when the UK was speculating on what powers a supreme court would hold. These types of books reach a specialized audience. They're small runs, but they can be particularly profitable. That one sold for fifty quid. We're pricing Betterton's volume at thirty-five."

"If my math is correct, that's about fifty-five dollars," I said, "an expensive book."

"Not for the right customer."

"Godfrey, is that Richard Mann over there?" Daisy asked, tugging on her husband's arm. "I've been meaning to talk to him about that painting I liked." She turned to me. "Would you please excuse us, Jessica?"

"Of course."

Left on my own for the moment, I briefly considered seeking out the lady judge to whom Tom had introduced me when we'd made our rounds of the room. But she appeared to be deep in conversation with the police commissioner, and I hesitated to interrupt.

"You're welcome to sit here, my dear," said a gravelly voice.

I looked over my shoulder to see an elderly black woman beckoning me from where she sat on a sofa in front of the fireplace. She had a pile of wispy white hair floating around her head like a halo. Ruby earrings hung from her ears and were a match to the necklace resting on the yellow and pink silk jacket she wore over a black skirt. Her long fingers were adorned with several rings, and her nails were neatly manicured.

"Come here, dear," she said, pointing to an armchair next to the sofa. "I sent my nephew off to bring me a drink and it appears I've been abandoned. He's probably been waylaid by one of the pretty girls, and I think I know which one."

"Would you like me to bring you a drink?" I asked.

"No. No. That's a job for a young man. You just sit here and give me a bit of company, if you would."

"I'd be happy to," I said, taking the chair she'd indicated and putting my champagne flute down on the glass-topped table between us.

"You know he's very clever, that boy," she said.

"What boy?" I asked.

"My nephew, Charles. He deposits me on this divan, knowing there's no way I can get up from these soft pillows without assistance."

"I know what you mean," I said. "They can trap you, those soft pillows."

"Exactly. Don't have strength in the back, or in the legs, for that matter, that I used to when I was your age. But as long as I have company, I'll accommodate him and sit quietly until he returns with my drink. I'm Agnes, by the way. Chudleigh-Stubbs is the last name, but it's a bit of a mouthful to get around, so Agnes will do."

"Nice to meet you, Agnes. I'm Jessica Fletcher."

"Oh, yes. The mystery writer. Well, wasn't I lucky to pick you out of the crowd?"

"That's kind of you to say. Are you a friend of the judge?"

"Tom? Everyone who's anyone is friends with Tom. He pours the best champagne and even serves caviar. Beluga, no less. You can hardly find it in the States anymore. It's considered an endangered species—not surprising, considering it's more than five thousand dollars a pound. Bermudians are no fools. We like our luxuries and the people who provide them," she said with a wink.

"That's quite an extravagance," I said, wondering how Tom could afford to serve his guests such expensive fare. Federal judges are certainly well compensated, but I'd never thought they were considered especially wealthy. In fact, I'd recently read that the chief justice of the Supreme Court had complained that federal judges were underpaid.

"Have you lived on Bermuda for a long time?" I asked.

"Just my whole life. Family dates back centuries. Not always the best people, mind you. I think there was a horse thief somewhere back there, but we've come up in the world now. My late husband, Stubby—his real name was

Algernon—don't blame him for sticking with Stubby—he was the first Afro-Bermudian magistrate. My nephew, Charles, grandnephew actually, is his sister's grandchild. Oh, there you are." She looked up with a smile as the man I assumed was Charles leaned over to hand her a glass. He had a handsome face, but affected the day's growth of whiskers so many of today's men in their twenties think marks them as sexy.

"Sorry for the delay, Aunt Agnes. The judge pulled me into the kitchen to help his man with one of the champagne cases. Stephen has made himself scarce, as usual. But there's your Dark and Stormy, just as you like it, heavy on the rum, light on the ginger beer."

"Good boy!" Agnes said, taking a sip from the glass. "Say hello to Jessica Fletcher." She waved her glass in my direction. "Judge Betterton's special guest tonight. Writes mysteries. Now, show your best manners." To me, she said: "My nephew, Charles Davis."

Charles shook my hand and smiled. "It's an honor to meet you, Mrs. Fletcher. My great-aunt must think I'm still a boy. She doesn't want me to embarrass her but doesn't hesitate to embarrass me." He winked at Agnes and excused himself, promising to check back in case she wanted assistance circulating in the room.

"I raised that boy right," Agnes said to me.

"He's charming," I said. "Does he live with you?"

"I wish he did, but no. He's in graduate school in the States. He's just here for the week. I had a feeling he'd arrive when I noticed Betterton's niece walking on the beach a few days ago. Charles takes every opportunity to court her, but

I'm not sure she's worth the effort. Don't tell Tom I said so. He dotes on her."

"My lips are sealed," I said.

"So, Jessica Fletcher, what brings you to Tucker's Town? Are you here to help the local constabulary with their murder investigations?"

"Heavens, no," I said. "I'm sure the Bermudian police don't need any help from a mystery writer. Not at all. I'm here because Tom offered me a week in one of his cottages and I accepted. I didn't even know that he was going to be here. In fact, I'd gotten the distinct impression that he wasn't able to take the time off. I came intending simply to sit in the sun and read a book."

"But you've heard about our scandalous murders, of course? The island is overrun with reporters. They say the killer is a reincarnation of Jack the Ripper."

"I did hear that."

"Foolish comparison. I wish those newspeople wouldn't play with the facts. They just like to upset the population."

"Why do you say that?" I asked. "From what I read in your local newspaper, there are some similarities between this murderer's actions and those of Jack the Ripper."

"Maybe so. Maybe so. But don't you think that if the killer finds himself compared to an infamous murderer that he'll go out of his way to truly imitate the original by killing even more young women? Give himself plenty of notoriety?"

"I would say that being a serial killer already imparts notoriety to the perpetrator, Jack the Ripper or not, but I understand your point," I said. "Unfortunately, you're dealing with an unbalanced person to begin with, an attention seeker."

"Well, imitating Jack the Ripper is certainly a way to attract attention."

I nodded.

"Oh, Agnes, are you on again about Jack the Ripper?" The speaker was a tall blonde in her midthirties, dressed in a gold cocktail dress that clung to her ample curves. She sank down on the divan next to Agnes, her weight causing the older woman to rise like a float on the water.

"A serial killer on Bermuda is news, Margo. I'm just keeping up with the times. Jessica Fletcher, this is Margo Silvestry, Tom's"—Agnes hesitated a moment—"significant other."

"How do you do?" I said.

"Fine, thanks, but I need a drink." She craned her neck and signaled to a uniformed waiter, who hastened over and held out his tray, where four tall glasses stood.

"Only champagne? Don't you have anything else?"

"What would you like?" the waiter asked.

"A sidecar, but I like it with Alyzé instead of Cointreau, and not so much lemon."

The waiter looked perplexed.

"You know what? Just find Adam and tell him Margo wants a sidecar. He knows how I like it."

The waiter left and Margo twisted around, crossing her long legs and tugging the hem of her dress in a vain attempt to keep it from riding up. "Tom told me about you. You're the mystery writer, right?"

"Yes."

"I don't know much about mystery novels, but maybe you can give me one of yours. I didn't bring anything with me to read."

"Actually, the only book of mine that I brought was a gift for Tom. Perhaps he'll lend it to you."

"I'll have to remember to ask him."

All the while she was speaking, Margo's eyes roamed the room as if searching for someone.

"She's not here yet," Agnes said to her.

"Who do you mean?" Margo said innocently, suddenly examining her red fingernails.

"Claudia. Tom's not interested in rekindling that relationship. I'm not even certain she was invited."

"That's never stopped her before," Margo said acidly.

The waiter returned with the same four glasses of champagne on his tray. "I'm so sorry, Ms. Silvestry. Adam said he can't break away right now, but if you can wait, he'll bring you your drink in fifteen minutes."

"Oh, how irritating. Then never mind." She extended her hand and wiggled her fingers at the waiter. "Help me up. I'll get it myself."

The waiter placed his tray on the glass table and assisted Margo to her feet.

"I'll be back," she said and flounced off.

"So that's Tom's girlfriend," I said.

"Yes. He's been seeing her for six months. Bit of an age difference, at least twenty years, but she seems intent on becoming wife number five."

"Number five? I'd no idea."

"My dear, you need a scorecard to keep track of Tom's love life."

"Who is Claudia, then?"

"Wife number four. She lives in St. George's. Their di-

vorce was big news on the island two years ago, nearly re-
sulted in assault charges."

"Against whom?"

"Tom, of course, although Claudia is strong. She plays
tennis every day. Spends the other half of her day in the
gym. She wanted the house and he wouldn't give it to her.
He managed to hang on to the house and the boat through
two other divorces and wasn't about to cave on that subject.
Told the judge it was all he had left. You can see that he won
that battle. It was quite the scandal for a while."

"And yet she comes to his parties?"

"This is a small island, dear," Agnes said. "We can't afford
to hold grudges. It would close off too many social opportunities. Margo doesn't understand that yet, but if she marries
Tom, she'll learn."

I looked across the room to where Tom Betterton
frowned down at his adopted daughter, Madeline, who was
telling him something and gesturing with her hands. He was
a tall man in his late fifties or early sixties, a bit on the heavy
side, face deeply tanned, his light brown hair teased and
combed to make it appear thicker than it was. He wasn't my
idea of an attractive man, yet he'd been married four times.

Agnes's gaze followed mine. "You're wondering how he
does it, aren't you?" she said.

"I don't really know him that well," I said, feeling that I
had to defend Tom if for no other reason than that I was his
guest. "He's certainly well spoken. The audiences we appeared before on our book panels enjoyed him. He's very
personable."

"And presumably rich."

"I don't know anything about his finances."

"Money is endlessly fascinating," Agnes said, sighing. "An inheritance from the first wife who died, I heard. Still, I can't imagine how he affords them all. He must keep a divorce lawyer on retainer."

I watched Tom and Madeline walk through the French doors to the broad terrace overlooking the ocean. They stopped to talk to a striking woman with short black hair, wearing a sleeveless yellow sheath. Even from my relatively distant vantage point I could see the muscle definition in her arms.

Margo, who had been on her way back to us, drink in hand, caught sight of the trio and immediately changed direction. She stepped onto the terrace, looped her free arm through Tom's, and leaned against him. I gathered from her body language that the newcomer was Tom's ex-wife, Claudia.

"It's a small island," Agnes commented. "Who was it that said, 'Keep your friends close and your enemies closer'?"

"Machiavelli, I believe."

"How apropos," she said with a little smile.

Chapter Three

The party was still going when I decided to retire for the evening. Agnes had convinced me to try a Dark and Stormy and regrettably the alcoholic concoction had simultaneously given me a headache and caused me to grow tired. I enjoy an occasional glass of wine or sherry, but I'm not accustomed to heavier drinks. Fortunately, Adam was available to escort me to my cottage, taking my elbow to guide me along the unfamiliar and winding gravel path down toward the beach.

Before leaving, I had bid Agnes good night and found her nephew Charles to let him know that she was alone.

"She's used to that," he said, scowling at me. "I don't have time for her right now." His rudeness took me aback, which he must have realized because he mumbled an apology before striding off in her direction. I now knew why Agnes felt it necessary to remind him of his manners.

Perhaps it was the freely flowing alcohol, but there seemed to be a change in the tenor of the party from convivial to combative. I saw Madeline and her brother, Stephen, arguing with Alicia. The younger woman tried to walk away and Madeline grabbed her elbow and forcefully turned her around. A moment later the woman I'd assumed was Claudia emerged from the kitchen carrying a box with an irritated Adam in pursuit, calling after her, trying to retrieve it. And when I made my excuses to Tom, thanking him once more for his generous offer of the cottage and for hosting the party, an inebriated Daniel Jamison, Betterton's litigious neighbor, came over to poke Tom in the chest and complain loudly that, unlike the judge and his cronies in New Jersey, he, Jamison, was not one to take a bribe.

Tom disengaged from his neighbor and waved to Adam, who quickly took my arm and ushered me across the terrace, eager to discharge his duty and get back to the man who employed him.

"You'll be all right, Mrs. Fletcher?" he asked as he deposited me on the porch of the tidy guest house that was to be my home for the week.

"Absolutely," I said. The briny aroma of the air and the echo of the waves softly rolling onto the sand were a balm to my aching head and a welcome distraction from the confrontational scenes I'd just left.

"Thank you for everything," I said.

"My pleasure, Mrs. Fletcher," Adam said. "I'd better get back. See you tomorrow."

I sank onto the canvas cushions of the porch swing and used my toe to propel myself into a gentle movement that seemed to keep time with the waves. I closed my eyes and let the sounds of the night wash over me. I heard Adam hustle uphill, the soles of his shoes crunching the pale gray gravel. Raucous noises from the party—laughter, loud singing, and some angry words—reached my ears, but they faded from my consciousness as the soothing sounds of the sea and the sway of the swing lulled me to sleep under a canopy of a million stars.

I awoke with a start some time later, disoriented to find myself still sitting on the swing. *What did I just hear?*

Stiff and sore, I made my way inside, locking the screen door behind me, but leaving the outer door open to let in the night air. I undressed, put on my robe, and brushed my teeth at the sink that served both the tiny service kitchen and the bathroom. The cottage was compact but held all the necessary amenities for a week's stay. A long counter, on which the sink sat like a glass salad bowl, also held a toaster, coffeepot, and miniature microwave oven. A half-size refrigerator was tucked under the counter next to open shelves of dishes, glasses, silverware, and pots and pans. The kitchen area was spare but surprisingly well equipped, I thought, as I pulled a paper towel off the roll to dry my hands.

My drowsiness had fled thanks to my unintentional nap. I stood at the screen door, took a deep breath, looked out, and listened carefully. Except for the soft beat of the waves on the sand, the night was silent. Whatever I'd heard—the cry of an animal or bird perhaps—was gone. My watch said it was two in the morning. I glanced longingly at the bed with its cool white sheets and comforter, but I was wide-awake and knew that if I lay down I would simply spend the next hours tossing and turning. Instead, I changed into a pair of gauze cropped slacks and a light sweater and walked down to the beach.

The sand was warm from the day's hot sun and my feet sank in with every step until I reached the verge where it became cool and firm. I slipped off my sandals and walked barefoot, dancing away from the higher waves but allowing the foam to wash over my toes. The moon had risen and its cold white light bounced off the waves, adding extra illumination to the night. I shaded my eyes from the moon and peered down the beach. To my right was Tom's second cottage, temporary home to his British publisher, Godfrey Reynolds, and his wife, Daisy. I couldn't see it from my quarters, but I noticed that it, too, had a porch swing and screen door. The Reynoldses' cottage was appropriately dark, its occupants probably sleeping off the caviar and champagne and other refreshments served at Tom's party. *If you were smart,* I told myself, *you'd be sleeping, too, instead of wandering a deserted beach in the wee hours of the morning.*

The contours of the beach curved to the left. A stone breakwater reached into the ocean; large rocks like offspring of the gray barrier littered the sand and blocked my view. Ahead of me rose two huge boulders, remnants of what once had been natural arches that were destroyed by a hurricane in the last century. I debated turning around. There was still time to get a good night's rest. No one would wake me in the morning. *I can sleep as late as I like,* I told myself, but of course I wouldn't. I've always been a lark, an early riser, up before the sun, preferably on the water with my rod and reel if a friend had offered a day's fishing. I weighed the benefits of returning to the cottage, but my feet kept moving forward.

A cloud slipped over the moon, dimming its brightness. I stepped between the large boulders and spotted a set of stairs leading down from a building on the cliff above. I couldn't see the whole house from where I stood, but it appeared to be another mansion overlooking the sea with a tower on one end. *The view from that tower must be spectacular*, I thought, turning toward the ocean and trying to envision how far its occupants might be able to see.

As I peered out, my eyes were drawn to what appeared to be a vague form near the water's edge, the muted light obscuring the details. Had some sea creature washed up on shore? Or was it simply flotsam thrown overboard by a careless boater that had floated in with the tide? I walked toward it and as I neared the form, the cloud parted and moonbeams shone down, breaking into a million flecks of light on the water. I stopped. A woman lay slumped on her side. The waves climbed up the beach; the white foam hugged her bare back, then receded into the sea with a sigh. Blood that had poured from her neck, black in the night's shadows, had stained the pink sand, but was fading as the ocean's relentless surge scrubbed it away.

I walked around the body to get a better look. Wet tendrils of blond hair covered her brow, rested on her cheek, and caught in the gaping wound below her jaw. The moon shone on a face contorted by the shock of the terrible death it had met. Her youth had been no protection. I longed to ask if her fascination with crime had been her undoing. But of course she couldn't answer. Tom's niece, Alicia, was dead.

Chapter Four

I wasn't there when police broke the news to the family. I was talking to some of the constables after I'd shown them where the body was. At least a dozen members of the police force had arrived on the scene, fanning out along the beach, hanging yellow crime scene tape, setting up lights, photographing the body. Two officers escorted me back to my cottage, where we could all sit and they could record the details in their notebooks by the light of a lamp rather than a flashlight. As a result, I never saw if they brought someone down to the beach to identify Alicia or when they took her body away.

After I'd recounted what I could remember, I was brought up to the main house and led to the other side of the breezeway. A pair of constables was stationed outside the door of a room I hadn't seen before, their tall rounded helmets reminding me of those worn by London bobbies.

The family was gathered in Tom's library, the space a reflection of the orderly mind of its owner. It was lined with pale gray bookcases with volumes of legal books perfectly aligned in size order. A large mahogany desk occupied one end of the room and held a regiment of pens and pads in size order next to the telephone on an otherwise pristine surface. At the opposite end of the room, closer to the door, was a stone fireplace flanked by two love seats. A pair of French chairs were positioned facing the empty hearth, in front of which was a potted bromeliad in full flower.

Tom Betterton rose from one of the chairs when I entered. His face was ashen beneath his tanned skin, and his hands trembled when he wiped his damp brow with a white handkerchief.

"Jessica, how awful for you. I'm so sorry."

"Tom, this is much worse for you and your family. You have my sincerest condolences. If there's anything I can do to help, you have only to ask."

"No. No. There's nothing anyone can do now. She was so young and vibrant. How could anyone—" He broke off, wiping his eyes.

Stephen, whom I'd only seen fleetingly at the party, put his arm around his stepfather. "C'mon, Tom. Sit down again. Adam will get you a drink." He beckoned Adam from behind Tom's back. "Do you want a Scotch?"

Stephen's face was somber, but the red rims of his eyes betrayed his emotional state. His sister, Madeline, sat shivering on one of the love seats, comforted by Tom's girlfriend, Margo. Adam, sitting next to her, had deep circles under his eyes.

Tom waved his hand back and forth. "No alcohol," he

said. "I want to keep my head clear. The police may still have questions."

"They've already interviewed each of us separately," Stephen said. "Since they've let us be together here, they're probably done with you for the night."

"Even so. I'll just have a little water."

Margo started to stand, but Adam put his hand on her shoulder. "Stay with Madeline," he said. "I'll get it."

"What time did the party end?" I asked Stephen, who'd taken a seat next to me across from his sister.

"I was back in my room by eleven thirty, but these evenings don't usually go late."

"Most people had left by midnight," Madeline put in.

Margo nodded. "That's when Norlene left. And the piano player, too."

"Just a few stragglers remained after that," Madeline said. "Once the music stops, people know to go home."

Adam returned from the kitchen with a pitcher of ice water and half a dozen tumblers, setting the tray down on a white table between the love seats. He poured the water and offered glasses to the others in the room.

I hadn't seen Daisy and Godfrey Reynolds, who were staying at the other cottage, or anyone else who may have occupied one of the guest rooms upstairs. The library held only those of us who'd had lunch together the day before, plus Margo, and minus, of course, the victim.

A million more questions swirled around my brain, but this was not the appropriate time to ask them. The family was in shock. Not only had their youngest member been murdered, she had been slain in a similar manner as three other women in recent months. But those women had been from the lowest social stratum on the island. They were recent immigrants, so poor and desperate that they'd turned to prostitution to support themselves. Alicia's circumstances bore little resemblance to theirs. She was a visitor, staying with a wealthy uncle. Had she just been in the wrong place at the wrong time? Or was the serial killer branching out?

I glanced at the people in the room and wondered what their relationships had been with Alicia. While Tom had boasted of her talents and Agnes had said that he was devoted to Alicia, I didn't get the impression that she inspired the same admiration and loyalty from the other members of her family. Madeline had called her the "favorite child" in an ironic tone, and Stephen had barely spoken to her at lunch. Both had argued with her at the party. Of course, family jealousies and squabbles rarely translate to murder, but these were the musings that occupied my tired mind until the police informed me that I would be expected at headquarters later in the morning.

"Please tell me again, Mrs. Fletcher, what time you happened to come upon the body."

The constable sat at a small table at police headquarters, a lined pad in front of him, as he wrote down my statement. A walkie-talkie perched on the shoulder of his black vest crackled, strong voices breaking through the static every so often. He reached up to turn down the volume. A blue-and-white checkerboard stripe and a blue patch with white letters on the front and back of the vest identified him as

POLICE. Worn over a light blue shirt with dark pants, it was the uniform seen on most of the men and women I encountered at the building outside Hamilton.

"I told you that it must have been about two fifteen or two twenty," I said. "I know because I looked at my watch before changing my clothes and leaving the cottage. And at that time, it was two o'clock."

"And why did you decide to take a walk at two in the morning?"

"I had fallen asleep in the porch swing after I came down from the party. When I woke up and went inside, intending to go to bed, I found myself fully awake. Rather than spend a restless night, I decided to take a walk in the hope a little exercise would make me sleepy again."

"So you found the body at two in the morning. Is that right?"

"Two fifteen or two twenty," I corrected.

"Two twenty, then. Do you frequently take walks in the middle of the night?"

"I can't say that I do, but—"

"How long did you know the deceased?"

"I only met her yesterday."

"And her name was?"

"Alicia. I'm not certain anyone ever told me her last name. She's Judge Thomas Betterton's niece."

"How old was she?"

"I really don't know. In her early twenties, I presume."

"And what was she wearing?"

"She wore a white sundress at the party, high in the front

and low in the back. I think she was in the same dress when she was killed."

"Shoes?"

"I didn't see her shoes."

"We found a pair of high-heeled wedges at the top of the stairs leading down to the beach."

"Perhaps they were hers."

"Could you identify them as hers?"

"No. Definitely not."

"And what did you do when you discovered the body of Ms. Betterton?"

"I ran back to the cottage and called the police."

"Did you touch the body?"

"No. I know better than that."

"Did you see anyone else on the beach?"

"No."

"No one at all?"

"It was the middle of the night and it was dark. I suppose it's possible the murderer was nearby, but I didn't see any evidence of anyone else. I couldn't see any footprints in the sand. The water was washing away my own footprints as I stood there. I was in a hurry to report the crime before the ocean pulled the body away. I told all this to the officers who responded to the scene last night."

"My inspector always likes us to interview witnesses more than once. You may have to tell your story to more people over the next few days."

"My story? I'm not telling you a story, Constable. I'm telling you the truth."

"Poor choice of words on my part. Sorry, ma'am."

"That's all right," I said, immediately contrite that I had answered so sharply. "I didn't get much sleep last night. I may be a bit testy."

"Perfectly understandable."

Another officer walked into the room. "The superintendent wants to see you about the press conference, Valentree."

"Please tell him I'll be there right away. We're just about finished for now." The constable closed his notepad and looked at me. "We will want you to stay in Bermuda for the time being. Is that going to be a problem?"

"I'm supposed to be here for the week," I said. "I don't know how much longer I can stay after that."

"We'll start with the week, and then decide whether we need you to stay longer. We can reach you at the judge's home?"

"I'd like to ask my host if he'd prefer it if I move to a hotel. This is a terribly upsetting time for him and we don't know each other very well. He may want only his family around him. I would certainly understand if he feels that way."

"We already spoke with Judge Betterton and he didn't express any objections to you staying in his cottage."

"Nevertheless, I'd like to make the offer. If I do move to a hotel, I'll be sure to let you know where I'm staying. I need to cancel my flight plans, too."

"Here's my card. Please call me or any of the other officers in the Serious Crime Unit if you remember anything that might be helpful."

"I'll do that," I said, tucking his card in a pocket of my shoulder bag, where I'd already placed cards from other police officers I'd spoken with over the last eight hours.

He came around and held the chair for me as I stood.

"Is the press conference about Alicia's murder?" I asked.

"That and the others," he said.

"Do the police believe they're linked?"

"I'm not at liberty to say," he replied, escorting me from the room. "If you go out the front door there will be a blue and yellow police car waiting. The officer can drive you back to Judge Betterton's. Thank you for your time, Mrs. Fletcher."

"You're very welcome, Constable Valentree."

He clattered down the flight of stairs and disappeared around the corner. I followed more slowly, holding on to the railing. I was tired, operating on the two or three hours of sleep I'd managed to snatch between police interviews.

Headquarters was full of activity, officers rushing up and down the stairs as I attempted to make my way out after my police interview. I paused on the second floor where a crowd was pressing into a room. Several people carried large cameras on tripods. Most wore badges hanging from strings around their necks that identified them as members of the news media. At first, I was amazed that so many press people were able to get to Bermuda so quickly, and then it occurred to me that most of them had probably already been there covering the serial killings. Although a nap was definitely on my agenda for that afternoon, I was curious to find out what the official position was on Alicia's murder and whether the authorities believed it was related to the other murders.

I joined a group of reporters who were pushing their way into the room. While I wasn't carrying any media credentials, the officers manning the doors were so overwhelmed by the numbers attempting to enter that they couldn't check everyone's identification, and I managed to slip past them.

Inside, a phalanx of video cameras and lights took up what little space there was on either side of the door. I squeezed over to a side wall, took an empty chair midway down a row, and tried to appear official, taking a pad and pen from my shoulder bag while reporters around me tapped into their cell phones or notebook computers, or held up miniature video cameras to capture the scene.

The police commissioner whom I'd met only briefly at the party the night before stood in the front of the room at a podium; several other officials were seated at tables on either side. Behind the commissioner was a large screen on which was projected the insignia of the Bermuda Police Service. I spotted Constable Valentree and another officer approaching the commissioner and hoped they wouldn't glance in my direction. As a precaution, I pulled out the pink ball cap Tom had sent to my home and put it on, lowering the peak to hide my face.

The commissioner tapped on his microphone and cleared his throat. "Ladies and gentlemen," he said, and waited for the room to quiet. He was a black man in his late forties with a shaved head and a narrow mustache. Standing erect in his dress uniform with his officer's cap tucked under one arm, he shuffled a sheaf of papers in front of him. After an audible sigh, he began again. "Ladies and gentlemen," he said to a chorus of camera clicks and flashes, "I'm Bermuda Police Service Commissioner Leonard Hanover, FCMI. We have some information for you. Please hold your questions until our literature has been distributed and you've had a chance to hear our official statement, after which we will endeavor to answer some of your inquiries."

Constable Valentree went up the center aisle and handed out copies of the commissioner's statement to the first person seated in each row, who passed the papers down the line. When Valentree reached the row before mine, I shifted in my seat and turned to the gentleman next to me so that my back was toward the constable.

"Did you have a question?" the man asked.

"No. Sorry. Just a crick in my neck," I said, raising one shoulder and rubbing under my collar. I sensed Valentree pausing and imagined his eyes on the back of my head.

"I get those, too," the man said. "Hazard of the trade, I'm afraid. My wife, Bergitta, used to recommend oil of eucalyptus. Worked like a charm, but no one wanted to sit next to me. Terrible strong smell, you see?" He laughed loudly. "By the way, I'm Gus Westerholm from Reuters."

"How do you do?" I gave him a weak smile, hoping he hadn't drawn Valentree's attention, and slowly faced forward, the constable having moved up to the next row by then. I accepted the pile of papers from the woman on my right, took one, passed the rest to Westerholm, put on my glasses, and concentrated on the press statement, hoping that he hadn't noticed that I'd neglected to give him my name.

"I want to begin by saying that it's early in the investigation and we don't have all the answers," Commissioner Hanover said, "but we want to give you an update of the incident that took place early this morning and try to correct any misinformation that has been reported so far. The Serious

Crime Unit continues to investigate the circumstances that led up to today's slashing of twenty-two-year-old Alicia Betterton. To the best of our knowledge, the murder took place between one and two a.m. on the beach adjacent to the house of the decedent's uncle, New Jersey Judge Thomas L. Betterton, on the south side of Tucker's Town Road in Saint George's Parish. The family has identified the body.

"The Bermuda Police Service was notified of the existence of the body at two twenty-nine a.m. by a house guest of Judge Betterton. Our crime scene team spent the remainder of the night and all this morning processing the scene and collecting evidence. We are waiting for a report from the Forensic Support Unit. Our investigators also spent the remainder of the night interviewing witnesses. We have approximately seven investigators on this case, led by Chief Inspector A. M. Tedeschi under the supervision of Superintendent Jonathan Bird and Deputy Commissioner Allan Mumford. As we are already working with Scotland Yard on prior murders here, our British colleagues will provide additional input and recommendations as relates to this case." He nodded toward a tall, strikingly beautiful woman who was standing in the corner. She had straight dark hair that curved toward her jaw; under thick bangs were a pair of large pale blue eyes outlined in black.

"It is important to note that we are still seeking information on this case, as well as the others, and ask the public's assistance," Hanover continued. "If anyone has anything to contribute, we ask them to call the following number, which is also on the screen behind me." He announced the number.

Two dozen hands went up when the commissioner concluded his statement and several reporters yelled out their questions.

"Is this another Jack the Ripper slaying?"

"Has the investigation changed in any way given the prominence of the family involved?"

"How long was Ms. Betterton in Bermuda?"

"Have you made any progress on the prior cases?"

"Was she a prostitute, too?"

The commissioner was patient, taking some questions, declining to answer others, and for the most part ignoring the aggressive outbursts. "We believe Ms. Betterton died from a loss of blood when her throat was slashed. An autopsy will confirm the cause of death. While on the surface it may seem similar to the manner in which the other victims have died, there are significant differences in the circumstances of the victims' lives and in the details of the murders themselves." He pointed to one reporter and declared with some pique, "We devote the same attention to all crimes on the island and do not alter our processes in light of the status of the individuals involved."

"Who did you say discovered the body?"

I hoped it was one of the questions that the commissioner would disregard, but my luck had run out.

"I didn't say," Commissioner Hanover replied, consulting the papers in front of him, "but the person who called in the incident was a house guest of Judge Betterton."

"What's his name?"

The commissioner looked up from his papers. "*Her* name is Jessica Fletcher. She's a crime writer from the States."

I slumped down in my seat and tugged on the bill of the

cap, dipping my head as far forward as I could. I must have resembled a turtle.

"Do you have a photo?"

"We don't, but I imagine in these days of Google that it won't be very difficult for you to find one."

The Reuters' reporter next to me stood up and called out: "Wouldn't we be better off with the FBI than Scotland Yard?"

The woman in the corner, who had been leaning against the wall, raised her head and glanced around the room, her pique at the question obvious on her face.

"As a self-governing British Overseas Territory, Bermuda, whilst independent, has access to all the government offices of the United Kingdom, including Scotland Yard," the commissioner replied. "The Yard is a world-renowned criminal investigation organization, easily on par with the Federal Bureau of Investigation in the States. I see no reason to reject the assistance of Scotland Yard, which has been so generously tendered. Any more questions will be taken by Superintendent Bird and Deputy Commissioner Mumford later today. Please check with the duty officer for the times of the briefings."

Commissioner Hanover gathered his papers and stepped down from the podium, flanked on either side and front and back by Constable Valentree and three others who pushed aside the reporters to clear a path for the commissioner to leave the room. I pocketed my pad and pen and stayed at my seat as the members of the press milled around, some interviewing one another, others standing before a camera and giving a recap of the press conference.

Wary of being recognized, I glanced around like a thief

about to be caught in the act, and saw a familiar face. It was the redheaded man from the airport. He was moving swiftly up the aisle, sliding between those who had paused to talk and cutting off others who were waiting patiently for an opportunity to exit their row. I tried to follow him but was stymied at every turn. By the time I was able to reach the landing outside the door, he was gone from sight.

Once on the street, I lingered until the throng of reporters had dispersed, my eyes searching in vain for the redheaded man. Frustrated, I turned toward a line of blue and yellow squad cars parked at the curb, approached one of the drivers, and explained in the most general terms who I was. The officer invited me to sit in the front, which I happily did, and he drove off.

Once clear of Headquarters Hill, I allowed myself to take a deep breath; however, my relief was not to last long.

Chapter Five

A television van, complete with a tower to accommodate a satellite feed, was already parked on Tom Betterton's street when I arrived at the house in the police cruiser. Fortunately, Adam had arranged for security men to block both ends of the circular driveway to keep the press from knocking at the door or walking around to the back. He had another man posted on the gravel path near my cottage to prevent any intruders, press or otherwise, from coming up by way of the beach.

Over the years, my experience with the press has been hit or miss. I've met many trustworthy reporters—Evelyn Phillips, editor of the *Cabot Cove Gazette*, for instance. We may butt heads over whether information should be published before the police have time to process it, but she's a sensitive and skilled journalist who honors the need for privacy by a victim's family and whose stories are always fair and unbiased. Unfortunately, I have also encountered reporters who were not so responsible, who lied to gain access to a witness or who presented "facts" that slanted the story, or whose lack of respect for the people they pursued for comments led them to behave in an aggressive, even un-civilized manner. I hoped that would not be the case here.

"The police don't want *me* to leave the island either," the judge told me when we sat down together later that after-noon in the white living room. Norlene had brought us drinks—a Scotch for Tom and a lemonade for me—and a plate of cold hors d'oeuvres left over from the party. Adam was outside instructing the guards.

I'd had an opportunity to grab a few hours' sleep at the cottage, leaving me greatly refreshed and more clear think-ing than I'd been earlier in the day. I'd canceled my flight home, and Tom had assured me I was welcome to stay.

"Do you want to go back to New Jersey right away?" I asked.

"I'm torn," Tom replied, jumping up and pacing in front of me. "I want to bury Alicia in the family plot at home, next to her mother and her father. She deserves that and I'll make sure it happens. But the police here won't release her body yet. That alone would keep me here even if they hadn't told me to remain on the island."

"What happened to her parents?" I asked.

"They were killed in a train wreck when she was still a kid. She's been with me on and off ever since, except when she was away at school, and for the last few years."

"Where has she been the last few years?"

"It's not important," he said, striding across the room.

The window coverings facing the street had been drawn to prevent anyone from seeing in. Tom parted the drapes with one hand and peeked through the slit he had created, then dropped his hand with disgust. "The press jackals are already circling their prey. I've been through this before and I'm not of a mind to accommodate them."

"Adam seems to have them under control," I said.

"He's a handy man to have around," Tom said. He stopped pacing to take a sip of his Scotch. "But this is a small island with few places to escape to. I don't want to feel like a prisoner in my own house. At least if I go back to the States I have the whole wide country and can disappear at will."

He seemed to be thinking out loud.

"Wouldn't your professional obligations keep you closer to home?"

"I can take time off, or if not, I can make sure the courthouse is so secure a mouse can't get in. I'm not about to let those vultures get near me or mine." His grief of this morning seemed to have transformed into anger at the press. I didn't know Tom well enough to determine if this was his way of dealing with a traumatic event, or if it was a more normal part of his personality.

"Where are Madeline and Stephen?" I asked.

"Maddy is upstairs sleeping. She's been sleeping all day. That's the way she deals with anything unpleasant. Margo drove Stephen into town with a grocery list from Norlene. We can't have delivery trucks coming to the house, not while those . . . those—" He broke off. "I'm trying not to use foul language in front of you."

"I understand," I said. "You think the press would use a delivery truck as a ruse to gain entry into the house?"

"I know they would," he said, pounding his right fist into

the palm of his other hand. "I'm not letting them in. I'm not talking to them. And as soon as I feel comfortable getting out of here, I'm leaving."

"Tell me more about Alicia, Tom," I said, hoping to draw him away from this rant about the fourth estate.

"She was such a cute little girl," he said, smiling at the memory. "Blond curls bouncing up and down. She was never still, never walking if she could run, never sitting if she could stand. A real pistol, that one."

"And as an adult? Was she just as active?"

"After my brother and his wife were killed, she was a bit of a wild one. Never totally outgrew that. Recently, she discovered her own beauty as a woman and the image she projected. I used to tell her to tone it down a bit. I didn't like all those men panting after her. You lead a man on and turn him down, you never know what can happen. You saw that dress she had on last night?"

I nodded.

"I made her go get a sweater, but she left it in the kitchen when I wasn't looking."

"Do you think it's possible that some man she'd rejected became violent?"

He sighed. "It's not out of the realm of possibility. Back in Newark, when I was coming up, people got killed for a dirty look. You can't play games with people's emotions. I tried to tell her that, tried to get her to listen to the wisdom I've accumulated after all these years on the bench, dealing with the lowlifes, dealing with life in general. But young people don't pay any attention. They all think they know more than you do."

"Then you don't think her death is related to the Jack the Ripper murders—for want of a better phrase—on the island?"

Tom took a gulp of Scotch and sank down into a chair. "I don't know, but who else would do such a thing? This weirdo must have been stalking around the beach and come upon her out for a midnight stroll. Crimes of opportunity, they call them." He paused. "She didn't fit his MO," he said, referring to the police term *modus operandi* or "method of operation." "Never would have happened if she wasn't in the wrong place at the wrong time," he concluded sadly.

There was a knock at the front door. Tom looked in its direction but kept his seat. The knocking became more insistent, but he sat unmoving, staring at the door.

Norlene emerged from the kitchen and hurried to the edge of the breezeway. She leaned over and cocked her head so she could see through the glass panels to the front of the house. "Oh, for goodness' sakes," she cried and opened the door.

Stephen came stumbling in holding a carton piled high with groceries. "I thought you were going to leave me out there forever," he said. "I had a devil of a time convincing the cops I live here. The press is everywhere." He cocked his head toward the door. "There's another one like this one in the car." He strode across the living room toward the kitchen. "Thanks for your help," he said sarcastically, flashing Tom and me a grim smile.

Norlene went outside to retrieve the second carton and returned, her arms full. "No, no. I have it," she said when Adam followed her into the house. She closed the door with her back, giving it a kick to make certain the latch connected.

Adam ran ahead and held open the door to the kitchen, then returned to where Tom and I were sitting.

"Anything you need right now, your honor?" Adam asked.

Tom shook his head. "No. Just keep those mangy animals outside away from me. If you do that, you've more than earned your money. I left you an envelope in the library."

"I'll make sure you're not disturbed," Adam said. He looked at me. "I just can't believe it. Can you?"

"What can't you believe?" I said.

"That Jack the Ripper would dare to come here." His eyes roamed the room. "Look at this place. If you can't be safe here, where can you?" He exhaled noisily and let himself out the French doors leading to the terrace.

"Good man," Tom said. "I never had a personal assistant before. Now I think everyone should have one, everyone who's in the public eye anyway."

"He told me he was replacing your law clerk," I said.

"He did?"

"I would think they have very different duties."

"They certainly do. He has it wrong. Just a coincidence I hired Adam when I let one of my clerks go. I must have a thousand applicants to fill that position. All tops in their classes. You need these people to research case law, check citations, write your bench memos. I keep two law clerks and sometimes they have interns working for them."

I didn't want to get Adam into trouble, so I decided not to mention that he had suggested the judge was upset when he'd learned his law clerk was copying documents and taking them home, or that Tom had given Adam the excuse that he liked to do his own research for why he had fired the clerk.

Stephen wandered into the living room and flopped down on the sofa across from me. He was very pale, had dark circles under his eyes, and there was a white bandage on his right hand.

"Where's Margo?" Tom asked.

"She decided to drive over to Hamilton. Something about a necklace, but I think she just doesn't want to hang around with us. Too gloomy here."

"Can't blame her," Tom said. "What happened to your hand?"

Stephen looked down at his palm. "Cut it trying to open a box."

I didn't recall seeing a bandage on Stephen's hand the night before when we were in the library. Was the injury recent? Or just the bandage?

Stephen sat up. "Oh good, you've got food," he said as he reached over and helped himself to a handful of canapés from the plate Norlene had left us. "I'm starving."

"You just left the kitchen," Tom said. "Why didn't you get yourself something to eat in there?"

"Norlene is putting away the groceries and she's angry as a bear. I wanted to get out of her way."

"What's her problem?" Tom said. "She didn't know Alicia all that well."

"It's still upsetting," I said in Norlene's defense.

"That's not it," Stephen said. "She says she doesn't know how she's supposed to make dinner without any knives."

"What do you mean?" I asked.

Stephen took another canapé before replying. "Between the cops and Claudia, the kitchen doesn't have any knives. Completely wiped out." He held up his bandaged hand. "That's why I got this. No knife to open the box."

"What does Claudia have to do with it?" Tom asked.

"Oh, you missed that little contretemps last night, did you?" Stephen said. "Claudia came in the kitchen and claimed the box of Wusthof knives were a gift from some member of her family, and she walked out with them. Adam tried to stop her, but she was too fast for him."

"Where was I when this happened?" Tom asked, clearly irritated.

Stephen shrugged.

"Do the police know about that?" I asked.

"I didn't tell them," Stephen said. "Frankly, I didn't think of it until now. Every time Claudia comes to the house, something else goes missing. Makes Claudia a prime suspect, doesn't it? She wasn't any too fond of Alicia."

"Neither were you," Tom said. "And I'll thank you not to speak ill of the dead."

"I'm not speaking ill of her," Stephen replied hotly. "I didn't hate her. I . . . well . . . I just thought she was a spoiled brat. She was. And I didn't kill her, if that's what you're suggesting."

"I'm not suggesting any such thing. I know you didn't kill her," the judge said wearily. "We'll have to let the police know about the knives. What a stupid, selfish thing Claudia did. I shouldn't be surprised."

"Yeah," Stephen said. "You were married to her."

"She wasn't so bad at first."

"She was always awful," Stephen said. "You just didn't recognize it."

"Maybe."

"No one was ever as good as my mother."

Tom heaved a sigh. "Your mother was one of a kind," Betterton said. He shook his head. "But she died and left me with her children to raise."

"C'mon. What do you mean, "raise"? I was practically in college. Just about."

"Well, your sister, Madeline, wasn't, and Alicia was just a kid."

"Are you telling me that you married all those women just to get us another mother? You would have been better off hiring nannies. At least you wouldn't lose half of what you have every time they walk out the door."

"We've been over all this before. I'm sorry they didn't work out. But you don't appear to be scarred by the experience."

"You have no idea what scars I have."

Tom looked up at Stephen from beneath his frowning brows. "Go wake up your sister," he growled. "I don't want her to sleep all day."

"Let her sleep. She's only going to fight with me."

"No. She needs to get up."

Tom started to heave himself out of his chair, then fell back into it, his eyes wet.

"Why don't I go wake Madeline," I said. "I'll try to coax her downstairs. Maybe she'll be more willing to listen to someone she doesn't know well."

"Thank you, Jessica," Tom said, shaking out a white handkerchief, wiping his eyes and blowing his nose. "She's in the second bedroom on the right at the top of the stairs."

The staircase was on the other side of the house, and I took a quick look out the windows of the glass front door as I crossed the breezeway's tile floor. Reporters were still camped out in front of the house, and there were policemen on the road directing traffic. I moved away from the door, wary of attracting attention, and climbed the stairs to the second floor. A long carpeted corridor linked both sides of the house. I followed Tom's instructions and found the second bedroom on the right. The door was open and I walked in.

It was a bright, airy room, obviously decorated by a professional in a yellow cotton print with large tropical leaves, but the room held few personal touches, apart from the clothing that had been draped over a chair at the dressing table or carelessly tossed across a turquoise chaise. On the left wall were two doors, side by side, and an unmade canopy bed. I opened the first door to find a large walk-in closet filled with clothing. The second door turned out to be the entrance to a Jack-and-Jill bathroom tiled in white with a narrow stripe in aqua running its length. On the other side was an open door, which led to the next bedroom. I walked through the bathroom and stood at the threshold.

Madeline sat in a chair by the bed, legs crossed on an ottoman, her arms wrapped around a pillow, her eyes focused on the view outside the window.

"It's her room," she said, without averting her gaze.

"Alicia's?"

She nodded, sighed, and slowly turned her head toward me. "Did they send you up to find me?"

"Tom did, yes. He doesn't want—"

"Me to sleep the day away. I know. It's a familiar refrain."

"May I sit down?"

"Sure," she said. She took her legs off the ottoman and kicked it in my direction. It rolled across the room.

I stopped it, moved it closer to Madeline, and sat on it. "I'm so sorry for your loss," I said.

She gave me a wry look. "You didn't know her at all."

"I know," I said, "but you did, and you're hurting. I'm sorry for that."

"She was the biggest pain in my a—in my neck," she said. "She was self-centered, spoiled, forever in trouble, which we had to bail her out of. I couldn't stand her. But she was my little sister, sort of, and I loved her in spite of it."

"Of course you did."

"Don't say 'of course.' Stephen hates her. Or hated her. They were always arguing. Not that I didn't fight with her, too. He wanted her to grow up and be responsible instead of living off Tom and whoever else she could wheedle something out of. She was a taker and Stephen's a giver." She gave a soft snort. "They weren't talking to each other recently. He had finally lost all patience with her. But I really think he loved her more than any of us."

"Did she have any friends here in Bermuda, anyone she might have been meeting last night?" I asked.

"You mean other than us?"

I nodded.

"Not that I know of. She was only down for the week. Oh wait. There's Agnes's nephew, Charles. They were pretty close. At least he wanted to be. Alicia was very good at attracting men and then dropping them. Even the older ones, Tom's friends. She would bat her eyes at them, and then tell them they were too old when they made a play for her."

"Why would she do that?" I asked.

"I think she enjoyed the game. For so long she was the baby, kind of the also-ran to Stephen and me. When she found herself grown up and suddenly the center of attention, she wanted to test her powers. Stupid! If that's what she was up to last night, it got her a terrible result." Madeline shivered. "I almost hope it was the Jack the Ripper killer."

"Why do you say that?"

"At least if it was him, killing her was always part of his plan, not something she brought on herself." She started to cry, but rubbed the tears from under her eyes and blotted her nose with a tissue.

"Did the police examine this room?" I asked.

"Top to bottom, I understand. I wasn't here at the time. I was being questioned."

"Do you know if they took anything?"

She shook her head. "Doesn't look like it. But Alicia didn't have much here other than her warm-weather clothes and a couple of books. Don't know why they would want any of those."

"Did she carry a handbag? Have a cell phone?"

Madeline straightened up and glanced around the room. "Now that you mention it, I haven't seen her bag. And of course she had a cell phone. The police must have confiscated them." She slumped down again.

"What about the book she was reading?"

"You mean this?" She reached behind her back and pulled out the paperback Alicia had shown me at lunch. "She had it hidden in this pillowcase. The police must not have found it, or if they did, they left it where it was."

"May I see it?"

"Sure." She handed it to me. "Ironic, isn't it? Her fascination with this monster, and then—" She broke off, unable to complete the sentence.

"Was she always interested in Jack the Ripper, or in true crime in general?"

"Yeah. She loved reading about crime. Never missed the police bulletin in our local paper. Used to pepper Tom with questions until he was ready to kill her. Oh God, I shouldn't say that."

"It's just an expression. I know you didn't mean it the way it sounds."

I paged through the book. Alicia had underlined or highlighted certain passages halfway through; it appeared as if she'd never finished reading it.

"May I keep this for a few days?" I asked.

"You can keep it forever," Madeline replied. "I was going to throw it out."

"Tom said Alicia lived with you on and off after her folks died. How old was she when they were killed?"

"I think she was ten. It's hard to remember because she was our cousin and she was pretty much always around. My mother was the one who insisted we take her in when Uncle

Mickey and Aunt Joanna died. Uncle Mickey was Tom's youngest brother."

"There were other brothers?"

"Yes. Two. Uncle Lee and Uncle Frank. I don't think they or their wives wanted to take in Alicia, but my mother wasn't about to let anyone reject her. She said that as the eldest Tom was the right person to raise her. I don't remember any hands going up in protest."

"That must have been a traumatic time for a little girl."

"I guess. But my mother felt so sorry for her that she spoiled her terribly. You can imagine how that sat with Stephen and me. We were not fans."

"Did she go somewhere else when your mother died?" I asked.

Madeline shook her head and sighed. "No. She stayed through two more wives, and got worse and worse. I think those women left Tom because of Alicia. Claudia changed all that."

"How did she do that?"

The beginnings of a smile played around Madeline's lips. "She sent her off to a boarding school." Madeline's eyes met mine. "We were all glad to be rid of her. Tom, too, I'm willing to bet. Not that he would ever admit it." She closed her eyes and covered a yawn with her hand.

"Tom wanted me to ask you to come downstairs," I said. "What shall I tell him?"

She sighed. "I'll be down in a few minutes."

As I left, she still sat with her arms embracing the pillow, a vacant, distant look in her eyes. She'd given me a snapshot into the Betterton family, and not a very pretty one. You never know about families. You view them from afar and all appears to be well. But within many there are jealousies, frustration, turmoil, ambitions, and egos at work that out-siders seldom see. I wasn't sure that I was pleased to be al-lowed into the Betterton family's inner sanctum, and under ordinary circumstances, I wouldn't have wanted to know anything.

But this wasn't an ordinary circumstance.

This was murder.

Chapter Six

Apart from the family and those who worked for them—and, of course, the police commissioner—I hadn't seen anyone else during the day who'd been present at the party the night before. I knew that Tom's British publisher, Godfrey Reynolds, and his wife, Daisy, who were guests in the other cottage, were among those asked to remain in Bermuda. But they had opted to go out to a restaurant rather than join the family for dinner. I didn't blame them. The meal had been a somber affair, and I had made my exit as soon as possible.

I hadn't had a chance to examine the scene of the crime in the daylight; policemen posted on the beach kept the curious away. When I returned to my cottage after dinner, the security guard Adam had hired cautioned me not to go down to the beach for a few days. It was a difficult instruction to follow with the sound of the waves rolling up the sand like a siren song.

I sat on the swing on my porch and replayed my discovery of Alicia's body over and over in my mind, trying to remember every detail. There had been a flight of stairs from the Jamisons' property leading down to the beach not far from where I'd stumbled on Alicia's body. The shoes that the police thought might be hers had been found at the top of those stairs. Daniel and Lillian Jamison were sparring with Tom over a building he wanted to construct that, according to them, would mar their view. If the shoes were indeed Alicia's, why would she have been at the Jamisons' house? She had direct access to the beach from her uncle's home.

Had Tom sent her over to their house to convince them to drop their suit? It seemed unlikely, particularly at that hour, and given that the last time I'd seen Daniel Jamison, he was drunk and trying to pick a fight with Tom.

Could Alicia have been planning to meet someone in secret? If she didn't want anyone at the Betterton house to see her go out so late at night, she might have walked over to the Jamisons' and used their access to the beach. That sounded like a more plausible scenario to me.

Of course, she could have walked down to the beach from Tom's house with one of the other guests and I might not have heard them. I was fast asleep on the swing. That was also possible.

The killer was either an acquaintance or a stranger, someone she planned to meet or someone who surprised her. Not much help there. But the killer had attacked her from behind. That much was certain. He or she would have had to move swiftly to catch Alicia off guard. There had been no indication that I could see that she'd fought off her assailant, although it had been dark when I discovered her.

I eventually climbed into bed with Alicia's book and paged through it, paying particular attention to the parts she had underlined.

The original "Jack the Ripper" was a product of late-nineteenth-century England. He'd operated in the Whitechapel district of London where poverty, crime, and violence were commonplace. Five grotesque murders sharing similar characteristics are attributed to this otherwise unnamed killer, although another six with variations on the distinctive features are thought to have possibly been his as well, but may have been the work of imitators spurred on by sensational news coverage.

In a typical case, the victim was a poor woman from the slums, most likely a prostitute. She would be found with her neck slashed and her body mutilated, in some instances with an organ removed. The crimes took place at night, within a few streets of one another, either at the end of one month or the beginning of another, and on or near the weekend, leading criminal profilers of the day to speculate that the murderer may have worked during the week and/or lived nearby. Others—including Queen Victoria—suggested that he may have been employed on a cattle boat, since Whitechapel was near the London Docks and cattle boats docked on Thursday or Friday and went out again on Saturday or Sunday. Those theories were never confirmed, nor was the one that suggested, given the killer's interest in the body, that he was either a butcher or a surgeon.

The investigation was shared by two police divisions—Whitechapel and the City of London—as well as the central investigating unit of the Metropolitan Police Service, or

Scotland Yard as it's known. Although thousands of people were questioned, hundreds investigated, and nearly a hundred jailed for varying periods of time, the killer had never been apprehended.

Alicia had highlighted a paragraph that referred to a volunteer citizen effort that arose when local businessmen, impatient with the authorities' progress, took matters into their own hands, patrolling the streets searching for suspicious individuals. Using the newspaper to advance its agenda, the Whitechapel Vigilance Committee hired private investigators to question witnesses, and encouraged the government to offer a reward for information, but was no more successful in identifying or capturing Jack the Ripper than the police.

I closed the book, intending to finish it the next day, and placed it on my nightstand. As I turned out the light, my mind ricocheted from fact to fallacy, from what I thought I knew to what was still a mystery.

The unsolved crimes of Jack the Ripper had inspired hundreds of fictional and nonfictional accounts in print, on film, on stage and television, in songs, poems, and games. Was this Bermuda killer a modern-day copycat? Could he have been reading the same book to learn the ways of his eighteenth-century predecessor? How were the Bermudian police going to track him down? According to the press conference, the police were already getting outside help, but what could someone who wasn't familiar with the island contribute? I was also curious about the beautiful woman whom the police commissioner had indicated when he spoke about help coming from Scotland Yard.

I must have dozed off during my reflections on the crime, but something interrupted my sleep. I opened my eyes and lay quietly trying to summon up what had awakened me. *It was probably unwise to read stories about Jack the Ripper before trying to sleep,* I chided myself. The images Alicia's book aroused were not the stuff of lullabies or sweet dreams. But I hadn't been having a nightmare. I knew that. I hadn't dwelled on the details of Alicia's death or the death of the other victims of a serial killer. No. Before I'd fallen asleep, I'd been thinking about the beautiful woman I'd seen at the police press conference. Was she really from Scotland Yard? What was her specialty? And did she know my dear friend George Sutherland, who was a chief inspector in the London office? It was likely that she did; I'd ask her if we had occasion to meet.

As I was reviewing my thoughts and recapturing my bedtime musings, I realized that someone was walking on the gravel path outside my window. Whoever it was made no effort to soften his or her footfall, or perhaps was unsuccessful. But what struck me was that he or she was still there. The footsteps hadn't faded away, neither moving toward the main house, nor down to the beach. Instead, it sounded as if someone was pacing in front of the cottage, or perhaps walking around it with a view to gaining entry.

I slid up to a sitting position, leaned against the pillowed headboard, and squinted at the door to see if I'd locked it before retiring. It was too dark to tell. The moon illuminated the landscape outside but left the details inside the cottage in shadows.

The sound of shoes on gravel stopped. While the knowledge that someone was walking nearby was unsettling, the silence that followed was worse.

I held my breath, reasoning with myself that this person was simply the security guard Adam had hired carrying out his patrol. But where was he? Why had he paused in his rounds right outside my cottage? And what if this wasn't the guard? What if it was the person who had murdered Alicia? What if he had indeed been in the vicinity when I discovered the body the night before? Was he worried that I might have had a glimpse of him? Had he come back to ensure that I wouldn't be able to identify him? Or was he just eager for another victim?

I groped around the nightstand for my cell phone, but when I opened it, no light came on. I'd left it on after notifying the police in case they needed to reach me, and had forgotten to charge it.

I heard a heavy step on the porch and had to stifle a gasp. Was this the way I would die? After all the danger I'd faced in my life, all the risks I'd taken, would my life end because I was trapped in a building with only one exit? No matter how fast I was, if I tried to flee through the door, chances are I would end up in the arms of the intruder.

I quickly debated my choices. Should I pretend to be asleep? Challenge him? Hide? There weren't many places to conceal myself in the cottage. Perhaps under the bed, assuming I could squeeze into that narrow space without making a racket. But what would that do if someone were determined to get in and attack me?

Was there time for me to barricade myself in the bathroom and yell for help? Confronting the intruder was out of the question. I was unarmed, and while in good shape for my age, certainly not up to doing battle with a man wielding a knife.

I slowly pushed the covers off my legs, trying to make as little noise as possible. I twisted toward the edge of the bed, catching one foot in the sheet and nearly toppling over. I forced myself to slow down and concentrate on extricating myself from the cotton snare, all the time listening closely for evidence of his next move.

The person on my porch shuffled forward. I caught sight through the window of the outline of a head and shoulders. I froze. Was he trying to see inside? Then I heard a little squeal from the springs on the swing as he dropped into it, and a thud as he put something down.

Cautiously, I put my feet on the wooden floor and stood, crouched over. Behind me in the corner was a golf umbrella. But to retrieve it, I'd have to climb over the bed and risk alerting the intruder to the fact that I was awake and aware of his presence.

Instead I decided on an alternative tactic. Creeping forward, I made my way toward the counter where the kitchen appliances were, stepping gingerly and praying that I didn't find a loose board to give me away. My target was the frying pan I'd seen on the shelf under the counter. If I could reach that, at least I'd have something with which to defend myself.

As I approached the door, I could see that the latch was engaged—one thing in my favor. The figure on the swing shifted his weight and drew in a lungful of air, wheezing as he let it out again. I pulled myself back against the wall out of any line of sight, even were this person able to see into the dark recesses of the cabin. My breath was shallow and the pounding of my heart was loud in my ears. Could *he* hear it?

I waited in the dark, deliberating what to do. I would need to cross in front of the screen door to reach the counter. He would surely become aware of me then. While we humans do not have the sharp senses of hearing and smell of the four-legged animals who share our world, we usually can sense when there is another person around. Even a slight motion might tip him off.

I heard someone coming in the distance, the crunch of the gravel a telltale sign. My intruder bolted from the swing and hurried down the path toward the beach. I swung around so I could see through the screen door as he ran off. The moon shone down on the retreating figure, his gait lumbering from the heavy suitcase that he carried and the thick woolen suit that hampered his speed.

It was the redheaded man.

Chapter Seven

The sun was shining the next morning and the sky was a spectacular blue. I was awake early, having barely slept the night before.

After my intruder had run away, I'd waited for the security guard to pass by my cottage but he never materialized. Twenty minutes later, I gave up listening for him and closed the outer door, securing it from inside. I pulled the shades on all the windows, plugged in my cell phone to charge, left the frying pan next to my bed, and made another attempt to sleep. I'd managed a couple of hours, but when the sun rose, so did I. I made a mug of tea in the cottage's efficiency kitchen and took it out to the porch.

This time, when I heard the sound of footsteps on the gravel, it wasn't disturbing. If anything, I welcomed the company.

"Good morning, Mrs. Fletcher. I thought you'd like to see this morning's newspaper."

"Good morning, Adam," I said from my perch on the swing. "That was very thoughtful of you."

"The judge sends his apologies."

"Whatever for?" I asked, looking up at the concern in Adam's eyes. I unfolded the newspaper. "Oh," I said. "I see."

There on the front page was my picture, one that had been taken for the back of my most recent book and which my publisher had posted on its Web site. I read the head-line aloud: *Mystery Author Stumbles Upon Ripper's Latest Victim.* "Makes me sound a bit clumsy, doesn't it?" I pe-rused the article and put the paper down, letting it rest in my lap.

"The judge is upset that you've been targeted by the press in this way," Adam said, carefully watching my expression. I imagined that he was trying to determine what he could report back to his boss.

"Please tell the judge that this is neither his fault nor any-thing he could have prevented." I sighed. "It's not the first time it's happened. I can't say that I'm used to it, but I'll make every effort not to embarrass the family further."

"Oh, no. He's not worried about the family. His concern was you, that you'd be distressed to be a focus of the press because of this Jack the Ripper business." Adam paused, a thought coming to him. "Unless, of course, the extra at-tention is more positive than negative." He cocked his head at me.

I felt a wave of heat rise in me. "Good heavens! What are you thinking? That I'd want to use Alicia's death to sell more books?"

"No. No. Of course not. You couldn't have known that

you'd find Alicia's body. Who could have imagined that Bermuda would have its own Jack the Ripper? I regret if you took it the wrong way."

"It wasn't I who took it the wrong way, Adam. The last thing I'd want to do is take advantage of such a tragedy."

Our conversation was mercifully interrupted by the sound of my cell phone ringing from the cottage. I excused myself and went inside, hoping Adam would make a hasty retreat. I looked at the screen on the phone and took a deep breath to calm myself before answering the call.

A familiar voice came on the line. "Hello, lass. I see you're up to it again."

"George! How nice to hear from you. How are you?"

"To tell the truth, I'm feeling a wee bit wabbit."

"Wabbit?"

"Sorry, lass, that's Scottish for tired."

Chief Inspector George Sutherland of Scotland Yard was a dear friend of many years. Our relationship teetered on the edge of something more, but never quite advanced. We were both busy, independent people at the top of our games in our professional careers, our lives filled with responsibilities, activities, and friends. Perhaps most important, our beloved homes were across an ocean from each other. Still, we held each other in great esteem and affection, and rejoiced when we had the opportunity to spend time together. Maybe someday . . . but not now.

"Have you been working late?" I asked.

"Late and long," he replied, "but I had a nice jolt some hours ago when I saw your face."

"Oh, dear. Was my picture in your newspaper, too?"

"Afraid so, lass. I imagine you're a bit of an international sensation."

"I'm sorry to hear it."

"Nothing you can't handle. You know that we've a team in Bermuda working on the case?"

"So I understand."

"The Bermudian police are doing a thorough job, but the governor is worried that if the case isn't solved quickly, the island will suffer economically."

"I don't doubt it," I said. "Having a serial killer roaming around isn't good for tourism."

"Precisely. I've got a strong trio of inspectors on it. Macdonald, one of our forensic experts, and Freddie Moore, a good lad, very knowledgeable, plus Gilliam, a profiler. Would you mind terribly if I told them to contact you? I'm overseeing from here, getting reports from those on the ground, but I'll always be happy to have your take on the situation, particularly with your intimate knowledge of this latest victim and her family."

"That's very flattering, George, but I only arrived on Bermuda the day before yesterday. I just met the girl and hardly know the rest of her family. And anyway, do you really think her murder is related to the others?"

"Tell me about the young woman."

"Well, she wasn't poor or a prostitute for starters, nor was she killed in an alley. She was a bright, very pretty twenty-two year old, well off, the niece of a judge, who was just learning how to be attractive."

"What do you mean?"

"Well, she didn't practice her wiles on me, but apparently

she was interested in drawing masculine admiration but not always happy when she got it. Her family loved her, but I have the distinct impression that some of them didn't particularly *like* her. Let's just say they were impatient with her behavior. Does she sound like any of the other Jack the Ripper cases?"

"She's a way apart from the others—I'll give you that— but I can't rule her out as a serial victim. The killer may be looking for more attention. So far, his actions have attracted only mild interest on Fleet Street. The case has been back pages and below the fold in our newspapers. But this time their ears perked up, I'm vexed to say."

"And my discovery of the body only made the situation worse."

"Not your fault, Jessica."

"No. But I'd rather not play a part in feeding the monster."

I heard George chuckle. "Meaning the press or the killer?"

"Either one," I replied through a smile.

"So you'll talk to my staff?"

"Of course, if that's what you want."

"You already have things to offer. I'll tell them to contact you. Meantime, you be careful, lass. This is a tricky one and he's been able to elude the authorities to date. I don't want to see your name on the front page again."

"Neither do I."

After we disconnected, I remembered I'd forgotten to mention Alicia's fascination with Jack the Ripper and the book she'd been so carefully reading. I made a mental note to tell his team when they got in touch with me and wondered when that might be. And was the beautiful woman I'd seen at police headquarters the forensic expert or the profiler?

I'd deliberately omitted telling George about my experience the night before. I didn't want to alarm him. He was too far away to do anything, and knowing about it would only frustrate him. I even questioned if I should mention it to his inspectors. Was it relevant? I was no longer sure. Given a night to speculate on his activities, I'd come to believe that the man was probably a ripperologist, one of the tourists fascinated by Jack the Ripper, about whom the police commissioner had complained. Perhaps the man had been discouraged from poking around the crime scene. Maybe he'd heard that I'd found the body and was curious to learn more, but—thank goodness—hadn't had the nerve to knock on my door in the middle of the night. Anyway, I had the feeling that my imagination had carried me away, inflamed by my prebedtime reading matter. I shouldn't have been so spooked and was determined that the next time I saw the redheaded man, I would buttonhole him and demand to know what he was doing on Bermuda, and why he'd chosen to give himself a rest on the porch of my cottage.

My rumbling stomach reminded me that I was hungry. Tea for breakfast was not enough to sustain me, but I was hesitant to take another meal at the main house. Instead, I decided to find a restaurant at the nearby village of St. George, or St. George's as it's often called. I could prevail upon Adam to drive me, but I wasn't eager to see that young man so soon again with his suggestion—still lingering in my memory—that I might benefit from the newspaper coverage of Alicia's death. Had Tom Betterton said that to him? How embarrassing if that's where he got the idea.

I could call for a taxi, but that would be awkward. How would the driver get through the throng of reporters and press vehicles still parked out front? I was certain there was a bicycle in the garage that I could borrow. I'm more than comfortable riding a bike since it's my main form of transportation at home in Cabot Cove. But it was at least six or seven miles to the opposite coast of the island, where St. George's was located, and I didn't know the roads well enough to find it. Plus, if I was spotted by the reporters, it would not be easy to escape them.

Regretfully, I walked up the gravel path to Tom's house, fearing that if I couldn't find a ride into town I would get roped into lunch with the family.

As I neared the rear terrace of the house, I spotted one of the security guards talking to another man. I approached them and posed my problem.

"I'm just going off duty, Mrs. Fletcher," said the guard, who introduced himself as Jock. "I'd be happy to give you a lift into town if you don't mind traveling by motorbike."

"Do you have an extra helmet?"

"That I do," he said, "and it's even got a shaded visor."

"Then I'd be delighted to take you up on the offer," I said. "By the way," I added as we walked to Tom's garage where Jock had parked his motorbike, "did you happen to see a redheaded man near my cottage during the night?"

"Can't say that I did," he replied. "Of course, I wasn't especially looking for anyone. My job was to keep people from approaching the judge's house from the beach. I pretty much stayed close to there. Did this fellow cause a problem for you?"

"No, not at all," I said. "It was just a little unsettling."

"A murder like this has us all on edge," he said. "My wife's afraid to leave the house at night. Of course, I told her that she wasn't the sort of woman who attracts a nut like this, but you know how women are." He realized he might have offended and laughed to soften the comment. I said nothing.

Jock backed his motorbike away from a shelf holding fishing tackle, and I climbed on. With me riding behind him, he rounded the corner of the garage, rolled down the drive and onto the road before any of the reporters had a chance to identify his passenger. I hoped. It was only when we were on Harrington Sound Road that I chanced a look back to be certain we weren't being followed. No one in sight. I sighed with relief and decided to enjoy the ride. The weather was warm, the sky clear, and I smiled as the breeze whipped my collar and ballooned the back of my blouse as we rode toward town.

We turned right at Blue Hole Hill and soon found ourselves on the causeway that leads to St. David's Island and the traffic circle to Kindley Field Road. One more traffic circle at Mullet Bay Road and we were on our way into St. George's.

Jock let me off at King's Square, and I traded his extra helmet for my pink ball cap and a pair of dark sunglasses. With so many tourists similarly attired, I hoped I could escape notice and enjoy a leisurely anonymous afternoon.

The closest restaurant was the White Horse Pub, which

promised a view of the water—and of a cruise ship docked at the nearby terminal. It was a little early for lunch when I entered the dark interior of the tavern; the throng of tourists that would certainly jam in at noon had yet to arrive. I asked for a table overlooking the harbor and was pleased to find myself the only diner in the covered area outside, at least for the time being. Since breakfast was no longer being served, I perused the luncheon menu and decided on an appetizer, conch fritters served with an arugula salad and Key lime mustard sauce, and a glass of iced tea. Not exactly eggs and bacon but a welcome meal for this hungry lady.

I removed the pink cap and the sunglasses and took a deep breath. This is what I had been looking for when Tom offered the use of one of his cottages for a week's stay: balmy weather, exotic dishes, and seven days to relax at the beach with few distractions and no demands on my time. I watched as the passengers from the cruise ship disembarked and walked toward King's Square. They were a colorful group, the men in plaid or pastel shorts and polo shirts, with ball caps shading their eyes from the sun, the women attired in similar colors, some in sundresses and with large floppy hats serving the same function. Years ago, the men would have had cameras dangling from straps around their necks, but these days most held up their cell phones or pocket versions of a video camera to record the street scenes and the town's beautiful old buildings.

Bermudian architecture owes much to English stone buildings of the seventeenth century. Originally built with Bermuda limestone—now in short supply—the houses are painted in soft hues approved by the government and feature distinctive whitewashed slate roofs, which are terraced to collect rainwater in an underground tank.

In my home state of Maine where fresh water is plentiful, thanks in part to its thousands of lakes, we never think about where the water that runs from our taps originates. Here in Bermuda the opposite is true. This beautiful island has no central water supply provided to residents. The cisterns that sit under its homes and apartment complexes—and groundwater pumped into holding tanks—must provide the population's needs. The government has a treatment plant that offers high-quality water to augment a homeowner's private supply, but this is a service for which its users pay a hefty fee. *The price for living in paradise,* I mused.

The outdoor dining area was filling up when I called for my check, donned my pink cap, and put on my sunglasses. The food had been delicious, and the peaceful interlude even more so. I walked through the restaurant and out into the sunshine only to have my mood shattered by a woman's screams.

What happened? There couldn't be a killer in so public an area, could there? I hadn't heard a gunshot or a bomb. Had someone been hit by a car or motorbike? Accosted by a robber? I heard the woman shriek again.

A crowd was gathered by the waterside and I hurried over. To my surprise, a wave of laughter greeted me as I pressed my way forward. A young woman in a lace-trimmed mop-cap, wearing a long blue skirt and blue vest over a white blouse was being pulled forward by a man in a blue frock coat and white pantaloons. It was a historical reenactment. I knew that St. George's was the oldest continually occupied settlement in the New World—it was founded in 1612—but had forgotten that the town used its colonial roots as one of its principal attractions. I looked around the square and noticed that tourists were taking pictures of one another with their hands and heads poking out of the holes in a stock, a form of public humiliation in colonial days. Apparently I was about to witness another form. I blushed at my foolishness and felt my heartbeat slow to its normal tempo. I certainly was jumpy these days.

"This wench has been accused and found guilty of being a shrew and a gossip," said the blue-coated man, holding his tricorn hat with one hand to keep the breeze from taking off with it.

"It's not fair," the actress playing the wench whined. "I didn't get no trial. You can't say I'm guilty."

"She had a trial, ladies and gentlemen. Don't you believe her for a second. Tried by three judges, count 'em, one, two, three." He held up three fingers.

"All incompetents," she shouted, "one, two, three," holding up three fingers to her audience, which rewarded her with a laugh.

"The judges have determined her punishment. She shall be seated in the ducking stool and be ducked, not once, not twice, but—" He raised a hand to cup his ear.

"Three times," shouted the crowd.

"Too few! I think we'll make it six times," the colonist called out.

"Noooo," shrieked the wench as she was led to the seat of the ducking stool, which she gamely climbed on before adjusting her skirts and crossing her bare feet.

"Do you repent?"

She shook her head.

"Ladies and gentlemen, this is what happens to an unrepentant shrew." With the assistance of two other costumed helpers, he pushed the long pole holding the ducking stool seat out over the water. "Last chance to repent."

"You're all a bunch of corrupt, incompetent fools, you and your judges," the wench replied.

With that the men released their hold on the pole and the wench was dropped into the water. She came up sputtering and shaking a fist at her punishers to a loud round of applause and laughter.

The scene was going to be repeated five more times, providing ample opportunity to pull myself away from the appreciative crowd and find a nice, almost-empty narrow street paved in bricks to explore.

Eager to recapture the serenity I'd felt on the deck of the White Horse Pub, I wandered around St. George's window shopping and kept my souvenir purchases small enough to fit in my shoulder bag. I came upon a bookstore down a short flight of steps and browsed their selections, keeping my sunglasses on even though the lighting inside wasn't at all glaring. While I doubted the tourists around me had read the local newspaper, it was certainly possible that the staff of the bookstore had, and I was anxious not to be pulled into a discussion of Alicia's murder.

Strangely, even though I had assumed that anything about a serial killer would discourage tourism, there was a pile of books on the front table about Jack the Ripper, including the one Alicia had been reading. I picked up a copy, as well as a guide to Bermuda, and approached the lady at the cash register. I paid for the guide and then, holding up the book on Jack the Ripper, asked, "Do you sell a lot of these?"

She looked at me over the top of her reading glasses and nodded. "Mostly to locals these day, but some of the tourists are interested."

"Do you happen to remember a young woman buying this book?"

"Do you mean Alicia Betterton, Mrs. Fletcher?" She pulled out a copy of the morning paper from under her counter.

"I guess I'm caught," I said, taking off my sunglasses.

"This is a small island, and there's not a lot that goes on that I don't hear about. Plus Alicia was a regular customer in our crime section, although I don't think she ever bought one of your books."

"Probably not gory enough for her," I said. "She told me she liked true crime, and my mysteries tend to focus on character rather than blood."

"We sell many of yours to other people."

"That's nice to hear. Do you mind if I ask you a question?"

"Not at all."

"Do you happen to remember when Alicia bought this book?"

"It was last week, right after the news came out about the latest murder in Hamilton."

"Do you remember if she bought anything else?"

She shook her head. "She was in a hurry. I think she

came in specifically for that book. I remember she told me someone was waiting to take her back home."

"Do you know who that was?"

"No. He was outside in the car, but the windows were dark. I couldn't see through them."

"And when she came in other days, did you ever see her with anyone else?"

"Her brother once or twice."

"Stephen?"

"Yes."

"Was she ever with someone younger, perhaps closer to her age?"

"Not that I remember. Excuse me." She turned to a lady who had brought a book to the register.

"Thank you for your time," I said, returning the book to its place on the display table and putting on my sunglasses.

"Oh, Mrs. Fletcher, would you mind waiting a moment?"

"Certainly."

She finished her business with the customer and came out from behind the register. "We just got in some copies of your latest hardcover. Would you mind signing them?"

I hesitated for a moment, thinking of Adam's remark that morning, but decided it would be worse to be rude to this bookseller, particularly if I wanted her to answer any questions I might have in the future. "I'd be happy to," I said.

Chapter Eight

The skies had clouded over while I'd been in the book-shop, and it looked as if a storm might come through. I debated removing my sunglasses, but since so many of the tourists on the street still wore theirs, I decided that keeping mine on wouldn't draw attention. While they hadn't served as much of a disguise—the lady in the bookstore easily saw through them—they still made me feel as if I were traveling incognito like one of the spies in a James Bond movie, or an actress hiding from the paparazzi.

Those of us who write for a living are rarely bothered by people on the streets stopping to ask for a picture or an au-tograph. With some exceptions—I'm thinking of someone like Jackie Collins or Maya Angelou—we don't fit easily into the celebrity mold. I often wonder how the truly famous cope with all the camera flashes popping in front of them or being trailed by fans or reporters waiting to catch them in an unflattering light. Some I suppose grow accustomed to it, while others hate the invasion of their privacy and fight back with lawsuits or assaults, often making the front page, which was exactly what they were trying to avoid. I'm pretty sure I would not want to be hounded by strangers were I ever in their position. But thankfully that wasn't something I needed to worry about. My encounters with the reading public were usually well organized in book panels and signing events, and the people I meet on those occasions are almost unanimously polite and kind, leading me to believe that book readers are a rare and wonderful breed. Of course, when your photo appears in a newspaper or on the Internet in connection with a salacious crime, all bets are off. It was recognition for that dubious privilege that I was trying to avoid.

I had just passed the broad steps of St. Peter's Church, the oldest Anglican church in the Western Hemisphere, when I felt the first drop of rain hit my head. I sprinted down York Street and ducked under the awning of an art gallery in a pink building just as another woman reached the same spot and bumped into me.

"Omigoodness. So clumsy of me. Oh, it's Jessica then, isn't it?"

"Hello, Daisy," I said to the wife of Tom's publisher, Godfrey Reynolds. They occupied the cottage down the beach from mine.

"Are you all right? I haven't harmed you, have I?"

"Not at all," I said, brushing drops of rain off my shoulder. "How are you? I haven't seen you and Godfrey since the party, which is remarkable since we're practically next-door neighbors."

"Oh, I know. We left you alone to deal with all that mess.

Godfrey said it was best to keep away, stay out of it as much as we could. We're actually planning to move to a hotel. Godfrey is over there now trying to make arrangements. I can't stand the idea of going down to the beach when, well, you know what happened there."

"Have you told Tom you're leaving?" I asked, wondering how he would respond to this rebuff of his hospitality.

"Not yet. Godfrey wanted to be certain we could secure a room before he gave him the news. There's some sort of conference taking place here, and the hotels appear to be full, even the second class ones."

"In that case, wouldn't you be better off staying where you are? You can always go to another beach."

"If Godfrey cannot find us a suitable room, we may have to. I don't mean to sound ungrateful. It was generous of Judge Betterton to offer the cottage, but this is the only time we could find to go on holiday. Britain has been so cold and rainy this year, and we were eager to find some sun. But a murder . . ." She shuddered. "If we weren't required to stay, I would insist that we be on a plane to somewhere else by now, Miami perhaps or Key West, or one of the Caribbean islands."

"I understand why the police asked *me* not to leave, but what reason did they give for wanting *you* to stay?" I asked.

Daisy rolled her eyes. "Oh, it was some such thing about Godfrey not being there when they knocked on the cottage door. It was four in the morning and I was so groggy, I'm not certain what answer I gave them."

At that my own eyebrows shot up. "If he wasn't in the cabin with you, where was he?" I asked.

"It sounds a lot worse than it is," she said, peering out into the rain, which was coming down in sheets now, providing a curtain of privacy. She looked at me again, her eyes pleading. "Please don't rush to judgment. He doesn't sleep well, my husband, and tends to get up at night and read. But it's a bit difficult in a one-room cottage. He didn't want to wake me. He's very considerate that way." She put a hand on my arm as if to steady herself. "He simply took his book outside with a torch—you call it a flashlight. He said he read for an hour and had just gotten up to stretch his legs by walking about for a bit and that's when the police came."

"Did he hear anything odd or see anyone else when he was walking around?"

"No. And that's what he told the constables, but they insisted we not leave, so here we are."

The door to the shop opened behind us, giving us both a start. A white-haired gentleman wearing a tartan vest and pale blue linen suit invited us in. "No use standing outside in the rain, ladies, even under the protection of my canopy. Others may wish to escape the rain, too. Please come in. I have an electric kettle if you'd care for some tea. Ah, Mrs. Reynolds, I didn't realize it was you."

"Hello, Mr. Mann," Daisy said, linking her arm in mine. "We didn't mean to block your door. Tea would be wonderful. I was just telling Mrs. Fletcher what lovely landscapes you have in your shop. Jessica, this is Richard Mann, owner of this gallery."

Evidently Daisy didn't want Richard Mann to know what we'd really been discussing.

"We didn't have an opportunity to say much to each

other," I said, "but you and I were introduced at Judge Betterton's party."

"Yes, yes," he said, ushering us inside. "I remember now. Poor fellow. What a sorry business." His face took on a forlorn expression, then brightened. "We do indeed have some wonderful landscapes. I'll be happy to show them to you. And we have some new pieces by an artist you ladies may be acquainted with—Stephen Betterton."

"I didn't know that Stephen was an artist," I said.

"I don't believe that painting is his occupation," Mann said, "but it is certainly his preoccupation, if you will." He closed the door behind us, *tsk*ing about the weather, and went to plug in his kettle.

I took Daisy's cue and began perusing the art on the walls. There were the to-be-expected beach scenes with turquoise water and pink sand and the views of the rocky remains of what had once been a natural stone arch on the shore. Several watercolors depicted a curved stone Moon Gate, a national symbol of good luck where honeymooners often posed for photographs.

"I see you're admiring the Moon Gate series. There must be at least a dozen Moon Gates on Bermuda," the gallery owner said. "Very popular."

"What are they for?" Daisy asked.

Mann shrugged. "A purely decorative gateway. They were brought to Bermuda by a sea captain in the 1860s. He'd seen one in China and had it copied for his garden. That's where most people have theirs, if they have one. According to Chinese legend, if a couple walks through one hand in hand, they will have everlasting happiness. It's a pretty story and has helped the island's wedding industry. The lady who painted these lives over in Hamilton. I have other landscapes of hers if you'd like to see them."

"No, thank you," I said, "but I would like to see Stephen Betterton's work."

"Most are in the back room," Mann said, leading us around a square pillar with narrow shelves on three sides holding small framed artwork. "This is where we have our one-man shows, or one-woman shows, as the case may be," he said, indicating the space with an open arm.

Seven of Stephen's paintings were hung on the walls, four Impressionistic depictions of Bermuda street scenes, one portrait and two still lifes.

"He works in acrylics, which many modern artists do," Mann said. "It lacks the subtleties and the richness of color you can achieve with oils, but it dries faster, making it a better medium for the prolific—and the impatient." He chuckled at his own joke.

"He's very talented," I said as I paused in front of the portrait. It was a three-quarter view of a woman gazing off into the distance, the blues of the background suggesting that she was looking at the sea. There was a large empty space on the wall next to the portrait and I wondered if the gallery owner had already sold the painting that had hung there. Probably not, however. Most galleries indicated that a work had been sold by placing a red dot on the frame, not by taking it out of the show.

"It looks like Madeline, doesn't it?" Daisy said, coming next to me.

"Yes," I said. "I like this work the best of what's here. It has the most feeling."

"I have another of his portraits I can show you, but I can't sell it to you," Mann said.

"Is it the one that used to hang beside this one?" I asked.

"Yes. Would you like to see it?"

"Very much."

"Do you suppose it's Alicia?" Daisy whispered to me when Mann left to find the painting.

"We'll find out," I replied. "If it is, Mr. Mann might have taken it out of the exhibit after her death."

"I'm not sure I want to see it."

"Why? It's only a painting," I said.

"Stephen probably wants it back as a remembrance," she said.

Mann returned a moment later, holding a small portrait. He placed it on an easel and the three of us stepped back to view it. Alicia had been a pretty girl, but the woman in the portrait was remarkably beautiful, eyes slightly downcast and pensive, expression serene.

"I didn't know the girl very well," Daisy said. "It certainly looks like Alicia, only different. I can't put my finger on why."

"Perhaps it's what he *wanted* her to look like," I said.

"Interesting observation," Mann said. "It is a bit idealized. When he brought it in, I told Stephen I'd never seen that expression on her face. He said it's what she was inside, a part of her that she didn't show to everyone. It's not for sale. I thought it wise to take it out of the show."

"That was sensitive," I said. "I'm sure the family will appreciate it."

"Oh, it wasn't done for them," Mann said. "Word would have gotten around and I don't want people coming in, wasting my time just to ogle the painting. Frankly, at this point, I would have found it distasteful had someone wanted to buy it."

I was tempted to take exception to his comment. The portrait of Alicia was an intriguing painting even without knowing the fate of its subject. That Stephen had painted his cousin with such sympathy made me wonder just how rancorous their relationship actually was. He'd been impatient with her bad behavior, yes, but he'd also seen beneath the facade she presented to the world. What did he really think about Alicia?

Daisy and I spent another fifteen minutes in Mann's gallery politely sipping tea that he'd gone to the trouble to make. Daisy had already bought a painting from him and weighed the purchase of another, finally promising to bring Godfrey with her for the final decision. We parted ways outside the shop. The rain had stopped, the skies were clear, and the puddles were drying in the sun.

"I hope I'll see you again before we leave," Daisy said, giving me a hug, "but if not, give us a call the next time you're in London. You do come to London every now and then, don't you?"

I told her that I did, and said I would call, but I wasn't sure that I would. My list of friends in the English capital had grown considerably over time and I invariably found myself torn when it came to making dates while there, an enviable but sometimes frustrating situation.

I walked back to King's Square where many of the tourists took pictures of the replica of the ship *Deliverance* while they waited to reboard their cruise ship. St. George's is a town steeped in history, and every few steps brought to life another piece of times gone by. According to the guidebook I'd just bought, the first *Deliverance* had been built on Bermuda by the shipwrecked survivors of another vessel bound for the Virginia colony in 1609. It took almost a year, but using salvaged materials from their original ship along with the natural resources provided by what was then an uninhabited island, they cobbled together an eighty-ton ship. After fourteen days at sea, they reached Chesapeake Bay.

Two of the shipwrecked survivors had elected to stay on in Bermuda rather than set sail. Since they were disreputable fellows—one was a murderer—the ship's company was probably happy to be rid of them. But ironically, they were the first inhabitants of Bermuda, and had the island all to themselves for two years before more settlers arrived to establish the town of St. George, named for the patron saint of England. William Shakespeare's play *The Tempest* is reputed to have been inspired by accounts of the shipwreck and the settlers' ordeal before they reached Virginia.

Beyond the *Deliverance* and King's Square was the ferry terminal that plied the waters between St. George and Hamilton. I would have enjoyed a ride on the ferry but Hamilton wasn't my destination, at least not that day. I needed a taxi or some other form of ground transportation to return me to Tucker's Town and my beachfront cottage. I saw where taxis were lined up and headed in that direction. It had been an interesting, yet relaxing day, a nice break from the turmoil in the Betterton household, although Alicia's murder had never been far from my mind.

The ferry was preparing to leave as I crossed the large car parking area toward the taxi line. Passengers had already boarded and crew members were starting to release the heavy ropes that tethered the boat to the dock. People leaned on the ship's railings on the open top deck and waved good-bye to friends and family below.

The ferry captain gave a loud blast on the ship's horn, alerting latecomers of its imminent departure. I covered my ears and laughed as the last two stragglers ran up the ramp to the ship. One of the latecomers wheeled his scooter onto the ferry. But it was the second one who gave me a start, the one person I had vowed to confront as soon as I had the chance. It was the redheaded man, hauling his heavy suit-case and still in his strange old-fashioned attire.

I hurried forward, not stopping to think how I would get on the ferry without a ticket and where it would leave me if I were successful in boarding. But I was too late. The lines were released, the ramp pulled back, and the ferry backed out of the dock and began its trip along Bermuda's north shore toward Hamilton, the capital.

Chapter Nine

Adam answered my knock at the Betterton house when I returned from St. George's. "Two people were here from Scotland Yard today, and they asked about you," he said.

"Did they leave their names and how I can reach them?"

"Yes. The judge has their cards in the library. He wants to see you." He hesitated. "Mrs. Fletcher, I want to apologize for my behavior this morning. I know I upset you. I didn't mean to do that."

"Why don't we forget about this morning," I said. "No harm done."

"Thanks." He looked relieved. "I was out of line."

"Tell me about the people from Scotland Yard. You say that there were two?"

"Yes. A woman inspector, a real doll. I never met a cop that good-looking before. I'd sure remember if I did. And a guy. I didn't get their names. The judge spoke with them."

"Did they question you?"

"Not today. The police asked me a lot of questions the night Alicia was killed, but I had nothing to offer," he said, as he led me toward the library. "I'm not important enough to be grilled again."

"You sound disappointed. Do you want to speak with them again?"

"No way! I'm just the PA. I'm not a member of the family. Anyway, how would I know anything about this Jack the Ripper guy?"

I stopped in front of the closed door to the library and turned to him. "But you certainly knew Alicia," I said.

"Yeah, but I didn't know her well."

"You knew her well enough to dislike her."

Adam's head snapped up. "Why do you say that?"

"Just a feeling," I said. "You didn't acknowledge her when we came in the other day. In fact, it appeared to me that you were deliberately ignoring her."

"Not any more than she ignored me all the time," he said, sounding annoyed.

"Why would she do that?"

"I was just the hired help to her—that's why. She considered me a servant. She never had a good word to say to me. Did I say *good* word? She never had a word of any kind to say to me. She was nicer to Norlene than she was to me."

"Norlene is also 'hired help,' as you put it, so I doubt that was Alicia's reasoning. Perhaps Norlene was nicer to her than you were."

"I was always nice to her. When I first came, I tried to do everything for her, but she wouldn't give me the time of day.

She could flirt and laugh with every man around, but not me. I couldn't even get a smile."

"Maybe she was sensitive to your working relationship with her uncle and didn't want to create the wrong impression."

"You can make all the excuses for her you want, but the reality is, she was just a nasty b—"

Tom's booming voice interrupted our conversation as he opened the door from inside the library. "I thought I heard you come in, Jessica," he said, stepping into the hall. "Would you like some tea or a cocktail?" He looked at his watch. "The sun is officially over the yardarm. Adam's going to bring me something. Right, Adam? Can he get you some refreshments to tide you over until dinner?"

"Actually, I had tea less than an hour ago, but thank you all the same," I said, realizing that I was not going to get out of dinner as easily as I had gotten out of lunch.

"Adam, please let Norlene know that Jessica will join us for dinner."

"Sure," Adam said sourly.

"I invited the Reynoldses," Tom said. "Wasn't sure if they could make it, but they accepted. They've been so busy since they came. Don't know how they managed to meet so many people on the island in such a short time."

"You introduced them to all your friends at the party," I said, deciding Tom's publisher had probably not yet found a hotel to move to.

"Yes, you're right, of course. Would you mind coming into the library for a moment? I won't keep you long."

"I'm not in a hurry," I said and followed him into the room.

The library looked as it had the first time I'd been there, the night Alicia was killed, the furniture grouped around the fireplace, the flowering plant in front of the hearth. But Tom's desk at the far end painted a different picture. Instead of the perfect still life it had been with pads and pens lined up just so, it was now covered with stacks of papers and files. More papers littered the floor around it, and the top drawer of a filing cabinet hung open, folders spilling out as if someone had roughly gone through its contents. I noticed several books had been removed from the shelves and put back but not in the perfectly neat alignment they had been in before.

"Excuse the mess," Tom said, waving me into a seat. "I've lost some important papers, probably left them home in Jersey, but I was sure I'd brought them here. They'll turn up. It's just that my mind is all a jumble since Alicia. I can't remember things . . ." He trailed off.

"Don't be so hard on yourself," I said. "You've had a great loss. And it's been such a short time."

"Yes, but—Did I tell you I received a condolence call from the White House?"

"No! When?"

"Today. The president was a classmate of mine in law school, but we haven't really been close since then. He was very gracious, very gracious indeed. His wife, too. She got on the phone to express her condolences. Just amazing! I don't know whether you're aware that I'm being considered for a higher office."

"I didn't know. That's wonderful. What position are you up for?"

"The truth is, Jessica, there's a possibility—and I stress that it's only a possibility—that the president will nominate me to fill a vacancy on the Court of Appeals for the Third Circuit." He crossed his fingers. "From there, the next step could be the U.S. Supreme Court. What an opportunity!"

"That's—that's big news indeed, Tom. Congratulations!"

"Don't congratulate me yet. It's not a given," he said. "It's been pretty hush-hush. There are others under consideration, obvious choices, but the president's staff responsible for vetting candidates recently contacted me." He laughed. "Of course, moving up from the appellate court to the Supreme Court is just a pipe dream. Too many things working against me, I think, starting with the fact that I've had four wives and been divorced three times. But hell, you never know. Reagan was divorced and he became the president."

But only divorced once, I thought.

"Like I said, it's not a sure thing. I'm not counting on it happening, but I'd be less than honest to say that I'm not flattered by the possibility."

I knew that most of the members of the Supreme Court had served in an appellate court before being nominated to the higher seat. Since the Supreme Court only hears about a hundred cases a year, the judges of the thirteen U.S. Courts of Appeals have a powerful influence on the law, handing down decisions on the remainder of the ten thousand cases filed with them each year.

Were Tom nominated by the president and confirmed by the Senate, he would have a lifetime tenure on the Court of

Appeals. Obviously having been the president's law school classmate played a role in his being considered for this spot, but having been a federal judge for many years also gave him the requisite legal background.

"I suppose the book I wrote caught people's attention," he mused. "It was controversial but still, it gave me a lot of good public relations, good exposure to those who don't read the law journals but who make those kinds of decisions. At any rate, Jessica, I've decided that while I don't want it made public knowledge, I do want to celebrate it with friends. That's why I wanted you and Godfrey and his wife to join us tonight, to share in some good news, rather than focus on a tragedy. You know what I mean?"

It struck me as strange that Tom was ready to pause in mourning his niece to celebrate something that wasn't a reality yet, but I've learned over the years never to pass judgment on how people respond to misfortune.

We're all wired differently. When my husband, Frank, died, it was many months before I could lift my head from the pillow in the morning without a wave of grief sweeping over me. I went on. I never let my friends know how I grappled with those feelings daily, although those closest to me suspected my unhappiness. I've seen some people who bounce back immediately, and others who weep openly until people lose patience with them. There are no rules. Each of us has to find his or her way to deal with death. To have to deal with a violent end is even harder; so I gave Tom a pass. We would toast his possible good fortune.

"Adam told me that there were people here from Scotland Yard today," I said, changing the topic.

"Oh yes. I knew I had something else to tell you." He looked around. "I've got their cards here somewhere. Wait! I put them in the top drawer."

As he went to his desk to find the business cards, Norlene knocked on the door and entered carrying a tray. She put it down on the table between the two love seats and offered me the cup of tea that I had declined. I took it from her anyway, placing the cup and saucer on the table, while she set out the glass of ice for Tom, and a decanter with a silver label that said SCOTCH. She poured some of the liquor into his glass, placed a dish of crackers and another of nuts on the table, and left.

"Here they are," Tom said. "Thought I might have lost them." He held up the business cards. "Thank you, Norlene," he called out although she'd already exited the room.

He handed me the business cards and I looked at them. They contained color photographs of the inspectors. One was for Inspector Veronica Macdonald, Forensics Unit.

"You'll find Macdonald's picture doesn't do her justice," Tom said. "Beautiful woman."

"So Adam said."

I hadn't told Tom about the press conference so there was no point in saying I'd already seen her at police head-quarters.

"Adam's eyes were nearly popping out of his head," Tom said, chuckling. "I thought he would fall all over himself when he brought them in. The other one is Gill something."

"Gilliam," I filled in, looking at the card. "John Gilliam. He's a criminal profiler." He had a pleasant face, not one you'd pay particular attention to, but perhaps that worked in his favor when he interviewed people in an attempt to ferret out the details that would inform his profile of the killer. He would want his witnesses to concentrate on the killer, not on him.

"Gilliam, that's it. No one probably pays him any mind when she's around. Anyway, they had a few questions, but they said that they didn't think Alicia's death was related to the Jack the Ripper killings." He sighed. "I don't know if they're right, but I'm not the expert there. I told them I didn't care if it was or it wasn't. I wanted them to find the guy and string him up. They assured me they're working on Alicia's case as well as the other murders."

"That's good to hear."

"Yes. They want to talk to you, of course, since it was you who discovered her body. I told them that I would have you call as soon as you got in. Do you want to use my phone?"

"No, thank you," I said. "It's too late now to go to police headquarters or to have them come here again. I'll call before I change for dinner and make an appointment for tomorrow."

"Whatever you say." He picked up his glass, took a long sip, looked at me over the rim, and smiled. "Here's to you."

I took a sip of my tea, wondering how long I'd have to sit with my host before I could go back to the cottage and make the call. As it happened, it wasn't very long. Madeline came into the room and asked to speak with Tom privately, the perfect excuse for my departure.

I took a quick shower in the cottage and dressed for dinner. I left a voice mail message for the Scotland Yard inspectors, brought Alicia's book outside, and sat in the swing. It was an hour and a half before dinner would be served. I idly flipped through the pages. Alicia had only read halfway through. The spine wasn't cracked for the second half of the book, nor were any sections underlined. She had, however, made a note inside the back cover. It said, "Fairy Fay, GD, 2, Tuesday."

Why hadn't I noticed that before? I was so busy reading the book that I hadn't looked at it thoroughly. I riffled all the pages to see if any papers fell out. I checked inside the front cover and went through the entire book page by page to see if she had left any other notes in the margins. I tilted the book in the light in case there was an impression on the cover of something she might have written on paper, using the book to lean on. Nothing more.

I pondered the meaning of "Fairy Fay, GD, 2, Tuesday." I assumed that the handwriting was Alicia's. To my knowledge, other than Madeline and me, no one else had handled the book. It sounded like an appointment. But who was this lady with an unusual name and when was Alicia supposed to meet her? Today was Sunday. Was she referring to last Tuesday or the day after tomorrow? Why had Alicia made an appointment with her? And had she hidden this information on purpose, or simply used the book because it was the only available paper to write on?

I went back into the cottage to retrieve my new guidebook and opened the folded map of Bermuda contained inside. If Fairy Fay lived here, where was GD? Was it a place in St. George's? A street? A store, perhaps? A hotel? A golf club of some kind? I studied the map, making a list of anything I thought might be helpful. There were quite a few places that started with a G—Gibbs Hill Lighthouse, Grassy Bay, Gates Fort, Governor's Island—but none that could be abbreviated GD. I was more successful in the restaurant listing. I found a place called Gardner's Deli in Hamilton. I made a note to myself to stop in at Gardner's Deli at two o'clock on Tuesday. Maybe Fairy Fay worked there, or perhaps someone knew where she could be found. I knew very little about Alicia's activities outside her uncle's house and it would be helpful to meet one of her friends.

I folded up the map, tucked Alicia's book into my shoulder bag for safekeeping, and left the porch. There was still time before dinner and I took a chance that the crime scene was no longer cordoned off. Shoes were needed on the gravel path, but once I reached the beach they were more an encumbrance than a help. I slipped them off and walked barefoot in the sand, retracing my steps the night I arrived, but this time with the advantage of a sun, rather than a moon, hanging over the horizon.

I ambled past the second cottage, the one still occupied by Daisy and Godfrey Reynolds. I remembered taking a look at that cottage the night of the murder and noticing that it matched mine with its porch swing and screen door. I hadn't seen Godfrey reading on the porch the night of the murder. I could hardly have missed him. I'd passed the cottage again, perhaps fifteen or twenty minutes later when I'd run back to call the police. If Godfrey had been sitting on the porch then, I wouldn't have noticed. My mind had been preoccupied with reaching the authorities before the surf washed away any more evidence, including Alicia's body. But had he been there, surely Godfrey would have seen me hurrying up the beach, or would have heard my footsteps when I reached the gravel path. Yet Daisy said that he'd told the police that he'd neither seen nor heard anything.

The sun was hanging over the rocky outcropping. The spray from the waves hitting the hard surfaces sent golden droplets up into the sky; they bounced off the gray stone, now gilded in the waning evening light. A piece of yellow tape affixed to the rock fluttered in the breeze, the only reminder of the violence that had taken place there. The beach was beautiful, romantic, serene.

I rounded a boulder and came upon the staircase that led up to the Jamisons' property. Someone was sitting on the bottom steps, his face turned away from me. He wore a pair of khaki slacks folded up at the cuffs; the arms of a navy blue sweater were looped around his shoulders. An aqua bandanna peeked from the open collar of his pink shirt. His black curly hair was tousled by the wind. Agnes's grandnephew didn't notice me until I was almost upon him.

"Hello, Charles," I said.

"Mrs. Fletcher!" He stumbled to his feet. "I'm sorry. I didn't see you coming."

"No need to apologize," I said. "May I join you?" I pointed at the stair on which he'd been sitting.

"Sure. I'm not going to stay very long, but please—" He untied his neckerchief and swiped at the sand on the step.

"Thank you," I said.

We were silent for a while, but I was aware of his eyes roaming the beach, taking in every detail.

"This is where you found her, right?" he said.

"Yes."

He sighed. "I . . . I might have been the last person to see her alive," he said, his voice choked with emotion.

"How do you know that?"

"We were supposed to meet after the judge's party. I had invited her to go with me to another party some friends were throwing in Paget. I knew it would still be going on. Those guys pretty much hang out until the morning."

"Did you go to the party?"

"I did, yes. Not Alicia. I wish she had gone with me. God, how I wish I had made her go with me."

"Why didn't she?"

"We argued. She was in a funny mood, picking fights with everyone. I'd seen Stephen and Madeline giving her a piece of their mind, but they couldn't contain her. She was high on something, maybe just a little drunk, I think. She was unsteady. She tripped and Mr. Reynolds had to catch her. That didn't sit very well with his wife. She practically shoved him out the door. Alicia just laughed. She was bragging how she was going to blow them all out of the water."

"*Who* was she going to blow out of the water?"

"I don't know. She wouldn't tell me. I asked her what she was planning to do. She said, 'You'll see.' Then she ran out on the terrace and was gone." He pressed his thumb and forefinger into the corners of his eyes and squeezed the bridge of his nose. When he spoke again, his voice was quavering. "Then next thing I knew, Aunt Agnes was shaking me awake and there was a room full of constables waiting to take me to headquarters."

"What time had you gotten home?"

"No idea. I went to the party, but I was so pissed at Alicia I just drank myself into a stupor. One of the guys threw my motorbike into his truck and drove me home. He told the cops he dropped me off at four or five. I really don't remember."

"That must have been a problem with the police."

"Yeah, my alibi's not the best. But my friend vouched for me. I never would have hurt her. Well, that's not entirely accurate. She made me want to strangle her. I sure was tempted, but I didn't do it. And I don't even own a knife."

"What does your great-aunt think of all this?"

He shook his head. "You'll have to ask her. She was never a fan of Alicia's. I knew that. But she never told me not to see her. She kind of goes with the flow. I think it's just something else for her to gossip about. She lives for gossip." He looked at me. "I know what you're thinking, but it's true. I guess at her age, there isn't a lot else to interest her."

I thought Agnes would not be pleased at her nephew's description of her life, but I wasn't in a position to contradict him. I didn't know her that well, but I couldn't help saying, "I'm sure she's not as cold as that."

He shrugged.

"How long were you seeing Alicia?" I asked. "Someone at the party said she had a boyfriend. Was that you?"

"I'm sorry," he said, sighing again. "I have to go." He pushed on his knees to stand, brushed the sand off the seat of his trousers, and put out a hand to help me to my feet. "I apologize if I was rude to you the other night. You caught me right in the middle of my argument with Alicia and I just wasn't thinking."

"I understand," I said. "Please send my regards to your aunt. I'd like to stop by and see her if she wouldn't mind."

"She'd love it. Just go. She's always there. Judge Betterton has our address."

"I'll do that," I said.

He turned and quickly climbed the stairs.

How odd to find him there, I thought, as I watched him take the steps two at a time as though eager to get away.

But from what?

From the scene of the crime?

Or from my questions?

Chapter Ten

When I returned to my cottage after dinner, there was a message on my cell phone inviting me to police headquarters early the following afternoon to meet with the representatives from Scotland Yard. I was certain my dear friend Chief Inspector George Sutherland had briefed them on what he and I had discussed in our phone call; I didn't know what more I could offer, but I eagerly looked forward to the meeting.

If I were being completely honest with myself, I would admit that I was curious to meet Inspector Veronica Macdonald, the forensics expert. Both Tom and Adam had commented enthusiastically on how beautiful she was, which I had seen for myself at the press conference. As a member of the team George had designated to assist the Bermudian police with their serial killer cases, she would have had to impress him with her knowledge and skills. Why else would George have chosen her for this assignment? Perhaps they had worked closely together on other cases in London. Did he find her as beautiful as the judge and his personal assistant so clearly did? I flinched at the direction of my thoughts. *Goodness, Jessica!* I chided myself. *Is that a twinge of jealousy you're feeling?*

As I got ready for bed, I forced myself to think about the evening I'd just spent. Neither the Scotland Yard inspectors nor one of the subjects of their investigation, the late Alicia Betterton, had been mentioned in the dinner table conversation. Instead, the meal was surprisingly convivial. We had been seven at the table: our host Tom and his girlfriend, Margo Silvestry; Tom's stepchildren, Stephen and Madeline; his British publisher, Godfrey Reynolds; Reynolds's wife, Daisy; and me. Adam apparently had been left off the guest list or perhaps had declined the invitation. I heard his voice in the kitchen once or twice talking to the cook, Norlene, but he never made an appearance in the dining room, which I found odd, given that he'd joined the family for meals before.

The judge, apparently buoyed by the contemplation of his potential nomination, was a congenial host, telling stories about his early days on the bench when he was first "learning the ropes," as he put it, and entertaining us with tales of his New Jersey boyhood and his hunt for the Jersey Devil in the state's Pine Barrens.

"Is the Jersey Devil an animal?" Margo had asked.

"More like a legend," the judge had replied. "You all know about the abominable snowman, or yeti." He pointed at Godfrey. "And I'm sure you've heard of the Loch Ness monster."

"Thought I saw it myself once," Godfrey quipped.

"Maybe you did," the judge said. "They didn't discover the mountain gorilla until 1901 or 1902. And it was less than a dozen years ago that Japanese fishermen took a picture of the giant squid."

"What's that got to do with the Jersey Devil?" Stephen asked, a slight smile on his face. It was obviously a familiar story to him, but he played along.

"Just that you can never be certain if a legend is false. There are hundreds of thousands of acres in the Pine Barrens, big enough to hide a rare specimen, particularly one that's shy. If there are creatures left to be discovered, one of them may just be my Jersey Devil."

"Have to admit I've never heard of it," Godfrey said.

"Me neither," added Margo. "What's it supposed to look like?"

Tom warmed to his tale. "It was kind of a cross between a horse and a pterodactyl. He was first spotted in the early seventeen hundreds, colonial days. A flying biped with hooves and a long tail is how it was described."

"Sounds horrible," Daisy said.

"Well, he was no great beauty in any of the pictures I've seen," the judge said.

"You've actually seen a picture of it?" Godfrey asked.

"Not a photograph, no. But over the centuries there have been lots of sketches, none of them exactly the same. Stephen used to make wonderful drawings of it when he was a boy." He looked over to his stepson. "Remember?"

"I remember."

"They say Napoleon's brother Joseph Bonaparte saw one when he was hunting in Bordentown," Tom continued. "That was in the eighteen hundreds. And even up to the early twentieth century, reports of strange footprints or odd sounds were attributed to the devil. I never did see one in person, but I had a lot of fun looking for it." He pointed his fork at Madeline and Stephen. "That would have made some trophy for my wall at home, eh, kids?"

"You've got plenty of those already," Madeline told him. "Anyway, you get to see the Devils all the time."

"Where?" Margo asked, looking at her.

Madeline smirked. "At the Meadowlands, of course. They named the hockey team after the Jersey Devil. The New Jersey Devils. You've heard of them, right?"

"Oh. I thought you were serious for a change," Margo said. Her face was flushed.

Stephen winked at his sister and smothered a smile. His right hand was no longer bandaged, but when he gestured, the angry red mark on his palm was visible. He noticed me looking at it and tucked his hand in his lap.

"When do you think you might hear about the nomination?" I asked, raising the topic of Tom's hopes for a seat on the Court of Appeals.

"Don't know. Don't know," Tom said, drawing in a breath between his teeth. "These things are so delicate; the least little thing can derail it."

Like the murder of your niece, I thought but didn't say, although her death was certainly not "the least little thing."

"A fortuitously placed leak in the press could do wonders for your book," Godfrey said, his eyes alight. "Might push it onto the bestseller list. Wouldn't that be a pip? I'd have to up the press run, then. We haven't printed that many volumes yet."

"No. No," Tom said, a worried look passing over his face. "Can't take that chance." Then he seemed to change his mind. "If it happens, well, I'm not responsible. But it can't come from anyone I know."

"There are ways to clue in the press without revealing the source," Godfrey said. "Why don't you let me run it by my public relations fellows in London and New York, see what they think. You want your name out there, don't you? Nothing like a book to boost your Q score."

"What's a Q score?" Margo said.

"It's a measure of familiarity and approval," I said, "but it's more commonly used to rate television shows and celebrities."

"Yes. And while Tom is neither a sports personality nor an actor, he is an author," Godfrey said. "Authors are celebrities. Politicians who've written a book always want to know their Q scores. Want to be a celebrity, Tom?"

"My reputation as a jurist is the most important element influencing those in power," Tom said, then added, "But it might be fun to be a celebrity."

"That would mean more paparazzi," Stephen said, cocking his head toward the front of the house. "We can do without that."

"God, yes!"

Tom's good mood lasted until dessert. When Norlene brought out her cassava pie, the air seemed to go out of him. Perhaps it was one of Alicia's favorites. No one else noticed, or at least they pretended not to. Godfrey held forth on how the "dreadful London weather" actually benefited his business. "Our distributor cheers when it rains," he said. "Means stronger book sales. Well, that's something, at least."

Daisy began to speak about the wonderful artist from whom she and Godfrey had purchased a painting, then stopped abruptly. My hunch is that she felt she shouldn't talk about another artist with Stephen sitting at the table and was hesitant to praise Stephen's work without mentioning the portrait of Alicia. She covered the awkward moment by choking on her coffee, at which her husband pounded on her back, and the dinner broke up soon afterward.

The next morning, with directions to Agnes's home in my pocket, I walked along the beach to the base of the stairs leading to Daniel and Lillian Jamison's house. Without stopping to reexamine the scene of the crime, I climbed up their steps to the top and walked across their expansive yard and the one next door. I saw no one and exited on Tucker's Town Road a quarter mile down from the Betterton property and its complement of press and security. From there it was less than a mile to the house of Agnes Chudleigh-Stubbs. I'd called ahead, of course, and she'd said she'd be delighted if I would stop by. She would be home all morning—all afternoon, too, in fact.

The day was warm, but not hot, and I relished the solitary walk. A few motorbikers rode past me, their owners giving me a friendly toot and a wave, but otherwise I was alone. Most of the homes I passed were hidden behind limestone walls, some with cascading flowers hanging over them. At one vine bearing red flowers, I spotted a ruby-throated hummingbird, the same kind that frequents the bird feeder at my neighbor's house back in Maine. Tina Treyz has put out homemade hummingbird nectar every year for as long as she's lived in Cabot Cove, and she's been rewarded by return visitors each spring. She swears they're the same birds she saw the year before, although I have no idea how she can tell.

Agnes's house was down a narrow lane off the main road, across the way from a pair of mini-mansions that might have been designed by the same architect, and landscaped by the same designer. A small car was parked on the grass in front. Her home, a modest two-story aqua rectangle with the classic white-terraced clay roof, was tucked away at the back of a garden behind a pink trumpet tree. The path to the house was lined with scattered flowering plants amid what looked like foot-high grasses with tiny blue flowers, which I later learned are called bermudiana. The wooden front door stood open and I knocked on the trim of the screen door. I could hear voices coming from the rear of the house, but my knuckles would take a beating before anyone would know I was there. Instead, I called out for Agnes.

"Just a minute," came a singsong woman's voice. "There you are. I thought I heard someone calling. We were out back. I'm sorry; the doorbell is broken." A tall woman in a tennis outfit with a white cap and dark sunglasses pulled open the screen door.

"I didn't even see a bell," I said, looking around the doorjamb in case I had missed something.

"No, of course you didn't. It's attached to the door, which is open. How do you do? You must be Jessica Fletcher. Agnes was telling me about you. We didn't meet the other night. I'm Claudia Betterton."

"How do you do," I replied.

She crunched my outstretched hand, turned around and trotted down a long hall to a screened porch in the back without waiting to see if I followed.

"Agnes, your guest is here," she sang out.

"Jessica, how good of you to come. I love company. Claudia has made some iced tea. Would you like a glass?"

"I would love one," I said.

"Claudia, would you be a dear?"

"Of course."

Agnes, who sat in an upholstered wing chair, waved me into a rattan settee with a flowered cushion, while Claudia poured me a drink from a pitcher on a white-painted sideboard. The porch was screened on three sides under a green plastic corrugated roof that protected it from the weather. The brick flooring continued under the screens to an outside patio, a short distance from a stone wall that marked the end of the property. The garden was all in front of the house.

"Here you go," Claudia said, handing me a glass and a paper napkin. "So how are things in the Betterton household, aside from the obvious? Margo having fun playing house?"

"Oh, you are bad, Claudia," Agnes said.

Claudia gave out with a bark of laughter. "I can't help it. I can't believe Tom is actually thinking about marrying her. She's dumb as a post."

"Well, some men like to be in charge," Agnes said, winking at me. "He tried a smart one; it didn't work out." She giggled at her own joke.

"He certainly went in the opposite direction from me, didn't he?" Claudia said. She folded her tall frame into an egg-shaped chair that hung from a rafter, and used one long tanned leg and sneakered foot to keep it from swinging. She turned her gaze on me. "Did Adam drop you off?" she asked.

"No. Actually, I walked here."

"You did? You're very brave. Those tourists on their scooters would just as soon knock you down as not. Isn't that right, Agnes? They're not used to driving on the left. My cousin visited from the States and got a doozy of a case of Bermuda road rash when some idiot on a cell phone ran into her bike and she toppled off. Her left arm and leg were scraped raw. You'd better be careful on your way back."

"Thank you for the warning," I said.

"Claudia was just telling me about the beautiful Scotland Yard inspector," Agnes interjected. "Have you met her yet?"

"I haven't," I replied, "but I expect to later this afternoon." I turned to Claudia. "Did she ask you what time you left the party?"

"Everyone has asked that. I left at one, and if you don't believe me you can ask the Jamisons. I gave them a lift home."

"But they live next door," I said. "Why would they need a ride?"

"Dan was so drunk, he could hardly stand. Lil begged me to drive them, promising that she would pay for the cleaning if he got sick in the car. Fortunately, he waited until he got out."

"Did you go home right away after that?"

"You're sounding like the Scotland Yard inspector."

"Sorry. I do ask a lot of questions," I said. "Must be the mystery writer in me. Did she ask you about the knives?"

Claudia laughed. "You mean *my* knives, the ones given to *me* as a gift, the ones I took from *my own* kitchen?"

"I thought the house was Tom's," I said.

She got a sour look on her face. "I redid that kitchen myself. You should have seen what a disaster it was before. Wasn't it, Agnes?"

"Yes, dear, and you tried very hard to keep it."

"I left some items there, fully expecting to be able to retrieve them whenever I wanted, but Tom has made it difficult. Well, no one is going to tell me I can't take what's mine."

"Did Scotland Yard confiscate them?" Agnes asked.

"No. The constables did. They said I could get them back at the end of the case, but who knows how long that will be."

"I guess the timing was unfortunate," I said.

She snorted. "You mean Alicia? I would never bother to slit her throat, the little witch. She wasn't worth my time. I knew what to do with her."

"Claudia, you should be careful what you say," Agnes said.

"Why? I never was before. I don't see starting now."

"I understand you sent Alicia off to boarding school," I said.

Claudia's smile reappeared. "I did. And everyone in that

house was really grateful. But did I get a thank you from anyone? I did not. All I got were complaints."

"From Tom?" I asked.

She shook her head. "From Stephen, who still doesn't know what to do with his life. And his sister, Madeline, who could win the laziest-girl-in-the-world contest if she got off her butt to enter."

"Is there such a thing, Claudia?" Agnes asked.

"No, hon, it was just a figure of speech."

"I liked it, though. I'll have to remember that." Agnes repeated softly, "laziest-girl-in-the-world contest." She chuckled.

I imagined the old woman telling the story to others, making the phrase her own.

Claudia raised her brows at Agnes, then looked at me. "Anyway, Tom's method of disciplining his children is to give them whatever they want. He calls it 'the path of least resistance.' I call it spoiling them. Look how they ended up. And the worst of them was Alicia."

"She wasn't that bad," Agnes put in.

"You only say that because your nephew Charles had a thing for her. Poor deluded boy. I'm telling you, she would have made him miserable. He could never have afforded her, for one thing."

"Probably not," Agnes said.

"A couple of months ago," Claudia continued, apparently happy to have an audience for her complaints, "Tom told me that Alicia asked him to buy her an apartment in New York City. She wanted to be an independent woman. Can you believe it? How is she independent if Tom is still paying her way? I told him he was a fool if he wasted his money that way. I heard he finally turned her down. At least he did one thing right."

She must have read my expression because she quickly added, "Of course, I'm sorry that she's dead. No one would wish that on their worst enemy. But it didn't surprise me. She was always asking for trouble. And this time she got it and couldn't get away from it."

Claudia, despite her disclaimer, seemed pleased that Alicia had been murdered. I'd never encountered someone so self-satisfied over the death of another person.

"Did you express these feelings to the police?" I asked.

"I'm not that stupid. But you're not the police, are you?"

I smiled. "No, I'm not."

"Are my feelings about Alicia safe with you, Agnes?"

"I've already been interviewed and I don't think they're coming back. Your secret is safe with me, although it's hardly a secret, Claudia. Everyone knew you didn't like Alicia."

I saw an opportunity and took it. "By any chance, do you know where Alicia was the last couple of years?"

Claudia shrugged. "Why do you ask?"

"Tom mentioned that she lived at home with him except when she was away at boarding school, and again the last few years. I wondered where she might have been. Did she go away to college?"

"That one? No way!" She shot a glance at Agnes and I got the feeling she was reluctant to discuss Alicia's whereabouts with our hostess. Agnes's nephew Charles had said his aunt lived for gossip. Perhaps Claudia wasn't eager to have Agnes know something more that might reflect poorly on Tom's family, or more important, on her.

Claudia consulted her watch, climbed out of her chair, and stretched. "I have to leave," she said. "I'm having lunch at the tennis club in half an hour."

"Thank you so much for visiting," Agnes said. She pressed a button on a remote control, and a motor started to hum.

"No need to get up," Claudia said.

"Nonsense! I can't stay glued to my seat all day. Do me good to walk you out."

The seat of Agnes's chair slowly rose and tilted on an angle until her feet touched the floor. She pushed off the arms and stood straight for a moment, letting her body adjust to the new position.

I stood as well. "It was nice to meet you," I said to Claudia, but I didn't offer my hand again; I didn't want my fingers crushed in her grip.

"I'll have to invite you over," Claudia said, but I was sure that she didn't mean it.

Agnes took her arm and they walked down the hall to the front door. I wondered if I should follow to help Agnes back to her chair, but she didn't ask, and I didn't want to offend her by making the suggestion. From what I gathered, she lived in the house alone except when Charles visited, and was able to manage on her own.

Agnes was gone for a while, and just when I began to be concerned she returned with a plateful of cookies. "Made these myself yesterday," she said. "Lost the recipe a while back, but I think I remembered it well enough. Been baking them for sixty or seventy years." She put the plate on a table between us and backed up to her chair.

"Nifty device, isn't it?" she said, holding up the remote. "It's a power lift seat." She leaned into the seat cushion, pressed a button, and the seat lowered back into the chair. "It's made a big difference in my life."

I took a cookie and offered the plate to Agnes. "They're delicious," I said.

She nodded. "Nice to know the brain still functions." She looked at me. "So, Jessica, do you think Claudia killed Tom's niece?"

Chapter Eleven

Adam let me off at police headquarters with a promise to pick me up when my meeting was finished. I gave the duty officer my name, showed my ID, and told him I had an appointment with the inspectors from Scotland Yard.

"What is it in reference to?" he asked.

I lowered my voice and said, "It's in reference to the murder of Miss Alicia Betterton." I evidently hadn't lowered it enough because a man who'd been leaning against a nearby wall strolled over while I waited to be admitted.

"Larry Terhaar, Associated Press," he said, holding up his media pass. "May I ask you a few questions, Mrs. Fletcher?"

"I'd rather you didn't," I replied. "I really have nothing to say."

"You found one of the bodies. That's hardly nothing."

I opened my bag and pulled out my cell phone, pretending I had a call. "Excuse me," I said as I put the phone to my ear and turned my back to him. "Hello?"

"This is a very important case, Mrs. Fletcher," he said, pulling on my arm. "The public wants to know what's going on."

"Hold on a moment," I said into the phone. I turned to the reporter. "I'll be happy to share anything I have to contribute with the authorities, not the press. Please excuse me. I have to take this call."

He chased around to confront me. "Your phony phone call won't cut it, Mrs. Fletcher. Don't you think the people have a right to know?" he said in a loud, confrontational voice. "This isn't one of your made-up stories. Real people are dying out there."

"And if I knew who the killer was, I would alert the police immediately," I said in my sternest voice. "But that's not the situation, and I don't care to speculate on so important a case. As you say, the public has a right to know, to know the *facts*, which they can get from their police department and their elected officials, not from someone who makes up stories, as you so nicely put it."

I saw a door open out of the corner of my eye and recognized Inspector Veronica Macdonald standing in the doorway. I snapped my phone closed, dropped it in my bag, and waved at her. "You'll have to excuse me," I said to Terhaar as I slipped past the inspector into the vestibule.

"Were you doing an interview?" she asked without introduction.

"I was trying *not* to do an interview," I replied, straightening up and trying to put my anger behind me. "I'm Jessica Fletcher. You are Inspector Macdonald, I believe."

She gave me a big smile and put out her hand. "It's a pleasure to meet you, Mrs. Fletcher. I've heard so much about you from George. He has only wonderful things to say."

"That's kind of him," I said, noting that she called George by his first name. "I think a great deal of him as well."

Her smile was smaller this time as she said, "Please follow me" and led me down a corridor.

Veronica Macdonald was dressed in a gray pin-striped jacket and matching skirt tailored to fit her curves, making the suit look more like a designer outfit than off-the-rack business attire. I estimated her to be in her late thirties, early forties at most. Her dark brown hair curved to the nape of her neck and hung slightly longer in front, curling toward her jaw. She wore dark eye makeup, which made her light blue eyes arresting, but the full lips of her mouth were without lipstick. She reminded me of a movie star, but I couldn't put a name to the image.

We entered a room at the end of the hall that was occupied by a man typing on a notebook computer. He popped up when we came through the door and extended his hands, taking one of mine in both of his.

"John Gilliam, Mrs. Fletcher. Please call me Jack. Thanks so much for stopping in. It's so good of you to give us your time."

He looked exactly like the photo on his business card: pale face, sandy hair, nondescript features, but when he smiled his whole face lit up and he immediately secured my confidence.

Veronica Macdonald held out a chair for me. "Freddie Moore is out at a meeting, but Jack and I would like to ask you a few questions."

"I hope I can be helpful," I said.

She came around the table and seated herself next to Gilliam so that they both faced me.

"Can you give us a recap of your experience in finding the deceased, Alicia Betterton?" Inspector Macdonald said. "We're aware that you've already told the Bermuda police what you know, and George has briefed us on your phone conversation with him, but it would be helpful for us to hear it in your own words. Do you object to our recording you?"

"No, not at all."

"We'd like you to start with your reason for being in Bermuda and how it came to be that you were at the home of the deceased," she said.

Gilliam tapped into his computer.

"Is your recorder in the computer?" I asked him.

"Yes, mum, both the video and audio. We're ready whenever you are." He gave me a reassuring smile.

I cleared my throat and began to speak, reviewing the whole event once more, how I had met Tom, his invitation to stay at his Bermuda property, and my evening at the party mingling with his family, friends, and acquaintances. I tried to remember everything I'd told George so that I could share it with them as well. I didn't want them to think that I was holding anything back.

"Chief Inspector Sutherland said that you'd told him the family had difficulties with the deceased."

This time she'd used George's formal title. Was it for the benefit of her colleague, or because we were being recorded?

"Do you suspect one of them might have murdered her?"

Macdonald added, tilting her head so that her dark hair fell on her cheek.

I wondered whether her beauty was a help or a hindrance when questioning people. I suppose it depended upon whether it was a man or a woman being interviewed. Some chauvinistic men would believe her good looks indicated that she wasn't intelligent. We've all met those types. Other more enlightened men would want to please her and might say things that weren't in their own best interests simply to gain her approval. I found it difficult not to look at her and admire her beauty. I also thought of George Sutherland and wondered what effect she had upon him.

I sighed. "I try not to suspect anyone until I have all the facts in front of me," I said. "It would be terrible to accuse a person and find out later that you'd been wrong. I'd rather say that I observed the behavior of those who were familiar with Alicia and tried to gauge her relationships with them. Sometimes what appears to be important at first turns out not to be relevant at all."

Gilliam nodded and looked up from his machine. "We're aware that you not only write bestselling murder mysteries, Mrs. Fletcher, but that you've also been . . . Maybe the best way to put it is that you've been involved in your share of real murders."

I couldn't help but laugh. "I wish you'd amend that," I said. "I've unfortunately been involved with real murder *cases.*"

Gilliam nodded and matched my laugh. "And you've helped to solve them," he said. "What I'm getting at is that in your experience as both a writer and someone who has been a keen observer of *real* murder, would you speculate whether Ms. Betterton's killer was a man or a woman?"

"Oh, my," I said. "Let me see. I'm hardly an expert. There are always exceptions, of course, but I have read that women are less likely to kill someone with a knife than a man. Men are generally more violent than women. A woman's preferred weapon of choice would be a gun, or she might poison her victim, since those methods of murder could be less messy and would put her somewhat at a remove from the unfortunate person. Those methods are less personal, if you can see it that way. That's presuming premeditated murder."

"And do you think Ms. Betterton's murder was premeditated?" Gilliam asked.

"I find it difficult to believe the killer was simply waiting on the beach with a knife for some lucky victim to show up," I said, my answer eliciting a smile from him. "Either Alicia meant to meet the person who turned out to be her killer on the beach, or the person who killed her followed her from the party and surprised her on the beach. People don't usually carry a knife if they don't intend to use it."

Gilliam shot a glance at Macdonald and raised his brows. I couldn't read what his expression meant.

"I'd like to ask you a question, if you don't mind," I said.

"Please do," said Macdonald.

"I understand you told Tom Betterton that you didn't think Alicia's death was linked to the serial killings here in Bermuda," I said. "May I ask why?"

Gilliam cleared his throat. "Miss Betterton does not fit the profile of the other victims."

"That's exactly what I told Chief Inspector Sutherland," I said. "She wasn't a prostitute, nor was she from a poor family. I read in the local newspaper that all three of the other victims were recent immigrants. Alicia was a visitor, not an immigrant. She was murdered on the beach, not in an alley in Hamilton. Aside from her neck, the rest of her body was untouched. It seems to me that her death doesn't bear any of the other hallmarks of the serial killer."

"You're right, of course," Gilliam said.

"I assume that those are the same reasons that you've concluded that she was not murdered by the island's Jack the Ripper killer?" I looked from Gilliam to Macdonald.

"There was one other reason," Gilliam said. He glanced at Macdonald and she gave him a slight nod. "Miss Betterton's throat was slashed, it's true, but that's not what killed her. At least it doesn't appear that way."

"I don't understand," I said. "If she didn't bleed to death from the cut, how did she die?"

"She was strangled," Macdonald said flatly.

"Really?" I sat back in my chair. "That certainly changes the picture, doesn't it?"

"It's our belief that whoever killed her tried to make it look as though it was the work of the serial killer here on Bermuda," she said. "The autopsy has proved otherwise."

"Is the autopsy conclusive?" I asked.

"Clear-cut and conclusive," she replied.

"Interesting, isn't it, how we jump to conclusions?" I said. "I'm always cautioning people about that. And here it never occurred to me that she hadn't died because of the knife wound to her neck. Of course, it was too dark for me to see clearly. I saw the cut on her throat and never thought for a moment that it might have been something else."

"We all made the same assumption," Gilliam said. He consulted a typed report on the desk. "The medical finding showed petechial hemorrhages in her eyes, and the hyoid bone in her neck had been broken. No question about it, Mrs. Fletcher."

I nodded. "Clear signs of strangulation."

"Oh, and I should mention that the knife cut was below the bone," he added.

I'd attended a few lectures on forensics, and was once allowed to be present at an autopsy conducted by a friend of mine in New York City. The island's forensic authorities, perhaps with the aid of Scotland Yard's forensic specialist Inspector Veronica Macdonald, had done a good and thorough job.

"So it's not the Jack the Ripper killer after all," I said. "I didn't think it was, but I'm relieved to hear that my hunch was correct."

"Now the question is: Who killed her?" Macdonald said.

"Will Scotland Yard stay on the case?" I asked.

"Frankly, it won't be a priority for us," she replied. "The Bermuda police are perfectly capable of investigating a homicide. They've done it before." She looked at her watch, and then at Gilliam. "He was supposed to be here by now." She turned to me. "Freddie is our Jack the Ripper expert," she said. "He had a meeting with the citizen group that has offered a reward for information about the killer, but he said that he wanted to meet you."

"I can wait, if you don't think he'll be very long."

"That's very nice of you, Mrs. Fletcher," Gilliam said, tapping on his computer and closing the top. "May we get you something to drink? Tea? Or water?"

"No, thank you," I said.

Gilliam looked over my shoulder and broke out in a big grin. "Ah, here he is now. Mrs. Fletcher, please meet Freddie Moore, our Jack the Ripper expert."

I turned in my seat with a smile that quickly faded. "Good heavens," I said.

It was the redheaded man.

Chapter Twelve

Freddie Moore pumped my hand and gushed about meeting me.

"It's a genuine honor, Mrs. Fletcher. I've been eager to make your acquaintance ever since the chief inspector told us you were here. What a bit of luck." He looked gleefully to his colleagues for confirmation. "I'd love to have a chance to shoot questions at you. May I take you for tea? Or coffee? You Yanks prefer coffee, don't you? I was so worried I'd miss you, I rushed out of my meeting. I'm afraid I left a very poor impression on the heads of the citizens' committee. Didn't assuage their worries very much. Will have to go back and apologize."

While he babbled on, I tried to school my shocked expression. He was in the same three-piece brown tweed suit I'd seen him wear at the airport. It must have been terribly uncomfortable in Bermuda's warm weather. His red hair, parted on the side, was damp. He mopped his brow with a handkerchief and then ran it across his mustache before pocketing the cloth.

Thank goodness I'd never mentioned my fear of the nighttime intruder or described him to George or to Inspectors Macdonald and Gilliam. I would have been red-faced.

Gilliam seemed amused at Moore's enthusiasm, but Macdonald appeared impatient to have this little scene end.

"It would be my pleasure to join you sometime for tea," I said to Moore. "I like tea every bit as well as coffee, probably more."

"Perfect! I have discovered a delightful tearoom in Hamilton. Can you come now? Tea begins at two thirty."

"Right now? Well, I suppose I could. I need to let Judge Betterton's personal assistant know. He was going to pick me up here"—I looked at my watch—"in five minutes."

"Let's go find him and give him his freedom. I have a car. I can drop you off at the judge's estate later. We have so much to discuss."

"Mrs. Fletcher, you've been very helpful," Gilliam said, shaking my hand. "Thank you for your time and all your observations. Please keep us informed if you learn anything new that bears on the Betterton case. Don't trust Freddie here to pass along the word. He stuffs his brain so full of information that he tends to forget to share."

"I'll make certain to keep you all in the loop," I said, waving at Macdonald, who conjured up a bright smile for my departure.

Adam was waiting outside and said he was relieved to have one less obligation. He had to pick up some supplies for the judge's boat at the Ocean Locker before going home.

Freddie, as he insisted I call him, led me to a tiny yellow Smart Car parked at the curb and helped me climb inside.

"How did you get a car?" I asked. "I thought only residents were permitted to drive a car on Bermuda."

"Perks of the office," he said. "We're supposed to divide its use amongst the three of us, but most of Macdonald's and Gilliam's work has been in headquarters, while mine has kept me roaming the island. I have first claim, although I have been known to take the bus or ferry on occasion."

Freddie turned the air conditioner on full blast and drove down the hill and into town, easily maneuvering the car around moped, scooter, and bicycle riders who failed to give way, as well as a horse and carriage carrying tourists, and other, larger vehicles. Since Bermudians drive on the left side of the road, as the British do, he hadn't had to make any adjustment to his driving style to accommodate his temporary assignment.

Bermuda's pastel buildings on Front Street were joined by a few more vividly hued exteriors, red and burnt sienna, to complement the yellow, pink, and aqua more commonly seen. Many of the shops had two stories and railed balconies or arcades overlooking the traffic, and the dockyards and harbor across the street. Multiple two-wheeled vehicles were lined up perpendicularly along the curb, adding their own colorful rainbow to the picture of downtown Hamilton.

Just outside town, Freddie pulled into the entrance of the Fairmont Hamilton Princess and parked his car in front of the hotel, flipping down the sun visor to display his police identification. "Handy placard to have," he told me as we got out, "rather like a disabled permit. Lets you park wherever you like."

He escorted me inside and through the marble lobby to the Heritage Court, a brightly lit restaurant with a coffered ceiling and polished wooden floor. A long bar took up a good portion of one side of the room and a skylighted corridor with huge windows overlooking a garden ran along the other. In between were tables set for tea, and small groupings of chairs and sofas arranged on oriental carpets, bordered by large square columns in Wedgwood blue with white trim. We took two green leather armchairs next to a window overlooking the garden and its bronze statue of a maiden dipping her toe in a stream. A cheerful waitress took our order and we settled in to get to know each other.

"I have a bone to pick with you," I said.

"Beg pardon? What a quaint Yank expression. Mind if I write it down?" He took a pad and pencil from his breast pocket and jotted a note to himself, then looked up and said, "What did I do?"

"You scared the daylights out of me the other night," I said, "and I've been looking for you, intending to grab you by the lapels and give you a good dressing down."

"Blimey! Thought I was meeting you for the first time, although you do look familiar. I chalked it up to the pic in the paper," he said.

"We've never officially met before, although I was behind you in the customs line at the airport."

He snapped his fingers. "That's it! You retrieved my book. Always been a bit of a clumsy bloke."

I smiled.

"But how did I brass you off?" he asked.

"You used the swing on the porch of my cottage to take a break in the middle of the night, and then you ran off when you heard footsteps."

He looked horrified. "So, so sorry, madam. I . . . I . . . I thought the cabin was empty. Even contemplated taking a peek round the place."

"If you had, you might have gotten hit over the head with a frying pan."

He sat back, eyes wide. "Fortunately, I was too knackered to be curious. You're a dangerous woman, I can see."

I laughed. "I suppose I am when I'm feeling threatened."

"Please accept my sincerest apologies for giving you a fright. Never my intention. I was just looking for a place to rest."

"But what were you doing there so late, and what on earth is in that suitcase that you carry around?"

"My files. My electronics. Don't trust anyone else with 'em. They're in the boot of the car. I can show you when we leave."

I cocked my head at him. He'd only answered one of my questions. "And what were you doing roaming around in the middle of the night?"

He leaned forward and lowered his voice. "I like to revisit the scene of the crime at the actual time it took place. Gives you a completely different vision. The moon was in a different phase and the tide was slightly off as well, but I crept around and found a place where the murderer may have hidden in anticipation of her arrival."

"You think that the murder was planned rather than spontaneous?"

He thought about my question for a moment. "It may also have been where the murderer hid following the crime," he said. "Maybe he heard you and chose to keep out of sight until you left."

I shivered to think the killer might have been so close—perhaps even watching me when I came upon Alicia's body. I hadn't considered it at the time. I was much more concerned that the tide would pull her body out to sea, and I didn't want to disturb the scene by moving her to higher ground or touching her in any way. It was obvious that she was dead. The most important step to take at that point was to alert the police, which I'd been in a hurry to do.

"If, as you say, the killer could have been hiding in the vicinity when I found her, then that pinpoints the time of the murder, doesn't it?" I said.

"Possibly. All this is merely speculation on my part," he said, "but I did see some disturbance in the sand behind a rock, and no footprints leading there from the land side. Therefore, he had to have approached his hiding spot from the water side of the rock, and the tide could have washed those prints away."

"If that's the case, he probably took the opportunity to escape when I ran back to the cottage."

"Yes, it's doubtful he would have risked following you down the beach. Too dangerous if you turned around and saw him. More likely, once you were out of sight, he fled up the stairs to the property above. I'm using the masculine pronoun to describe the killer, you understand, but it could have been a woman."

"What makes you say that?"

"No evidence to the contrary at the moment. And we have yet to identify the owner of the shoes the constables found at the top of the flight of stairs. Apparently the woman of the house up there doesn't claim them, and the family of the victim was unable to identify them as hers. Ronnie—uh, that's Macdonald—was going to run some tests to see whether the soles held on to anything helpful, such as sand, grass, seeds, etcetera."

"If they were the killer's shoes, and she fled up the stairs, wouldn't she have picked them up when she got to the top?"

"Panic does not always lead to logic," he said. "Despite the attempt to put the blame on the serial killer, I do not believe that this perpetrator is experienced, nor a professional."

"Why would you say that?"

"He or she used a blunt knife."

"Blunt? Do you mean dull?"

"Dull means boring," he said with a twinkle in his eye. "I don't know that I would apply that to a knife. The murder weapon wasn't *sharp*."

I laughed. "I thought we were speaking the same language, but every now and then, I wonder."

"Perhaps we should invest in a British English to American English dictionary."

"It would be a help."

"Please stop me if there's anything I say that's not clear," he said.

"All right. Getting back to the Jack the Ripper killer's knife, is it always sharp?"

"Always. Or, I should say, it has been three times. And unlike the cases of the other victims, the blade used on Miss Betterton was not serrated—possibly a kitchen knife or a hunting knife, and perhaps one that was not used very often. They've found a bit of rust in the wound."

"Rust. Well, we're on an island surrounded by water," I said. "If a blade isn't water resistant, I imagine it could rust pretty quickly. The one I use for fishing does."

He shrugged.

"Did you have a chance to see all the Bettertons' household knives that the constables removed following the murder?" I asked.

"Wasn't one of them," he replied, waving his hand in front of his face. "The constables were working on the theory that the killer may have washed off the knife and replaced it in the cupboard."

"And you don't think so?"

"My hypothesis has the slayer flinging the murder weapon into the surf, probably not right in front of the scene itself. It may turn up, but by the time it does, it will likely be scoured of all trace evidence. Between the salt and the sand, the ocean can be a very efficient cleaner."

"Would it clean off fingerprints, too?"

"Hard to know. Plus, the killer may have worn gloves. I would have liked to have found the weapon, but it's a moot point now. It doesn't bear on my duties here. I'm looking for a different person."

"The Jack the Ripper killer," I said.

"Yes."

The waitress returned, temporarily interrupting our conversation. She took china cups and saucers from her silver tray and set them down on the small table in front of us, along with a pot of steaming tea. "Would you like me to pour?" she asked.

"I'll pour," Freddie replied.

The waitress left but was back moments later with a multitiered serving piece holding an assortment of finger sandwiches and, under a silver dome, two scones with Devonshire clotted cream. I remembered from my visits to London that afternoon tea is a meal in itself, and a wonderful one at that. Freddie poured the tea and we helped ourselves from the selection.

Despite the fact that the topic of conversation would discourage the appetite of most, we ate heartily. The first sandwich I tried was ham and cantaloupe, an unusual and refreshing combination, but my favorite was minted cucumber and goat cheese on a tiny onion roll.

Freddie concentrated on the plate in front of him, every now and then raising his head to roll his eyes and nodding to show how much he relished the food. I got the impression that considering his odd attire and distinctly special interests, here was a man who threw himself into whatever activity was at hand, which at this moment was enjoying the refreshments that were part of afternoon tea at the Fairmont Hamilton Princess.

Apparently he also threw himself into the role of Jack the Ripper expert, right down to dressing the part of a gentleman who lived in the nineteenth century. Still, he was not above using twenty-first-century technology as an aid, though he stored whatever it was in an ancient valise. I wondered what had inspired this passion, and proceeded to ask.

"Interest, mainly. Anyone can become an expert on anything if they stick to it and do all the necessary research. I did have one advantage, though. My father was a Ripper follower, had a whole library on the subject. Even named me after the chief inspector on the case, Frederick Abberline. Used to read to me about the investigation when I was a lad."

"That's certainly unusual."

"I guess it was fated that I'd become a policeman and work in the CID. That's the criminal investigation department."

"I know that London's Jack the Ripper was never found, but did the inspector you're named for have a likely suspect?"

"He did. Abberline was certain Jack the Ripper was actually George Chapman, the name taken by a Polish immigrant who had been apprenticed to a surgeon in his native land."

"Why him?"

"Well, for one thing, the early Ripper murders were assumed to have been perpetrated by an expert surgeon. Chapman had the requisite training. Perhaps more compelling, the murders coincide with Chapman's arrival in London and ceased when he emigrated to America, where oddly enough, a similar murder occurred at about that time."

"I didn't know that!"

"Further, Chapman was a true misogynist, having multiple wives and lovers, all of whom he abused terribly, perhaps revealing a motive. And he had opportunity; he worked as a barber in London at the time of the killings, in Whitechapel in fact, where the Ripper murders took place."

"And barbers don't use *blunt* blades in their work," I put in.

Freddie smiled. "We'll make a Brit of you yet."

"Do you agree with Abberline?"

"About Chapman? Sadly, I don't. Chapman killed three of his wives and was hanged for his crimes. But he poisoned them all. We don't only know a lot more about forensics these days; we're also more informed about psychology than when Abberline was investigating."

"Ah, so you believe that a man adept at poison wouldn't be likely to change his manner of killing," I said.

"I do, yes, although Abberline did not agree. He argued that Chapman was known to be a serial killer, and that fact was more important than the manner he may have used. He saw no reason why a man with professional knowledge, as Chapman surely had, would not be capable of changing his methods. Plus, since the wives he eliminated were of a different class than the Ripper victims who were prostitutes, Abberline postulated that Chapman may have fancied that they required a different method of dispatch."

"Interesting theory."

"I still cling to the idea that a killer with so specific a manner as the Ripper followed would not be likely to change his technique, so to speak. There were eleven women killed at the time the Ripper was operating, but only five of them— the 'canonical five,' they're called—share all the distinctive features he was known for. I don't want to go into the details. We're about to be served our sweets."

While we'd been speaking, the waitress had cleared our sandwich and scone plates and replaced them with fresh ones. The desserts, a selection of petits fours, came accompanied by sorbet. I chose a tiny pear amandine tart, while Freddie went for the black forest chocolate cup.

He smiled as the waitress poured more tea, waited for her to leave, and then continued. "The murders here are striking in their similarity to the Ripper cases. It's possible the Bermuda three, as I call them, may have been followed to the island by their killer, but I suspect he's home grown."

"How did you come to that conclusion?"

"Several things. All three were found in Hamilton, and the city is covered with CCTV cameras."

"Closed circuit television cameras?"

"Yes. Sorry. The jargon comes too easily."

"If there are surveillance cameras almost everywhere, the killer would have to be intimately familiar with Hamilton to know where he wouldn't be recorded during the murders," I offered.

"Bravo, Mrs. Fletcher! Even your sterling reputation doesn't do you justice. That's exactly my reasoning. And given the high alert the island went on following the second murder, it seems to me the man has to be knowledgeable about Bermuda's daily social and business schedule to have committed the crimes without anyone noticing anything out of the ordinary."

"The original Ripper crimes took place on or near the weekend. Has that been the same here?"

"Within a day or two either side."

"Do you have a theory as to why these women were targeted?"

"I do," he said, leaning forward. "See if you agree. What we know is that the women all originated from the Dominican Republic."

"What's the connection?"

"There's been quite a bit of *romantic* tourism to that country on the part of older Bermudian men. There are even Web sites promoting 'dating vacations,' as they're labeled. For the men, it's enticing to think that a beautiful young Latina admires them. For the young women, marrying these men offers a way for them to escape poverty."

"Are there a lot of marriages?"

"The government is trying to crack down on them, making the newcomers apply for visas. It's a volatile issue. There have been articles in the press and letters to the editors. Yet they continue. The ladies come here on the promise of a good life, but when they arrive, their men find they can't communicate with their new fiancées or wives."

"Who only speak Spanish," I inserted.

He shook his head sadly. "A few women have even been abandoned at the airport. Without any means of support and no way to return home, they turned to what they viewed as their only option."

"But surely the men knew these women didn't speak English when they met them in their homeland," I said.

"They did, but perhaps they were blinded by the idea that an attractive young woman would be willing to marry them and bear their babies. So these sham marriages take place and after that, things go pear-shaped."

"Is that the same as downhill?"

"The very same. And while one can argue they should have known this would happen, people who are desperate to change their lives—and that goes for both the men and the women—will take desperate measures."

"And the three victims, did they follow this pattern?"

"We believe so. We are cooperating with the police in Santo Domingo to trace their backgrounds."

"If they all share this background, the killer must have a reason for why he chose to act now," I said. "What do you think triggered the crimes?"

Instead of answering my question, Freddie posed one of his own. "This is really Gilliam's specialty; he's the profiler amongst us. But put yourself in the mind of the murderer. What could his motives be?"

I mentally reviewed what I knew from reading the local newspapers and the little I had seen on the Internet. "The women are vulnerable, probably alone, definitely without the support system they would have had at home. That makes them an easy target," I said, thinking aloud.

"Yes. And they're on the lowest rung of society. They're street walkers, not upstanding citizens."

"The killer could be attacking them on moral grounds, trying to eliminate an element he sees as corrupt. He's angry—"

"Anger often plays a part in these scenarios." A small smile played on his lips.

"This person may have had homicidal tendencies to begin with," I said, "but circumstances have conspired to focus his anger on these young women. As outcasts, they are easy to dispense with. He rationalizes that no one will miss them."

"He thinks: Who in Bermuda really cares what happens to them? They're outsiders. Immigration is a hot topic in all countries that attract foreigners. Bermuda is no exception."

"I think I see your theory," I said.

"Go ahead."

"He's furious that foreigners are coming in. He thinks they're 'ruining' his country. And he not only kills them," I said, "he marks them in a way that serves as a warning to other potential immigrants to stay away from his land."

Freddie sighed. "You have it spot on. I'm impressed. Would you like to accompany me on some of my rounds?"

I smiled. "I'm supposed to be here on vacation," I said.

"I would adore having you work with me, Jessica Fletcher. Together we could solve all the cases in the world."

We both laughed.

"That's very flattering," I said, "but I'm already committed to my other work."

The waitress approached us again. "Are you Inspector Moore?" she asked Freddie.

"Yes."

"There's a telephone call for you at the bar," she said.

Freddie patted his pockets. "Cor! I must have left my bloody mobile in the car. Would you please excuse me?"

"Of course," I said.

He followed the waitress across the room to the bar where a young man handed him a telephone. When he returned to our table, his expression was somber.

"Is something wrong?" I asked.

"Yes," he replied. "They've found another victim."

Chapter Thirteen

A crowd had already formed outside the yellow tape that the constables had strung across the alleyway at the latest crime scene. The victim's body had been covered to shield it from prying eyes, but the edges of the pool of blood in which the corpse lay were visible. The police had put traffic cones around the stain to prevent investigators from treading in the blood.

Gilliam and Macdonald were already there when Freddie and I pushed our way through the throng to gain admittance to the cordoned-off area. The Scotland Yard inspectors were standing apart from the constables, talking to the police commissioner.

Commissioner Leonard Hanover's eyebrows rose when he saw us walk into the crime scene together, but he greeted me cordially. "Mrs. Fletcher, I believe we met at Judge Betterton's the other evening."

I shook his hand.

"I must apologize, Mrs. Fletcher," he said. "You're not seeing the best side of Bermuda at this unfortunate time."

"No need for apologies, Commissioner. Bermuda is always beautiful. I'm sorry you're having to deal with such terrible crimes, and I'm sorry these poor women have been targeted by a madman."

"Who found her?" Freddie asked.

"Some men from Works and Engineering," the commissioner replied. "They were collecting trash and moved those bins." The commissioner pointed to a row of large-wheeled garbage containers. "Her body was behind them."

Freddie addressed Inspector Macdonald. "Was she killed here or was the body dumped here?"

"From the volume of blood, I'd say this is the site of the murder," she replied.

"Same perp," Gilliam added. "Same MO."

"Do we have an ID?" Freddie asked.

"Not yet," the commissioner said. "My boys are tracing her. She's wearing some kind of fancy bracelet. They're checking jewelry merchants. If she purchased it here, we may get a make on her. Superintendent Bird's team is inquiring with its undercover officers to find out if any of the prostitution ring bosses and madams are missing a girl."

"Anything from the Dominican community?"

The commissioner shook his head. "Nothing."

Gilliam turned to me. "It's a very touchy subject, as you might imagine. The Dominicans who work here are sensitive to any talk of prostitutes coming from their country. They're afraid they'll all be tarnished with the same label."

"I'm ready to take a look," Freddie said, his face grim. He

put on latex gloves and walked over to the body, gingerly raising a corner of the tarp high enough so he could see the face of the victim. He circled the corpse, carefully avoiding the puddles of blood, and checked under the covering at intervals before discarding his gloves and returning to us.

I wavered between curiosity about what he was seeing and relief that he hadn't invited me to view the remains. I was grateful that he'd made the decision for me, but I wondered if I should have asked.

"No need," Freddie said, reading my mind. "It would just upset you, and I don't see anything new to change the picture we discussed today." He wandered away to consult with an officer, leaving me standing with his colleagues and the commissioner.

A flash of light from behind the yellow tape alerted us to the fact that the press had arrived and were taking pictures. The commissioner excused himself and walked over to confront the photographer. I heard him say, "We have scheduled a briefing for eighteen hundred hours. We ask that you please allow the authorities to complete their work unimpeded." He signaled to some officers in police vests and tall helmets and they pushed back the crowd.

A reporter called out to me. "Mrs. Fletcher! Mrs. Fletcher!"

I turned at the sound of my name and the photographer's flash went off again.

"It's Larry Terhaar, AP." He beckoned to me. "We met earlier. Can we have a word with you?"

I ignored the appeal, and the constables began lining up the garbage bins in a row across the alley entrance, effectively obscuring the scene so the crowd couldn't see us, and we couldn't see them.

"You have to stay away from those fellows," Veronica Macdonald said, not bothering to lower her voice. "We can't have information about the investigation leaking out to the press."

I looked at her sharply. "Any leaks about your investigation didn't come from me," I said. "It may have been my misfortune to discover Alicia Betterton's body, but I've never spoken about it with the press."

"They certainly seem to know who you are."

"I can't help that my photograph appeared in the newspaper. I didn't invite this reporter's attention, nor have I responded to it. And I don't appreciate being accused of something I haven't done."

"I wasn't accusing you," she said icily. "I'm merely warning you to be careful who you speak with. Any casual remark can be passed along and blown out of proportion."

"Has that happened to you?" I asked, making an effort to tamp down my rising indignation.

She pulled back her shoulders. "It has not. I'm very mindful of keeping mum on my work. I don't share information with anyone outside my team and I don't associate with the islanders beyond the office."

I wondered whether Freddie heard her comments. Clearly she didn't approve of his discussing the Bermuda Ripper cases with me.

"I'm a guest of one of the islanders," I said. "I can hardly avoid communicating with my host and his family when I'm taking advantage of their hospitality. And, yes, we certainly have discussed the terrible tragedy that they're experiencing. But I don't see how I could have revealed anything about the Ripper cases, since I didn't know anything other than what I've read in the local paper."

"Unfortunately, you do now. Please don't take this the wrong way, Mrs. Fletcher, but while you may be a very talented amateur, you are not a police official, and it is imperative we do nothing to jeopardize the safety of others like this girl." She waved her hand at the body that was being wrapped for removal.

"And just how do you think I have jeopardized anyone's safety?" I demanded, no longer concealing my annoyance.

Gilliam, who had been standing by silently, jumped in. "Now, Ronnie. That's going a bit far, don't you think?" he said. "The CI wouldn't approve."

Macdonald eyed him coldly. "George is a professional, as am I. He would not want us to breach security, even in the name of friendship."

Freddie, who'd caught the drift of our conversation—if so gentle a word can be applied to our exchange—hurried over to try to calm the waters. "Mrs. Fletcher is a trusted associate, Ronnie. I have total faith in her discretion, as I know the chief inspector also does. No need for worry. Perhaps I shouldn't have brought her along just now, but what's done is done. I'm going to take Mrs. Fletcher back to her host right away." He aimed a smile at me. "Are you ready?"

"I'll be happy to leave with you," I said. "However, I just want it made clear"—I looked directly at Macdonald—"that 'talented amateur' or not, any involvement I might have with the cases you are investigating came at your request. It was not something I looked for, but a favor Chief Inspector

Sutherland asked of me." I purposely used George's formal title. "And in response to the invitation from you and your colleagues, I came to headquarters today to provide whatever help I could offer."

"And you provided very good information, indeed," Gilliam put in, clearly hoping to draw this discussion to a close. He glared at Macdonald, who seemed taken aback.

"I apologize if I said anything to offend you, Mrs. Fletcher," she said stiffly. "This case has been very difficult, and . . ." She trailed off, her gaze dropping to her shoes.

"Apology accepted," I said, although it was difficult to get the words out. Pulse up, I wrestled with my irritation as Freddie and I walked out the far end of the alley.

"Oh, my dear, dear lady," Freddie said. "I hope she didn't upset you. Ronnie is very competent, but she's also a little blinkered . . . that is, only sees her own point of view. Perhaps a bit guarded as well. She didn't mean any harm."

"She may not mean any harm," I replied, stopping to face him, "but she appeared to me to be fending off what she sees as an intrusion into her territory by an outsider."

"No. No. You're no outsider."

"I just don't want to be put in that position."

We walked in silence to where he had parked his car, and—thank heavens!—didn't encounter any more press people.

Once we were strapped into our seat belts, and on the road to Tucker's Town, I voiced the thoughts that had been churning in my mind. "Freddie, I hope you won't think that I'm stating the obvious or that I'm uncaring, but the Ripper murders are your responsibility, not mine."

"Absolutely they are, Mrs. Fletcher. I didn't mean to burden you."

"You didn't burden me. I enjoyed our talk and I learned a lot more from you than you learned from me."

"It's a great boon to have someone to bounce ideas around with, someone who approaches an investigation in the same way I do."

"You have two colleagues with you from Scotland Yard. Can't you do that with them?"

"They are consummate professionals—no skin off them—but they don't immerse themselves in the case the way I do. And the way I believe you do."

"I'm flattered. If I think of anything that could possibly be useful, I'll happily pass it along to you, but—"

"Yes, your input is always welcome," he put in before I had a chance to finish my thought.

"I don't think we had better work together, even in an informal sense. There's too much risk to you," I said.

And to me, I was thinking but didn't express. I wasn't concerned about a physical risk, but I didn't care to give Veronica Macdonald another opportunity to take me to task.

"I don't see how I hazard anything consulting with you," he said.

"You could endanger your reputation. And clearly it upsets your colleagues."

"My reputation is secure," he said. "Please don't let Ronnie's intemperate remarks keep us from sharing confidences. I know that you would never compromise our investigation, and I value your opinions. And our chief trusts you implicitly. Otherwise, he never would have suggested we take heed of your views."

I hated to say it, but I knew it was what his colleague was thinking. "I'm afraid Inspector Macdonald suspects that our personal friendship—George's and mine—may color his judgment."

"You can't believe that for an instant. Our chief is the soul of professionalism."

I was grateful to hear that, but didn't change my mind. "I have the utmost confidence in Chief Inspector Sutherland," I said. "However, even the smallest appearance of inappropriate special treatment is just as perilous as the reality."

Freddie refused to acknowledge that my input into his investigation exposed him to criticism, but I was not convinced. He argued with me all the way to the Betterton house and, against my better judgment, extracted a promise from me not to make a decision about working with him just yet. He would "ring me up" in a day or two.

I thanked him for the tea, told him how happy I was to make his acquaintance, and said I would give his arguments careful consideration. What I didn't know was that the choice would soon be taken out of my hands, and that my participation in the Ripper cases would have an impact on more than Freddie's good name.

Chapter Fourteen

S tephen Betterton had invited me to see his studio. We'd been the only ones at the dinner table the previous evening because Tom, Margo, Madeline, and Adam had taken the Betterton boat out and were not expected to be home until later in the day. The Reynoldses were eating out. I didn't know if they'd resigned themselves to staying in Tom's cottage or were still hunting for a hotel, but they evidently hadn't informed the cook of their planned absence because Norlene had prepared an elaborate meal including enough food for all. She was obviously disappointed when only Stephen and I showed up and questioned whether we wanted to have dinner in the dining room. We decided that we did, if only not to see her efforts wasted.

Over a delicious dish of baked lobster and spinach, accompanied by a salad of potatoes and Bermuda onions and a sweet biscuit, Stephen and I had found ourselves discussing life and art. I was pleased to have the chance to spend time with him alone. There had only been limited opportunities to get to know various family members and I'd pledged to myself that I'd seek out those moments.

"How's your hand?" I'd asked during dinner.

He glanced down at his palm. "Healing." He made a fist. "Aches a little, but it'll be fine. Hasn't gotten in the way. What about you Mrs. Fletcher? Have you had a chance to see much of the island since you arrived? I know it hasn't been much of a vacation." He gave a soft snort. "Getting involved with the Bettertons is always complicated."

"It certainly isn't the kind of week I'd planned for," I said, "but Daisy Reynolds and I did get to visit St. George's and happened to see your works at Richard Mann's gallery."

"Oh?"

"Actually," I said, "Mrs. Reynolds and I hadn't intended to go to the gallery, but ended up there when we bumped into each other, literally, while we were both escaping the rain."

"You must be among the very few who've seen the show," Stephen said. "What did you think of it, if I dare to ask?"

"I was very impressed with your talent, and was particularly taken with your portraits of Madeline and Alicia. I was sorry there weren't more of them."

"Mann has been after me for a while to give him enough pieces for a show," he said. "It's ironic in a way. He obviously thought that he could capitalize on our family's name and that all the people we know on the island would bring in customers for him."

"That didn't happen?"

"I don't think that all the gossip surrounding a murder is exactly what he had in mind. He changed his plans about taking an ad in the paper to announce the opening."

"Then that was foolish on his part," I said. "Art should be able to stand on its own and shouldn't need to have a family name or long story behind it."

"I agree with you, but Mann is a businessman as well as a gallery owner. No people coming in to see the show, no sales. Not good for him *or* the artist. What about my street scenes, Mrs. Fletcher? What did you think of them?"

"They certainly show your skill," I said, "but you obviously put all your emotion into your portraits."

"It's that obvious, huh? A lot had to do with the model. Madeline is a good one. Alicia was . . ." He shrugged. "I couldn't paint her."

"Yet you did."

"Only that once."

"What made her a poor model?" I asked.

"She was too fidgety, couldn't sit still. Her mind was always hopping from one thing to another, from one scheme to another."

"Scheme?"

"Maybe the wrong word to use. Anyway, she never could hold one expression for any length of time."

"But Madeline can?"

"Maddy's a daydreamer. She's easy to paint. Just give her a mental image to focus on and she can hold a pose for hours."

"Is painting what you want to do with your life?" I asked. Richard Mann had indicated to me that art was Stephen's hobby rather than his vocation, but perhaps Mann had been putting his own interpretation on Stephen's intentions.

"At the moment, it's the only thing I'm good at," Stephen

said with a shrug. "Tom doesn't think that being an artist is a manly profession. He's told me that many times. He'd have preferred that I study law or medicine, something he could brag about."

"But he seems proud of your artistic abilities," I said. "He praised your drawings of the Jersey Devil the other evening."

"To Tom, my artistic skill falls into the category of amusing talent, like juggling, or balancing a ball on my nose," he said. "That's why, even with all the trouble she caused him, Alicia was his favorite."

"Why was that?"

"I don't know. Maybe it's because she argued about everything. She had one of those mouse-trap minds. She'd catch you in an inconsistency and throw it up in your face. Tom wanted her to study law and follow in his footsteps, and she even considered it for a while. But she lost patience with all the memorizing of minutiae it required."

"So what did she end up studying?" I asked.

"She never really focused in on anything."

"What did she do after boarding school?"

He shook his head. "Drifted, I guess you could say. I wouldn't know how else to describe it."

I didn't press him, although I was interested in knowing more. His tone reflected that he was not particularly eager to delve into the question any further. Alicia's whereabouts after boarding school remained a tantalizing mystery. When I'd asked Tom, he had sloughed me off, saying it wasn't important. His ex-wife Claudia had avoided the question, too. Now Stephen would only define that time as "drifting." All their evasion and obfuscation only increased my curiosity as to why no one was willing to talk about that period of Alicia's life. Not that it necessarily had a bearing on her death, but it was one of those loose strings I dearly wanted to tie up.

Before leaving the dinner table and going our separate ways, Stephen told me that he was working on another portrait, this one from an old photograph he'd found. "You're welcome to come tomorrow and take a look," he said, to which I readily agreed. It would give me another opportunity to broach the topic of Alicia and hopefully get a more definitive answer.

The next morning, fortified with a cup of tea and a Bermudian doughnut—Norlene told me that it was called a *malasada*, a confection that had been brought to the island by its Portuguese-speaking population—I climbed the stairs to the second floor of the Betterton house and walked softly to the end of the hall. I hadn't seen anyone else downstairs and presumed they were still sleeping. The door was open and I knocked on the frame before entering what was obviously a bedroom that had been converted into an artist's studio.

Stephen, who was barefoot, wore a pair of ripped and paint-dappled jeans, a similarly paint-adorned T-shirt, and a red bandanna tied over his hair. He stood on a rumpled tarp, anchored in place by his easel while mixing paints on a palette in his left hand.

"Good morning," I said.

"Hi," he replied. "Have a look around. I just want to finish this little piece I'm working on."

"Is that the painting you were telling me about last

night?" I asked, coming around behind so I could see over his shoulder.

"Yeah."

A long narrow table next to the easel held his painting paraphernalia. He had propped a color photograph against a coffee can that held brushes in various sizes, their bristle ends poking up. The photo showed a pretty woman looking over her shoulder at the camera with a bemused expression, as though someone had unexpectedly called to her. The frame that once held the photo was in pieces on the table top. Stephen had transferred the outlines of the subject in the picture to his canvas and was filling in the large background area with color.

"Who is she?" I asked.

"My mother. For some reason, we don't have many shots of her, and those that we do are these tiny prints where you can barely make out her face. She wasn't alive when digital photography was invented, or at any rate popular. This is the only good-sized picture I could find. I would have preferred to paint her when she was a little older, but I guess by then she was usually the one behind the lens taking pictures of the rest of the family."

I gazed around the studio and imagined what it would have looked like if it had been the bedroom it was intended to be. Large windows overlooked the water and sunlight streamed in from a skylight above. Instead of a bed, there were canvases, some finished, some blank, and a few empty frames leaned against the long wall. Charcoal and pencil sketches and pieces of paper that he'd torn from magazines—inspiration perhaps?—were pinned to a standing corkboard where I saw the perfect space for a double dresser. Appropriately, a pair of battered upholstered armchairs faced each other under a window. I would have used that spot for seating, too. A pile of sketchbooks and drawing pads sat on the floor next to one of the chairs.

I wandered around examining Stephen's paintings, and peered into a bathroom with a sink that had once been white, but was now a dingy gray from who knew how many years of paint being washed down its drain.

The bathroom reminded me of questions I wanted to ask him.

"That building Tom wants to put up, the one the Jamisons object to so much. I heard someone say that it's supposed to be a new studio for you."

"That's right. Every time Tom sees that dirty sink, he gets upset. He wants me out of the house, but more than that, he wants this room back. I think it was originally the master suite, but it'll take a bit of work to get it back again to what it was."

"A new sink at the very least," I said.

"That'll make him happy. He offered me either of the cottages, but they don't have good light, not for painting anyway." He smirked. "I have to admit that he took me by surprise when he talked about building me a studio."

"I'd say that Tom supports your painting more than you give him credit for."

"And I'd say that he wants me out from underfoot, but if it results in my own studio, I'll take it. Of course, if the Jamisons have their way, it won't happen."

"I'm told that they object to a new building because it would block their view of the ocean."

"So they say. But even when Tom relocated the proposed site to the other side of the property, away from their house, they still made a fuss."

"Why do you think that's so?"

"There's some bad blood between Tom and Dan Jamison, but I don't know what's behind it. Tom's always trying to patch things up, but the fact is that they don't like him."

"Why would they accept his invitation to a party if they don't like him?"

Stephen put down his palette and wiped his hands on a piece of toweling. "Tom knows all the influential people on the island. I guess they don't want him to get ahead of them, socially that is. Excuse me."

He took his brushes into the bathroom and turned on the faucet.

I sat in one of Stephen's old armchairs, idly picked up a sketchbook, and lifted the cover. The first image surprised me. I turned to the next and then the next, my attention now totally captured. Page after page were drawings of Alicia—Alicia reading in a chair. Alicia peering into the telescope. Alicia smiling. Alicia frowning. Alicia sleeping. I closed the sketchbook and pulled out another one. It was more of the same.

"Did you get any breakfast?" Stephen called out from the bathroom. "Don't answer that. I won't be able to hear you with the water running."

He turned off the tap and reentered the studio. The second sketchbook was still open on my lap.

"Norlene made *malasadas* this morning. Did you get one?" he asked. "She . . ." He stopped when he saw what I was examining.

"I thought you said she was a poor model," I said, looking up from a drawing of Alicia with her head cocked to the side.

Stephen lay his brushes down on the table, took the chair across from mine, and gently pulled the sketchbook out of my lap, turning it so he could see the picture I was referring to. "No," he said as he slowly turned the pages. "*You* said she was a poor model. I just didn't correct you."

"Why not?"

"How can I put it? The truth is that I couldn't *paint* her. As I said, she didn't have the patience to sit still for a painting, but she was a perfect subject for the quick sketch, the kind when I want my impressions to be loose and spontaneous. I used charcoal, sometimes pastel, even crayon. I tried to capture that effervescence, that quixotic nature of hers. I never knew when she would run off." He sighed.

"You were in love with her," I said gently.

His laugh was rueful. "It shows that much?" he asked.

"I'm afraid so," I replied, smiling.

He exhaled, sat back and shook his head. "She was practically my sister," he said, slapping the book closed and tossing it on the pile of other pads. "There was no way we could ever be together in that way."

"But she wasn't a blood relative," I said. "You're Tom's stepson. She was his niece."

"Yeah, I know. I think a lot about whether Alicia would accept the fact that I had certain feelings for her. But even if she did—and I was never sure—Tom would never have stood for it. He'd think it would have made *him* look bad."

"How so?"

"Even though we weren't related by blood, she was still family, and to Tom, having members of the family marry each other wouldn't look *proper*. A proper appearance is everything to him. His reputation stands on it. But it's all just conjecture now. Alicia's gone." His eyes filled with tears, but he willed them away and stood abruptly. "I'm going to take a walk," he said. "I've got to get out of here."

"May I come with you?" I asked.

"Sure. Why not?"

I followed him down a back staircase I hadn't seen before that led to the kitchen. We left the house by a side door and took a different path to the beach than the one I was familiar with. This one was steeper, winding in and out of patches of sage and palmetto, with no gravel to prevent one from slipping on the sandy soil. Stephen sprinted down it like a mountain goat, sure of his footing. I trailed him more slowly.

Could this have been the route Alicia had taken to the beach? If so, it was not surprising that I hadn't awakened to the sound of footsteps on the gravel, or that Godfrey Reynolds hadn't heard anyone passing by his cottage. Of course, he hadn't heard me either when I'd walked down to the beach and run back. It was something to ask him about at another time.

The sandy soil gave way to beach and my feet sank down into the sand, the warm silky grains filling my sneakers. I half-trotted, half-trudged over to where Stephen was throwing shells into the surf like miniature Frisbees, the bottom of his jeans wet to the knees. I picked up a broken scallop shell, flipped it into the water, and watched a rolling wave return it to the sand.

Stephen took a deep breath and stretched his arms wide above him before heading along the water's edge in the opposite direction from where I'd found Alicia's body. I joined him and he slowed his pace.

"Stephen, do you mind if I ask you a few questions?" I said.

"You can ask," he replied.

"I saw you and Madeline arguing with Alicia at the party. Would you care to tell me what that was about?"

He pulled off the bandanna and ran a hand through his hair. "You know, Mrs. Fletcher, I'm not even sure. Alicia had been taunting us all day and evening about a surprise that she had planned."

"Do you know what it was?"

"No idea. Maddy thought maybe she was going to marry Charles Davis. He's the nephew of Agnes Chudleigh-Stubbs. Did you meet her?"

"Yes, and Charles as well."

"I didn't think that was it. Charles is a nice guy, but he's, well, he's weak, not in the physical sense but in his nature. He's just not strong enough for her. He would've been miserable if he ever married her. She would have eaten him alive."

And you wouldn't have been very happy either, I thought. I wondered if Stephen was giving me a true picture of Alicia and Charles's relationship or simply what he hoped was the case. How far would he have been willing to go to prevent Alicia from marrying Charles? He obviously loved her. There was no question about that.

Had they walked down to the beach together that night? Could she have tormented him with the idea that Charles was about to propose? Was it even true? Had he strangled her in a jealous rage and then attempted to pin the crime on the island's Jack the Ripper killer?

Stephen didn't strike me as a violent man, but when passions come into the picture, the calmest of us are capable of actions we never thought possible.

We continued to walk for fifteen minutes without another word between us, turned and started back toward the house, each of us caught up in our own reveries. The sea air and the exercise had conspired to make me hungry.

"I hope Norlene has some *malasadas* left," he said, echoing my thoughts. "I could eat a dozen right now."

"I think I could, too," I said, smiling.

"Speaking of Norlene," he said, shading his eyes with his hand and waving at the cook, who stood on the bluff above.

We tramped up the sandy path we'd taken down to the beach until reaching Norlene.

"Mrs. Fletcher, I've been searching all over for you," she said.

"Sorry, Norlene," Stephen said. "I dragged her off for a walk."

"Why are you looking for me?" I asked.

"You have a visitor."

"I do?"

"Yes. An Inspector Sutherland."

Chapter Fifteen

"My goodness, George. This is a surprise," I said. Britain's Metropolitan Police Service Chief Inspector George Sutherland rose from the sofa where he'd been sitting and came to greet me. He took both my hands and gave me a soft kiss on the cheek, his eyes smiling. "Always good to see you, Jessica."

"When did you arrive?" I asked. "Why didn't you let me know you were coming? I would have met you at the airport. Have you been to headquarters already? You know about the fourth murder? Of course you do. Where are you staying?"

"One question at a time, lass," he said, chuckling. He led me to the chair by the window where Alicia had sat reading when I first arrived, and took the seat across from mine next to the telescope, laying his raincoat over the arm of the chair. "I apologize for not alerting you to my pending arrival. As you may presume, it was a late decision, prompted by circumstances."

"Murder number four," I said.

"Precisely so."

"Were you waiting very long?" I asked. "Had I known you were here, I would have come up from the beach earlier."

"Not long at all." George patted the top of the telescope next to him. "I entertained myself with this while I was waiting for you," he said. "Thought I might see you wandering along the shore."

"And what did you see?" I asked. "I haven't looked through it myself." I stood and leaned over to peer into the viewfinder.

"Just a portion of the beach," he said. "It's locked, and I didn't want to change someone's settings."

"A very important portion of the beach," I said, sitting down again. "That's the scene of the crime."

"You'll have to show it to me before I leave."

George looked tired. There were circles under his eyes and lines next to his mouth that I didn't remember seeing there before. Travel can do that to you, especially a trip that hadn't been planned in advance. He must have rushed to make his transatlantic flight, and if he was unlucky enough to sit in the middle seat in coach, it would have made the trip torture. For someone his height—well over six feet—those seats are a tight squeeze, making a lengthy journey seem even longer. Put that together with grabbing meals on the fly from airport fast-food outlets, not to mention the pressure to make his connecting flight to Bermuda, and he had every reason to look worn out. But I suspected there were stresses I wasn't aware of contributing to his weary demeanor. Even so, he was still one of the handsomest men I knew. Of course, my fondness for him might color my view.

"I caught the first flight out after the news arrived, barely had time to pack a bag. As you can see, I'm still carrying my mackintosh"—he patted his raincoat—"even though the climate here is quite lovely."

"You'd be surprised," I said. "You'll probably find plenty of use for it. I got caught in a downpour just the other day."

"Did you? Well, then, I won't complain," he said. He cocked his head. "Met your host, the judge, leaving with his man as I was coming in. Seems a decent chap."

"Tom has been very generous, continuing to entertain his guests even though this has got to be a terrible time for him and his family. I feel a little guilty that my being here is preventing them from having a private mourning period."

"They could have asked you to leave. Perhaps they're grateful for the distraction. Some people would prefer to ease into their grief, rather than having it beset them all at once."

"I hope you're right," I said. "My staying near the scene of the crime does have its advantages. I wouldn't confess to Tom that I've been conducting my own investigation, but it's difficult not to think about his niece's murder while surrounded by those who knew her, and in particular those who disliked her."

"Are there many who disliked her?"

"For someone so young, she seemed to have approached the world with a scorched-earth policy, gleefully alienating people, although I haven't uncovered many details of how she managed to accomplish this so easily."

I turned at the sound of someone clearing her throat.

"Excuse me, Mrs. Fletcher," Norlene said, coming into the room with a heavy tray. "I thought the gentleman might like a little something to eat."

George rose from his chair and relieved her of her burden. "Thank you, madam. You're very kind."

"How thoughtful of you, Norlene." I pulled a small table closer to us so George could set down the tray. "This is more than a little something," I said, smiling at her. "This is a feast."

In addition to a pot of tea and its accompaniments, Norlene had piled up two sandwiches on the plates, and even included a couple of her *malasadas* for George.

"If you'd be more comfortable in the dining room, I can set you up in there," she said, a question reflected in her voice.

"Please, *dinna fash* yourself on my account," George said, slipping into his Scots dialect. "This is wonderful exactly as it is. You are an angel come to a starving man's rescue." He put his hand over his heart and gave her a big grin.

Norlene blushed and aimed a small smile in my direction, clearly charmed, before returning to the kitchen.

It was his considerate manner that had captivated me for so long as well. George was certainly the consummate professional Freddie had said he was, but he also had a personal warmth that set people at ease and made them want to please him. I imagine that such charisma was helpful in drawing out suspects, encouraging them to give away the information he sought. And I saw firsthand how loyal his staff was—the respect and admiration they felt for him.

With George, such appeal was not something he turned on and off. It was his nature to be kind and courteous. Yet everyone who met him knew there was a will of steel beneath his manners and refinement.

I withheld my questions while George ate. I poured tea for both of us, shared one of his sandwiches, but left the other and both the *malasadas* for him to enjoy. When he had finished his meal and picked up his second cup of tea, sighing with contentment, I was confident my curiosity wouldn't be out of line.

"Is there a problem with the investigation, George?" I asked. "I had the impression it was going well. Why did you need to rush over here?"

"It's a long story, lass," he said, peering into his cup as if the tea leaves could divulge the future.

"Do you have time to fill me in?"

He sat forward, set his cup down on the tray, and reached out for my hand. "I do. But why don't you take me down to the scene. We can talk along the way."

"Are you sure?"

"Yes. I'm fully content." He patted his stomach. "Please thank that lovely lady again for me."

We exited by the terrace doors after I had notified Norlene that we were leaving and passed along George's and my gratitude for the food. We took the gravel path, stopped at my cottage so George could drop off his raincoat on the swing of my porch, and talked all the way to the beach. George gave out with a belly laugh when I told him the story of my encounter with the intruder who turned out to be Freddie Moore.

"The redheaded man! Sounds like a great title for one of your books," he said. "Freddie would love to be a scary character."

"I certainly felt foolish once I met him and we had a chance to talk," I said. "He's not scary at all."

"People often mistake Freddie for someone other than who he is. No, he's not scary, but he's nobody's fool either. Very shrewd, that one. It's easy to dismiss the costume and the bumbling manner, but his method of getting into character in his own way has been very efficient at solving crimes."

"I thought that's what he was doing. He's dressing like Inspector Frederick Abberline to think through Bermuda's version of Jack the Ripper."

"Or he may be impersonating Jack the Ripper himself. If it helps him to get into the mind of the murderer, it's fine with me. I don't question whatever works for him. Plus, he's a whiz with electronics. One of the best we have."

"He was going to show me what he carries in his suitcase," I said, "but we were interrupted by news of the fourth murder."

"Plenty of time for that. He's scheduled to give a class to the Bermudian police before he leaves. Perhaps you can sit in."

"I'd like that," I said.

I led George to the place on the beach where I'd found Alicia's body. Under the azure sky, boats bobbed in the water, and with the sun bouncing off the wet rocks and the foam washing up the sand, it was a beautiful setting with no sign of the terrible act that had taken place there.

George examined the rocks, and looked back to the window in the house where he'd seen this portion of the beach through the telescope. I showed him the spot that Freddie had revealed to me, where my red-haired friend had found evidence of a hiding place that may have been used by the killer.

There was little more to see, so George and I sat together on the bottom step of the flight of stairs that led up to the Jamisons' property, and that Charles and I had occupied two days earlier. As we watched a motorboat cruise along the shore just beyond the breakers, I gave him a rundown of all my activities to date, my suspicions and my lack of conclusions, plus the few trails I still wanted to follow. He listened carefully, nodding at intervals, until I fell silent.

"You've gathered a lot of productive information," he said. "Unfortunately, my team is not free to pursue Miss Betterton's killer."

"So Freddie told me."

"We have to be careful what toes we tread on here. Our duties are clearly circumscribed with no room to improvise or to expand our investigation."

"It sounds as if the Bermudian police are upset that Scotland Yard is here," I said. "I thought they had specifically invited your help."

"They did," George replied. "But it's a complicated relationship we have."

"I'm sure you can simplify that for me," I said.

George laughed and took my hand in his. "Let me try. You see, we train many of their officers. Their system is very similar to ours, almost a copy of it. Yes, they want our help, but only on their terms. And they've basically given us a time frame to put up or shut up, as you Yanks like to say."

"Why would they be so impatient?" I asked. "They must know an investigation takes time."

"They don't trust us, you see."

"I'm afraid I *don't* see. Why don't they trust you? They asked you here, didn't they?"

"They did, but they've invited us in before with spectacularly unfortunate results." George paused and I waited for him to continue. The topic was evidently one he found difficult to explain.

"This is not the first time the Yard has been called in on a difficult case on the island," he said. "In the seventies, not so long ago that I can't remember hearing about it, we were called to help investigate the murder of the island's commissioner of police."

"No!"

"Ironic, isn't it? But that was not the worst of it. Later, we were called again when the island's governor and one of his aides were assassinated. In each instance, to our great irritation and to the Bermudian government's frustration, we were unable to determine the perpetrators or effect any arrests. We returned home with a blot on our record."

"How embarrassing."

"Complete humiliation," George said. "There was a good deal of racial tension in Bermuda at the time, and the authorities made no headway in drawing out witnesses despite offering a *crackin'* reward."

"But those things will happen," I said, looking out at the water before turning back to him. "Not every case is solved, even though the popular media make it seem as if they are."

"You are very sweet, lass," George said, putting his arm around my shoulder and giving me a squeeze. "But that was not the end of it. We were called in again when two shopkeepers were murdered with equally unsatisfactory results. After we'd returned home defeated for the third time, the local boys arrested a pair of bad apples—two lifelong petty criminals—and accused them of the murders. They were hanged for the crimes, setting off a major riot, millions in damage, and the deaths of three more people."

"Oh dear," I said. "I hope they were truly the guilty parties."

"They were involved somehow, but there must have been others behind them. When we were here, our boys had continuously come up against walls, not only from the communities in which these men lived but from the top echelons of Bermudian society. They were satisfied with simply pinning the crimes on these two thugs. They didn't want any scandals to threaten the entrenched establishment or to tarnish Bermuda's reputation as an island paradise."

"So Scotland Yard has a lot to prove with these Jack the Ripper cases," I said.

"We have indeed. I wasn't in the service when those other crimes took place, but several colleagues who've since retired were among the investigators. We asked them to brief us. They were reluctant to discuss the case—not exactly a red-letter day for the Yard—but they did sit down with the team."

"Did they give you helpful information?" I asked.

"It remains to be seen. It's another island now, with a new regime and far more integration, both in government and in the police ranks, than was true before."

"And, of course, the case is completely different," I put in. "The victims are not officials or even part of the establishment."

"Far from it. They're poor souls whose lives don't touch the majority of the populace, except for those who have sympathy for them—or who might have engaged their services."

"Or those who are afraid their killer will look beyond such easy targets."

George slapped his hands on his knees and stood. "I have to motor into Hamilton. I'm due at headquarters for a meeting with the team." He put out a hand to help me up. "I'd be pleased to give you a lift into town."

I smiled up at him as I took his hand. "I'm going to take you up on that offer."

I stood and brushed the sand off the seat of my slacks. "I have some errands to run fir . . ." I said, trailing off as I eyed the motorboat, which was slowly passing in front of us for the third time. "Do you see that boat?" I asked.

George shaded his eyes with his hand and looked out to sea. "Yes."

"It has been up and down this portion of the beach several times."

"Do you think they're spying on us?" George said, amused.

"I don't know," I said, "but they're not dragging a fishing line. I have a bad feeling about that. Why would they crisscross the same piece of water?"

"Curiosity seekers? One of your literary fans? Or they may know that this is where a body was found. Not our problem today," George said, taking my arm as we walked up the beach toward the gravel path.

And it was true. It wasn't our problem then, but it was to become our problem very soon, and I would be sorry I hadn't taken note of the boat earlier and acted on my suspicions.

Chapter Sixteen

George dropped me off in downtown Hamilton, where I planned to do some shopping and then find my way back to the Bettertons.

A cruise ship must have been docked at the island because Front Street was filled with tourists wandering in and out of the stores. I followed a group into the Irish Linen Shop, a favorite stop of mine on a previous trip. The shop features linens from Ireland, of course, and brings back warm memories of my family and visits to the land of my heritage. I remember my mother shaking out the crisp white sheets, making them billow over our beds when she made them, and feeling the cool linen on the pillow under my cheek at night.

The store also carried tablecloths from Provence in France, sparking another sweet recollection. Their yellow, red, and blue hues were colorful enough to liven up even the dullest of dinners, not that my dinners there were ever dull.

I leisurely perused the shop's offerings, reminding myself

that this—or something like this—was why I had chosen to come to Bermuda in the first place. There were many tempting items that would have overburdened my one suitcase, but I couldn't escape without buying a handkerchief. Made by women on the Portuguese island of Madeira who specialize in the traditional skill of embroidery, there were several with delicate patterns around an initial. I chose one without any letter, thinking it would make a wonderful gift once I decided to whom to give it. If no deserving giftee presented herself, I would be happy to keep it for myself.

Around the corner on Queen Street was a lovely little park next to one of the island's most popular historical sites, the Perot Post Office. A whitewashed building with black shutters on the windows and front door, it was named for Hamilton's first postmaster. The bustle of Hamilton is left outside when you enter the charming room, with its shiny wooden beams and warm scent—was it cedar?—a throwback to days when William Bennett Perot designed Bermuda's first stamp. That penny stamp would cost a pretty penny at auction today.

Several people lined up in front of the polished wooden cage to mail postcards home, and I did the same, stopping first to admire the simple furniture from Perot's day, and the shelves displaying pottery and lamps from Bermuda's past. I felt the tension in my shoulders begin to melt away.

Farther up Queen Street, I turned onto a small lane and window-shopped while keeping a weather eye on the clouds. They had begun to gather while I was in the post office. A sign above a marine supply store, Ocean Locker, caught my eye, as did the display in its window. I stood in front of the shop, scrutinizing the sample tackle box, which was open to show the tools that would fill it. My eyes moved to a card that read "Just In" next to an array of fishing knives arranged in a circle. Their handles were scribing the outer edge of the arc and their open blades were almost touching in the middle.

Freddie had said that the murder weapon was not among the household knives that the constables had taken away the night of the murder. He'd also mentioned that the autopsy had detected a bit of rust in the wound on Alicia's neck. I'd wondered if the knife used may have been a fishing knife. Knives around water tend to rust easily. I know my fishing knife does. The police wouldn't have found it in the house, especially if, as Freddie suspected, it had been thrown into the ocean. Members of the Betterton family had been out on their boat recently. If a fishing knife was missing from their tackle box, Adam would be the one asked to replace it.

The judge's personal assistant had mentioned coming here the day before to pick up supplies for the family's boat, and his errand had given me an idea. Could Adam have bought a new knife to replace one that was missing? If he had, it could suggest the missing knife had been used to slash Alicia. I'd seen the fishing paraphernalia in Tom's garage when the security guard had retrieved his motorbike and given me a lift into town. Any member of the family would have had access to it, and come to think of it, so would anyone at the party who might have known where Tom's fishing equipment was stored.

Finding out if Adam had bought a new knife was not

going to be easy. In my experience, merchants tend to clam up when asked about their customers' purchases. I studied the knives and wondered how effective my argument would be. Sometimes a little subterfuge was called for.

I pushed open the glass front door and looked around. On one side of the shop, an older man, perhaps the proprietor, was helping a couple trying on windbreakers. Across the room, a younger man sorted fishing lures. He had them spread out on the counter in groups of three and four. I decided to approach him.

"Aren't those pretty," I said, looking over the bright silver fish-shaped pieces with multiple hooks hanging from them. I reached out a finger to touch them but withdrew it when the man said, "Please don't, ma'am. You need to be careful. Those barbs are very sharp."

"Okay," I said, holding up my hand. "See. No touching." I gave him a lopsided smile.

He returned my smile. "My boss is taking care of other customers right now. Do you mind waiting?"

"Well, I am in a bit of a hurry. Can't you assist me?"

He sighed and put down the lure he was holding. "Sure. I guess. What do you need?"

"Well, I'm not sure if I need anything yet, but I think you're the one who can help me figure out if I do," I said, trying to act like the scatterbrain many young people assume an older person is.

He looked at me skeptically. "I can?"

"I have to admit I have this funny favor to ask."

"Maybe my boss should help you."

"But he's busy, and besides, you're right here."

"I'd like to help you, ma'am, but I can't unless you tell me what you want."

I lowered my voice as if I were about to tell him a secret. "A friend of mine was in yesterday, picking up some supplies for his boat."

"And?"

"And, I need to know if he bought one of those new knives you have in the window." I giggled.

He raised one eyebrow and scowled at me. "Why do you want to know that?"

"Because I want to get him one as a gift, of course."

"I don't know, ma'am. You know that's private information, what a person buys. I don't think my boss would like me to—" He looked over to where his boss was helping a customer into a jacket.

"But however am I going to give him that gift?" I said, interrupting his excuse. "He was moaning about losing his fishing knife." I pouted. "I want to get him one of those pretty orange ones you have in the window, but how do I know he hasn't already bought it for himself if you won't help me?"

"What's your friend's name?" he asked.

"Adam Wyse."

"Adam's your friend?" he asked, clearly surprised.

"Well, not a friend exactly," I said coyly, "but I'd like him to be. I told the judge if he was thirty years older or I was thirty years younger, he wouldn't be safe from me. He's just the most charming man."

"The judge?"

"No, silly. Adam."

I could see the gears working in his head. *Poor Adam*, he was probably thinking. *This loony old broad has a crush on him.*

"Hang on. I'll check for you," he said. He went to the register and keyed in some information.

I leaned over to the counter to see if I could view the screen.

"Step back, ma'am. I'll give you the information you want."

"You're such a dear," I said, batting my lashes.

"Let's see," he said under his breath. "Wax wing jigs, fifty yards monofilament, leader line, double J hook. Here it is! Sorry, ma'am. I'm afraid you're out of luck."

"I am?"

"He bought a Benchmade Griptilian with a corrosion-resistant steel blade."

I gave him a sad look. "I guess I'll have to think of something else."

"I guess you will," he said.

"Well, thank you, young man," I said, perking up. "You're very handsome, you know." I winked at him. "I appreciate your help."

"Sure, um, anytime."

I could almost hear his sigh of relief as I exited the store.

Chapter Seventeen

According to my guidebook, Gardner's Deli was the newest incarnation of a restaurant that had previously been a Mexican cantina and before that a French café. The stucco walls had once been an intense ocher, and the subsequent pale blue paint didn't quite cover the deeper hue. The resulting color was not exactly guaranteed to aid digestion.

The new owners tried to mask the decorating faux pas by hanging large posters evidently provided by their food purveyors. Above my table was an image of a giant hot dog on a bun with mustard and sauerkraut, and farther down the wall was a poster showing a large ham with slices curling off the front. Others pictures were akin to these, in hopes, I assumed, that customers would be inspired to order a similar item from the menu.

It was a bit late for lunch, but the half sandwich I'd eaten with George was not enough to keep me satisfied until dinner. I perused the menu and ordered a tuna platter with a side of coleslaw and an iced tea. When the waiter returned with my food, I asked, "Does anyone named Fairy Fay work here?"

"That's a different name, isn't it?" he said. "I'm only a part-timer. I'll check in the back for you."

I observed the few other patrons sitting in the deli. Only two other women were there and neither appeared to be someone who might have been a friend of Alicia's. One was an older woman sitting with a man, presumably her husband. The couple spooned up their soup in silence. The other woman sat across from two children of about five and seven, and rocked a baby in a carrier she'd set on the chair next to her.

Of course, who was I to judge who Alicia's friends might be? It wasn't that I didn't know her well; I hardly knew her at all. I'd been looking for another young woman, but Alicia could just as easily have made friends with someone older, perhaps with children. From the little I did know about Tom's niece, however, she seemed to be too self-centered to befriend people whose lives were so different from her own. But I scolded myself to keep an open mind.

I'd finished my late lunch when a lady in a starched apron, and whose gray hair had been dyed a bright blue, emerged from the kitchen. She surveyed the dining room and made a beeline for my table. "Are you the one looking for Fairy Fay?" she asked, poking a pencil into the tight curls above her ear.

"Yes," I said, sitting at attention. "Does she work here?"

"Never heard the name before. And I would've remembered that one." She laughed.

"Oh," I said, a bit deflated. "Perhaps she's a customer," I offered.

"Maybe. I don't know the names of all my customers. Too many tourists and onetimers. I know my regulars though. She isn't one of them."

"Was Alicia Betterton one of your regulars?"

"That name sounds familiar, but I can't put a face to it. What's she look like?"

"Young, slim, pretty, about twenty-two with long blond hair."

She gave out a bark of laughter. "You're describing half the white girls on the island."

I smiled. "I know. She was supposed to meet her friend here today, but couldn't make it. Did you happen to notice if anyone who came in waited for someone and then left?"

"Can't say that I did," she said.

I checked my watch. It was a quarter past two. "Maybe she just hasn't arrived yet."

"You're welcome to wait. We're open until ten. Can I get you anything else?" She picked up my plate and passed it to the waiter who had just delivered a dish to another table and was on his way back to the kitchen.

"No, thanks," I said. "I think I will wait a while longer, though."

"Happy to have you." She left me and stopped at the other tables, greeting her customers. At the table where the mother sat, she drew two lollypops from the pocket of her apron and presented them to the children, then moved on to the older couple.

The mother reached across the table and took the lollies

from the children, who watched her solemnly. She peeled the paper wrapper off the candies and gave them back. Big smiles replaced the serious expressions and I smiled, too, noticing how such a small gesture made them happy.

I watched the door, hoping that someone who might be Fairy Fay would walk in. *You're wasting your time*, I told myself. *They must have met last Tuesday. Or if the appointment was for today, she wouldn't bother to come, having heard about Alicia's death. Why would she keep an appointment if she already knew Alicia wouldn't be here to meet her?*

Still, I waited on the slim chance that word had yet to reach this friend. I didn't want to lose the opportunity to meet someone who could provide insight into Alicia's life from a perspective outside the family.

At three o'clock, disappointed, I paid my bill and left.

Only one photographer still lingered across the street from the Bettertons when I returned. He seemed uninterested in me, thank goodness, but kept a wary eye on Adam's security detail when the guards met me in the driveway. I saw him raise his camera and snap off a few shots, but otherwise I was able to enter the house without being accosted.

"Would you like some tea, Mrs. Fletcher?" Norlene asked when she opened the door and welcomed me inside. "I can bring it to your cottage."

"A cup of tea sounds like a great idea," I said, "but why not let me make my own in the kitchen? I don't want to interfere with your preparations for dinner."

"It's no trouble," she said. "Dinner's all ready to go into

the oven. I made individual casseroles for whoever's here tonight."

"Wonderful! Then you have time to join me for a cup."

Norlene may have been a little uncomfortable inviting a guest into her kitchen, but she hid it well, leading me through a swinging door into a bright sunny room that overlooked the front of the house. Tom—or perhaps it was his ex-wife Claudia—had outfitted the kitchen with the latest professional appliances and a giant rack over the center island, where copper pans and various utensils hung. Six stools were pulled up to one side of the long island, allowing visitors to watch, out of the way, as the cook worked. It would have made an excellent schoolroom to teach cooking classes, I thought, provided there were not more than six students.

I took one of the stools and watched while Norlene put up a kettle to boil water, rinsed a teapot using the hot water tap over the stove, and poured tea leaves into a mesh basket.

"I like fresh-boiled water for my tea," she said.

"It must be wonderful working in a kitchen as nice as this one," I said.

"It's a lot fancier than my kitchen at home." She looked around with approval.

"It's a lot fancier than mine, too," I said. "And about ten times larger. But I do love my little kitchen. It's full of warmth and wonderful memories."

"My kitchen is full of noisy children and a messy husband," Norlene said, chuckling. "Doesn't have a lot of room, either, but sometimes I make dinners for my family here and take them home. The judge doesn't mind. He's a nice man."

"Have you worked for him for a long time?"

She nodded. "Ever since he moved here. Of course, he's not here all the time, but he pays me anyway," she said proudly. "And when he's away, I can still use the kitchen. I do more of the housekeeping then. I make sure the place is ready for the family whenever they have time to come."

"Do his children stay here without the judge when he's working in the States?"

"Oh, yes. Stephen is here all the time, but he takes most of his meals out. Madeline comes over on weekends and stays for a month every holiday."

"And Alicia, did she stay here as well?"

"Some," she said, pouring the water over the tea and setting the pot on the island while she took down two cups and saucers. "Would you like a biscuit? I made some fresh this morning."

She put four triangular cookies on a plate and placed it in front of me.

I took a bite of one. "These are delicious," I said. "You're some baker, Norlene. The *malasadas* this morning were terrific, too, and I'd love to get the recipe for these. Would you mind? I'll understand if you do. Some people don't like to share their recipes."

"I don't mind. I'll write it out for you," she said, pleased. "These here are butter almond biscuits, but some people call them Bermuda triangle cookies."

"Bermuda Triangles? Very clever," I said, taking another bite. When I finished the cookie, I asked, "May I ask you another question? You let me know if you're uncomfortable answering. I'm just trying to get a feeling for the family relationships."

She shrugged. "I guess it's okay. Is it for a book?"

"Not one I'm working on right now," I answered honestly, "but it could be for another one, perhaps later on."

"Okay. I'll help you if I can."

"Thank you." I took a sip of tea and put my cup down. "How long does—did—Alicia stay when she came to Bermuda?"

"Not long. She and Madeline didn't get along."

"Why do you say that?"

"Because they were always screaming at each other. When Alicia got out of the hospital, she stayed here during her recovery and I thought they'd shout the walls down."

"How long was Alicia in the hospital?" I said carelessly, not wanting to alert Norlene to the fact that this was news to me.

She thought for a moment. "A year and a half, maybe two. I don't recall exactly."

It was unlikely that a physical disease or even a drug problem had put Alicia in a hospital for that length of time. But a mental illness could take a long time to treat. It would also account for the family's hesitation to talk about where Alicia had been after boarding school and before she moved back with her uncle. The pieces of the puzzle were falling into place.

"Had she been out of boarding school long when she was hospitalized?" I asked.

"Wasn't out of it at all. Went straight from school to the hospital. Had some kind of breakdown, I heard." Norlene *tsk*ed and shook her head. "She was always an angry child, that one. Knew how to get her way, though. She could work the charm when she wanted to."

"So I understand," I said.

She lowered her voice. "You know that she and Madeline had a big row that night."

"Do you know what it was about?"

"Uh-uh, but I heard Madeline say she'd kill her if she did that."

"Did what?"

"I don't know. I didn't hear that part."

"That's a fairly common expression," I said. "People threaten to kill without ever meaning to carry it out." I took another sip of my tea. "You don't think Madeline killed Alicia, do you?" I asked, deciding to be direct.

"I hate to think she would, but she could. She was that mad. And she's a good one with a knife, Madeline. She can scale and gut a fish as good as Adam."

Chapter Eighteen

The next morning Adam didn't bring me the newspaper as he had before. I assumed that the family was lingering over their morning meal and still reading it. I made myself a cup of tea and ate the last of yesterday's *malasadas*. Norlene had kindly wrapped them up and insisted I take them back to my cottage.

The sky was a beautiful blue and there was a slight morning chill in the air when I walked down to the beach with a towel and a book, hoping to get in an hour of reading before the sun's rays became too strong.

The beach was almost deserted when I spread out my towel on the sand. I wore my sunglasses and the pink hat Tom had sent me, and for the first time my bathing suit covered by the long skirt and white shirt I'd worn to the party. I sat facing the water, my book open and propped on my knees, but the air was so refreshing, the view so peaceful, that I hated to take my eyes from the water.

A couple walked along the strandline off to my left, bent at the waist and obviously beachcombing. He carried a small bucket like a child's toy and each of them stopped at intervals to drop a find into the pail. I had to smile. Beachcombing is as pleasurable for adults as it is for children, and I've done my share of it back in Cabot Cove.

As the couple neared, I recognized them as Daniel and Lillian Jamison, Tom's next-door neighbors, the ones who objected to his building a studio for Stephen because they claimed that it would impair their view, the same couple whose stairs to the beach may have been used by the killer to escape the night Alicia was killed. We'd been introduced briefly at the party but hadn't had an opportunity to talk. I wondered if they remembered me, and if so, would be willing to talk a little about the victim. I was thinking of how to approach them when Lillian hailed me.

"Hello! You're the writer, aren't you? The judge's guest?"

"That's right," I said, scrambling to my feet to shake hands.

"Oh, you don't have to be so formal down here," she said, but she took my hand. "Please, sit. Do you mind if we join you for a few minutes?"

"Not at all."

Lillian threw herself down next to me, pulled off her moccasins, and dug her feet into the sand.

Her husband took his time getting into a sitting position and I recognized the signs of sore knees.

"Here, give me that bucket," Lillian said to her husband, reaching across me to grab the little pail. "Put both hands on the ground and swivel around," she told him. "Dan had a knee replaced last year," she said to me. "He needs the other one done, but hasn't gotten up the nerve to do it yet."

"It's not a matter of nerve, Lil. I'm just too busy to take the time it requires."

"They say that the reason people have both knees replaced at the same time is that after you've gone through the pain of one, you'll never go back for the second," I offered.

"I've heard that, too," said Lillian. She turned to her husband, saying, "You remember Jessica Fletcher, don't you, Dan? Tom introduced us at his party."

He smiled and shook my hand. "Nice to see you again," he said. "Everyone doing okay up there?"

"As well as can be expected."

"Terrible thing," he said. "The cops better find the killer before all of us start selling our homes here."

"It won't be so easy to sell if there's a serial killer on the loose," Lil said. "Anyway, I'm not going anywhere. I love it here and this so-called Jack the Ripper will never scare me away. He'll have to make me his next victim if he wants me gone."

"Pfft," said Dan. "He's not interested in you or me for that matter. He likes 'em young and easy." He turned to me. "Not to say Tom's niece was easy, mind you. Sorry, didn't mean to imply that. Hope you weren't offended."

I ignored his remark and asked, "Did either of you hear anything that night or see anyone down here on the beach?"

"Better ask Lil," Dan replied. "I was three sheets to the wind. Boy, haven't had that much to drink in an age."

Lillian rolled her eyes. "You were awful, Dan, and I think we'd just as soon not relive your behavior that night."

"A man's got a right to get drunk every now and then," he said. "I was having a good time, that's all. It's not like I do it every day."

"Never mind that." She looked at me. "No, I didn't hear or see anything after Claudia helped us home. I felt foolish being driven such a short distance, but considering Dan's condition, it made sense. He could barely walk. Do you know Claudia?"

I nodded. "We've met."

"We got Dan into bed and then sat outside for a while."

"Claudia helped put me to bed? I didn't know that," Dan said.

"You didn't know *anything*."

"That's embarrassing."

"There's nothing you have that she hasn't seen before," his wife said.

"How late did Claudia stay?" I asked, interrupting what seemed to be the beginning of an argument.

Lillian shrugged. "Maybe another half hour." She giggled. "Claudia left her shoes by the pool and the constables took them. I didn't know who they belonged to; I only knew that they weren't mine. I forgot that she'd complained about how uncomfortable they were."

"I'm sure the police will return them if she asks," I said, wondering whether the police ever did identify the shoes' owner. I made a mental note to tell them if they hadn't. I then wondered why Claudia hadn't told the police about the shoes, so I asked.

"I think she's afraid that they'll accuse her of killing Alicia," Dan offered. "They never got along. The kid resented her big time. That happens with stepmothers all the time. Hard for a kid to accept a new woman in the house."

"I understand that she was a difficult child," I said.

"Difficult? That's putting it mildly," Lillian said. "If you ask Claudia, she can go on for hours about her. I don't think she'll miss Alicia at all."

"Tom will, though," Dan said, adjusting his legs so they stretched out in front of him. "Feel a little sorry for him. He was attached to her."

"Just a *little* sorry?" I said.

"I don't know how well you know your host, Mrs. Fletcher, but the judge is not the greatest guy in the world. Not the sharpest knife in the drawer either. I could tell you stories."

"Dan!"

"What?"

"That's not a very kind thing to say, Dan, considering what's happened to his niece."

"What'd I say that was so bad?"

"'Sharpest knife,'" his wife reminded him.

"Aw, it's just an expression. What I mean is that he's not so smart for a judge."

"Now, Dan, don't get off on that topic."

"That's all right," I said. "Why do you think he's not smart?" I asked. "After all, he is a district court judge. You have to have a lot of knowledge to hold that position."

"You have to have a lot of contacts," Dan corrected. "He's

shrewd—I'll give him that. But shrewd isn't the same as smart. He's a politician, knows the president. If he'd never been appointed to the bench, he'd probably be running Ward E campaigns in Jersey City or some other place."

"I think you may be underestimating him," I said. "Tom wrote a book about judicial reform, which I understand was very well received."

"It's ironic, isn't it? Of all people."

"Dan, that's enough," Lil said.

"She should know who she's dealing with, Lil. Tom is not the Honest Abe judge he makes himself out to be."

"How do you know this?" I asked.

"I just know," Dan said, struggling to get to his feet again and moaning in the process. "I'm too old to sit on the beach," he groused, dusting sand off his pants.

"We'll bring down a chair next time," Lil said.

"You were talking about Tom," I said, not wanting him to leave without explaining his comments.

"Look," he said, "I don't have to present anything in court, make a legal case out of it, but I know who I'm dealing with. I don't trust him as far as I can throw him. Please excuse me, ladies," he said as he limped off in the direction of their stairs.

"Sorry for Dan's outburst, Jessica. He's not a fan of Judge Thomas Betterton."

"That's easy to see," I said. "I'm just curious what Tom did to make Dan so angry with him."

"My son from my first marriage is a lawyer. There was a disagreement about something between him and the judge. I don't know the details."

"Lawyers and judges often have disagreements," I said. "That goes hand in hand with the judicial process."

"I told Dan he should stay out of it; it's between Barry and the judge. Barry is a grown man now and has to fight his own battles." She shook her head and sighed. "Unfortunately Dan doesn't forgive easily."

"Did you and Dan know Alicia well?" I asked.

"I don't think anyone knew her well," she replied. "After all the stories I'd heard from Claudia, I avoided her as much as I could, and she didn't go out of her way to make a friend out of me. Claudia said that was typical. As far as Claudia was concerned, Alicia was your standard spoiled brat, and she felt that Tom enabled her through his generosity. I think she spent half their marriage trying to convince him to let her grow up, go out on her own, fight her own battles like we all have to."

I had no idea whether Lillian was right. After all, she was only repeating what Claudia had told her, and from what I'd gathered, the relationship between Claudia and Alicia was a poisonous one.

Lil said that she had to get back to the house, but before leaving, she showed me the beach glass they had collected, the little shards of blue, white, and brown glass that had been softened into pebbles by the action of the ocean. "Come over anytime," she said before walking away. "We're not leaving for another week."

When she was gone, I gathered up my towel and unread book. The breeze had dropped off and the sun was getting too high to remain on the beach. I looked over to the cottage where the Reynoldses were staying. Funny how they'd been unable to find a hotel room on an island filled with hotels. Or perhaps, I speculated, Godfrey had never made a sincere effort and had only been placating his wife with his supposed search for an alternate place to stay.

As I debated whether or not to knock on their door, Godfrey came outside with a beach chair and unfolded it on his porch. I waved at him and called out "Hello." He returned my greeting and I took the opportunity to approach him.

Tom's publisher had been unable to account for his whereabouts when the police arrived following my emergency call, and the constables had insisted that he and Daisy remain in Bermuda until further notice. While he'd obviously been reticent in speaking with the authorities, I hoped I could coax him into answering *my* questions. He was too smart a man to have gotten lost on the property. Besides, it hadn't been that dark; there had been a moon out that night. Even if he was simply stretching his legs, as his wife said he told the police, he must have seen something. I wanted to know what that was.

"Still here, I see," I said, climbing onto his porch.

"Yes," he said as he got to his feet. "No rooms at the inns, so to speak."

"Not even one?" I asked archly. "Not *anywhere* on the island?"

"Well, those that were available were outrageously priced, but don't let my wife know. I told her they were all full up, and innocent that she is, she believed me. Why should we abandon a perfectly lovely room with a view, and one that is gratis to boot?"

"Speaking of your wife, is she here?"

"I'm afraid she isn't. Daisy went shopping with Madeline, some sale or other."

"How nice for her," I said. "May I talk to you for a moment?"

"Would you like me to get you a chair?"

"This is fine for me," I said, sitting on the swing that was a match to the one on my porch.

"What are you reading?" I asked.

He held up the thick volume. "Tom's book."

"Is it as good as I've been told?"

"I'll tell you after I've read it."

I laughed. "I would have thought that you'd read it by now," I said.

"I have people for that," he said, smiling. "Seriously, I can't read everything I publish, now, can I? I'd never get out of the office. One of the smart young fellows in my acquisitions department recommended that we publish it. It was already out in the U.S."

"Did Tom actually write it?" I asked. It was a question I'd never put to Tom.

He chuckled. "Spoken like a woman in the book business. I understand that he paid a ghostwriter to help him. Very wise decision. Just because people are experts in one area doesn't mean they can put words together mellifluously, although I understand your American judges have to write opinions and such."

"Often they have people for that," I said, echoing him.

"So they do," he said.

"Just the same, writing a judicial opinion is like running

a short race," I said. "Writing a book is more like a mara-
thon. They take different skills."

"Well put," he said. He cocked his head at me. "Why do
I get the feeling that you didn't climb on my porch to chat
about writing or to discuss the publishing business?"

"Because I didn't."

"Thought so."

"Godfrey, you weren't in the cottage when the police
came the night of Alicia's murder," I said.

"And where did you learn this little tidbit of information?"

"From your wife."

He frowned and shook his head. "How indiscreet."

"Please don't scold her," I said. "I asked her why the police insisted you stay on the island and she confided in me.
It's not something I've discussed with anyone else."

"Thank you for that."

"You're welcome. But I would like to know what you saw
when you were supposedly 'stretching your legs.' I never saw
you reading on your porch while I walked down to the
beach and back. Had you been here, you surely would have
seen me, likely heard me running up the gravel path. But
you never mentioned that to the constables because, unlike
what Daisy told me, you weren't reading on your porch.
Where did you go? And why?"

He took a deep breath and let it out, obviously weighing
what was safe to tell me.

"I'm only asking so I can understand what happened that
night. I think you must have seen something but you didn't
tell the police about it. I can't help but wonder why."

"I didn't tell the constables because I cannot afford to be stuck on Bermuda indefinitely," he said with irritation, "or get called back here as a witness at a trial. That could tie me up for months and I simply cannot leave my business for that length of time."

"What did you *see*, Godfrey?" I pressed.

He sat back and looked out over the water as though pondering how much to tell me. Finally he came forward and said, "I didn't see anything at first, but then I heard that tidy package, Alicia, talking with someone. She'd swished her bottom in my direction all night, actually fell into my arms at one point, and I thought I'd go see who she was enticing now."

"And did you see who it was?"

"No. When I went inside to get my torch, Daisy told me to mind my own affairs. We'd had a row about Tom's niece. Daisy thought I'd been flirting with her and I probably had, but so what? I knew the young woman wasn't about to take me up on any offer I might make. I told Daisy as much. She was furious. She told me to get out, and stubborn as I am, I stayed inside just to spite her."

He paused, annoyed with himself, or maybe with Daisy.

"How long a time was it between when you heard Alicia's voice and when you went outside again?"

He shrugged. "An hour, maybe a little less." He looked out to the ocean again and I had a feeling that he was retracing his steps that night.

"Go on," I said. "What did you see when you went outside?"

"Actually, I saw you, Jessica. You went around the rocks. I crept forward and saw what you found. I have to admit I got a little sick to my stomach and retreated behind one of the boulders. When you ran back up the beach, I stayed hidden until you got to the gravel path."

"Then what did you do?"

He raised a hand. "It's not what I did—it's what I saw."

"Which was?"

"Tom's manservant."

"His manservant? You mean Adam? Where did you see him?"

"I spied him running up the stairs over there." He gestured with his hand.

"And did you follow him up the stairs?"

He hung his head. "I did. To be truthful, I wanted to avoid you in the event you decided to return to the beach. I didn't want you to see me there."

"So you followed Adam up the stairs to the Jamisons' property, and both of you crossed their backyard to the Betterton house."

"I didn't see him doing anything other than running away, mind you. I'm not accusing him of killing that poor girl. I figured that he was probably in the same position that I was, seeing you find the body and not wanting to get involved. If the police asked him, his story could be identical to mine."

"Is that what he told you?" I asked. I was guessing, of course, assuming that Adam would have looked around to see if he was being followed.

Godfrey looked startled. "Yes. But how did you know that? I can't imagine that he told you about it."

"There was a bright moon that night," I said, "and I doubt very much whether you could have followed him that far without his having caught sight of you."

He smiled ruefully. "A woman's intuition," he said.

"Just putting two and two together," I said.

Chapter Nineteen

Adam had left the folded newspaper on my swing, secured with a rubber band so that the wind wouldn't blow the pages away. I slipped off my sandy shoes at the door and tossed the paper on the bed, my mind preoccupied with all that Godfrey had told me.

He was right. He and Adam could have told the same story to the police, each one pointing to the other and accusing him of having killed Alicia, or at least of having been at the scene of the crime.

What a busy night it had been on the beach! And I had been completely unaware of all the company I was keeping other than the deceased. I wondered what George would make of it. Or if Freddie would say that one of these men surely must have killed Alicia. But, I reminded myself, Scotland Yard was no longer interested in her murder. Their center of focus was on the Jack the Ripper killer and she apparently was not considered one of his victims.

I took a bottle of water from the tiny fridge, sipping a

little before I changed out of my bathing suit, showered, and put on clothes more suitable for a trip into town. I was hoping to see George again; perhaps he would even have time to share another lunch where I could fill him in on what I'd discovered. I checked my cell phone. The message icon indicated voice mails, probably one from him.

I took my phone, the newspaper, and the bottle of water and went outside to sit in the swing. I pulled the rubber band off the paper and let it flop open on my lap as I dialed in for my message.

"Oh, no," I gasped, hanging up on my voice mail. The headline in huge letters went across the entire front page: "Business or Pleasure?" Underneath, the subhead asked: "What is Scotland Yard's chief inspector doing here?" And below it was a large photograph of George and me sitting on the step, George with his arm around my shoulder. The caption read: "Cuddling at the scene of the crime."

I groaned.

The article that accompanied the photograph was filled with innuendo, suggesting that the Scotland Yard team was merely enjoying an extended vacation at the expense of the Bermudian government, given their usual inability to actually solve any crimes. Not surprisingly, there were no details about what they had already uncovered since that information had been withheld from the press. Instead, the reporter took George to task for using the occasion to meet his "sweetheart" when he should have been exhorting his team to accomplish something, anything.

I could feel my face flooding with a combination of fury and mortification. I'd had a hunch there was something odd about that boat that kept traversing the same area of the ocean in front of us. George had kidded that the people aboard were spying on us, but that was precisely what they had done. We were victims of the paparazzi.

Clearly the Bettertons had read this article and perhaps even hesitated about letting me see it. But it would have been hard to keep it from me for long.

I looked at my cell phone and dialed voice mail again to get my messages. There were three. The first one was from a reporter who wanted a comment. I don't know how he got my number, but I quickly erased his request.

The second call was from Seth Hazlitt back home: "Hate to tell you this, but a picture of you and Sutherland was in the Bangor paper this morning. The article was none too flattering. Sorry about that. Send my regards to the inspector. Hope you're planning to come home soon."

The third call was from George. I listened with trepidation. "You were right about that boat, lass. I have an appointment with the commissioner at noon to 'explain myself'—his words. I knew I was taking a chance coming here, but I never believed it would involve you in this nasty business. Terribly, terribly sorry."

Oh, George, I thought. *It's not your fault some reporter starved for news would twist our meeting into something ugly.*

Adam was in the kitchen with Norlene when I went up to the main house. The cook gave me a sympathetic look. Adam's expression was unreadable.

"Adam, I need to get to headquarters for a meeting," I said. "Is there any chance you can give me a lift?"

"I'm busy right now," he said, looking down at a catalogue that was open on the counter. He turned a page.

"Can you call a taxi for me, then?"

"I can try, but I doubt they'd be able to get through all the reporters out front. Take a look." He cocked his head at the window that overlooked the front of the property.

I went to the window and carefully lifted the curtain. All the press that had deserted the Bettertons' house the day before were back again, and more, including the television truck with its satellite pole.

"Norlene, do you have the Jamisons' number?" I asked.

"I'll call them for you," she said. "You go over there by the beach and I'll have a taxi waiting for you in front of their house."

"Thank you so much," I said, giving her a fast hug.

I left the kitchen without saying goodbye to Adam, who refused to look at me again as he continued turning the pages of his catalogue. He must have been reflecting the family's annoyance with me, and I couldn't blame him—or them—yet the situation had not been created by me but by a reporter stretching the truth beyond recognition. Nevertheless, it was the second time the family's problems had been complicated by my presence, both times via a photograph of me in their local newspaper. I wondered how long it would be before Tom withdrew his offer of hospitality and asked me to leave. And when he did, what would I do?

Chapter Twenty

Whatever members of the press weren't loitering in front of Tom's house were milling about headquarters when I arrived. Sunglasses firmly in place, I walked swiftly through the crowd, hoping to reach the duty desk before I was recognized.

"Hello, Mrs. Fletcher." It was Larry Terhaar, the reporter from the Associated Press. He'd spoken my name softly, perhaps in hopes of keeping me to himself before the other reporters got wind of my presence. But the moment he turned my way, his colleagues pursued me as well.

"Who's that?"

"Is that the writer?"

"Mrs. Fletcher, just a minute."

"Did you come to Bermuda to have a tryst with your lover from Scotland Yard?"

"What do you have to say for yourself?"

My face was flaming by the time an officer in the front room of headquarters grabbed me by the elbow and used his

ID card to open the door to the corridor inside. "I don't know who you are," he said, chuckling, "but if those hounds are after you, you need our protection."

"Thank you so much, Constable—?"

"Andrews," he replied.

I brushed imaginary dust off my skirt and tugged at the hem of my jacket. "I'll have a lot more sympathy from now on for those pursued by the press," I said, forcing a laugh.

"As I tell my wife, everyone's got a job to do, not all of them with clean hands and shiny shoes. Now, who are you looking for?"

I debated asking to see the Scotland Yard team first, but decided to address the commissioner directly, hoping to head off any misplaced anger at George.

"I'd like to see Commissioner Hanover," I said.

"Do you have an appointment?"

"He's not expecting me, but I believe he'll be willing to see me."

"Write your name and direction on this page," he said, giving me a notebook.

I did as instructed.

"I'll have to call his office. You wait here. Don't go anywhere else, or I'll be in a lot of trouble for letting you fend for yourself."

"I promise I won't move," I said.

Constable Andrews trotted down the hall and turned the corner.

I leaned against the wall, listening to the shouts and arguments outside in the front hall, and caught my breath for the first time since I exited the taxi. *How can I make this right?* I wondered. *Was I even wise to come here?* I asked myself. George might be upset to find me defending him when he'd done nothing wrong. And he hadn't. Neither had I. But we both knew that the appearance of wrongdoing was every bit as damaging as the actual act. How did we end up in this thorny situation?

Constable Andrews returned, waving a paper name tag at me. "Here, wear this," he said, handing me the badge, which I stuck on my jacket. I followed him to the stairs and climbed to the second floor, passing the large room where the press conference had taken place. "The commissioner is in a briefing room right now, but he said you could come up."

The constable opened the door to a small conference room where three men sat around the table with Hanover. It was obvious to me, judging by their dress uniforms, that they were all senior management in the police service.

"Good afternoon, Mrs. Fletcher," Commissioner Hanover said, rising. "Come in. These men are part of the team working on the cases." He didn't need to specify that the cases were the Jack the Ripper murders. He introduced me to Superintendent Jonathan Bird, Deputy Commissioner Allan Mumford, and Chief Inspector A. M. Tedeschi. "Is there something that we can do for you?" he asked, holding out the chair next to him.

I had been hoping to speak with the commissioner privately, but it seemed he was not going to allow that to happen. I took the seat and composed myself.

"I appreciate you gentlemen seeing me on such short notice," I began.

"On no notice at all, you mean," Hanover said. "One caveat for our courtesy, Mrs. Fletcher. What gets said in this room stays in this room. Understood?"

"Yes, of course."

"Please proceed."

"I asked to see you, Commissioner Hanover," I said, "in hopes I could set the record straight before this story—and that's what it is, just a made-up story—before this story gets blown so far out of proportion that the real focus of the investigation gets lost."

Hanover sat back in his chair and smiled. "You're referring to the headline and picture in today's newspaper, I presume."

"Yes! It's terribly embarrassing but completely without merit. Chief Inspector Sutherland and I are old friends, it's true, but we were not 'cuddling' on the beach. In fact, I had brought him down to show him where I had found the body, and we had been discussing the investigation."

"Didn't you see the photographer?" Deputy Commissioner Mumford asked. He was a large white man with a bushy mustache and black hair combed straight back.

"I did notice the boat passing by us several times," I replied, "but unfortunately, at the time I didn't realize what those on board intended."

Superintendent Bird laughed. "Sneaky curs, aren't they?" he said to his colleagues. He removed his glasses and polished them with the hem of his white shirt.

"We're sorry you had to go through this, Mrs. Fletcher, but there really isn't anything we can do for you," Commissioner Hanover said.

"You could voice your support for Scotland Yard, and specifically for Chief Inspector Sutherland, who doesn't deserve the drubbing he's taking in the press."

"I'm sure the Chief Inspector can fend for himself," Mumford said. "He's hardly a novice at dealing with the media."

Chief Inspector Tedeschi raised his hand. "'You lie in your throat if you say I am any other than an honest man,'" he said. *"Henry the Fourth, Part Two."*

His colleagues groaned.

The officers seemed to be in a relaxed and cheerful mood. They certainly didn't appear to be upset with me, nor with George. If anything, they were sympathetic. It occurred to me that by drawing the focus of the press to George and me, we had taken pressure off the police department. So long as the reporters had something they considered scandalous to pursue, no matter how false the accusation, attention was taken away from those on the Bermuda Police Service, who continued to work on the investigation.

"I'm sorry for interrupting your meeting," I said. "I thought you were angry with us about the article, although we had no control over how the newspaper portrayed us."

"We're not angry with either of you," the commissioner said. "We wish the Yard would make more progress in helping to solve these cases, but our expectations are not high, given London's lack of familiarity with the island."

"Not to mention its utter failure in prior cases," Superintendent Bird put in. He made no effort to suppress a smile.

"We fully expect that the Bermuda Police Service will

find the perpetrator or perpetrators, as we have in the past," Hanover said to me.

"Then why bother to call in Scotland Yard at all?" I asked.

Hanover looked around the table as if seeking the answer.

"Frankly, it was a public relations move," Deputy Commissioner Mumford said.

The others nodded.

"The government was getting a lot of pressure from the hospitality industry. They worried about losing business, that the tourists would cancel reservations. They wanted to see progress. We gave them Scotland Yard," he said.

"Not our fault if the Yard are no more successful than our boys," Superintendent Bird added. "Gives us a bit of wiggle room to run our investigation with less pressure."

"Of course, if you tell the press we said this, we'll deny it," Chief Inspector Tedeschi added.

"I have no intention of speaking to the press on any matter," I said. "My intuition tells me a denial will only inflame them more."

"Very wise, Mrs. Fletcher," Tedeschi said. "They'll only see it as 'the lady doth protest too much.'"

"Are you quoting Shakespeare again, Tony?" Superintendent Bird said.

"*Hamlet*, act three, scene two," he replied. "Comes in handy."

"Thank you for your time, gentlemen," I said. "I appreciate your seeing me." I started to rise, but the commissioner put a hand out to delay me.

"Before you go, Mrs. Fletcher, do you have information

on the Betterton murder that you can share with us? Like who the killer might be?"

He released my arm and I sat down again.

"We are not unaware of your reputation, you know," he continued. "The police are always happy to have more information."

"The only new information I've uncovered," I said, "is that the shoes found at the top of the stairs on the Jamison property belong to Claudia Betterton."

"Isn't that just like a woman to concentrate on the shoes," Bird said, smirking.

"We were hoping for information more in line with identifying the person behind the crime," Hanover added.

"I can't deny I've been talking to people and trying to figure out why Alicia was killed and who her murderer might be, but I wouldn't say I'm ready to accuse anyone."

The commissioner rose from his seat and I stood as well. "You be sure to let us know when you can pinpoint the culprit," he said. He winked at his fellow officers as he escorted me to the door.

Perhaps he thought I hadn't seen his expression, or maybe he didn't care that I had. As he closed the door behind me, I heard Tedeschi say, "All's well that ends well." The men laughed.

Constable Andrews was waiting for me in the hall. "Get what you need?" he asked.

"Not exactly," I replied. "Would you mind if I stopped in to see the Scotland Yard team before I leave?"

"Have a go," he said. "Know where their office is?"

"I know where I met with them before."

"Let's see if they're still there," he said. "If not, I can sneak you out the back door where you're less likely to be accosted by those fellows out front."

We descended the stairs to the first floor and I walked ahead of him to the room where I'd been interviewed by Inspectors Macdonald and Gilliam. It was empty.

"Do you mind if I wait a little while in case any of them return?" I asked Andrews.

"I don't mind, as long as you don't wander about." He looked at his watch. "They may be out for lunch. I'll give you fifteen, twenty minutes before I come to collect you. Is that enough?"

"I hope so," I said.

Andrews left and I grabbed a chair, arranging it so that I could look out into the hall, but wouldn't be immediately seen unless someone came into the room. I dug in my shoulder bag for something to read—I am never without some kind of reading material—and found Alicia's book on Jack the Ripper. I started from the beginning again, reviewing the information on the "canonical five" Freddie had told me about, looking for Alicia's highlights and underlines. There were six more victims who'd been killed either by the Ripper himself or someone imitating his style. There was a footnote at the end of the sentence that discussed the eleven victims, and I turned to the back of the book to find the reference. Alicia had put a little star by it.

In one case, it is unclear whether or not the Ripper attacked the victim. The murder was alleged to have taken place the day after Christmas 1887, yet

Whitechapel police have no record of a murder on that date. Nevertheless newspapers gave the mystery victim a nickname, "Fairy Fay." Most authorities agree she never existed.

"Good grief!" I said aloud. "She never existed?"

Chapter Twenty-one

"Ah, Mrs. Fletcher. How wonderful to see you," Freddie said, coming into the room lugging his battered suitcase in one hand and juggling a pile of letters and a package in the other. "I was afraid we'd lost your assistance." He parked his suitcase under a table, put his mail down on top of it, and said, "I heard your voice just now. Who are you saying never existed?"

I looked up at him. "Fairy Fay."

"Quite right," he said, stroking his red sideburns. "She was a figment of the press's imagination. Possibly they meant Emma Elizabeth Smith, who was attacked the prior Christmas in 1886, but she lived. Why does she interest you?"

I opened the back cover of Alicia's book and showed Freddie the note in her handwriting. "I took it to mean Alicia had an appointment with this Fairy Fay. I went to Gardner's Deli in Hamilton yesterday at two o'clock looking for her. No wonder no one knew the name."

"That's a fairly cryptic message," he said. "Interesting

how you worked it out. Perhaps she played a game with a friend where they traded the victims' names."

"From what I've learned about Alicia, she was flirtatious, provocative and at times capricious. I'm not surprised she would choose the name of a nonexistent victim if she were playacting. I'm just not sure that's what this is." I closed the book and returned it to my shoulder bag.

"Well, I'm delighted you're here, whatever the reason. And by the by, what is the reason? Oh, sorry to be so gormless. Chief Inspector Sutherland, of course. Dreadful piece in today's newspaper. Don't take it to heart."

"I came here hoping to prevent the commissioner from thinking poorly of George, only to find out the police service is actually happy to have reporters move their focus onto someone else."

"Isn't that always the case?"

"Was he very distressed about the piece?"

"Chief Inspector Sutherland? I would say he was more concerned about how you would react than how he was portrayed, although, I must say that it's not a good image for the higher-ups in London to happen upon. Doesn't reflect well upon him."

"Oh, dear. That's what I was afraid of. Where is he now?"

"I believe they were stopping at the laboratory after lunch. Should be back soon."

"Have you made any more headway on the case?" I asked.

"Not enough," he said. "I keep thinking there's something I'm missing that would help break it open, but I can't think of what that might be."

"If the murderer really wants to be taken for a modern-day Jack the Ripper," I said, "what elements of the nineteenth-century investigation have not been replicated yet?"

"Many, I would say. While we have the misfortune to see volunteer citizens patrolling the streets at night—and there have been quite a few false leads we nevertheless must pursue—no one has come forward claiming to be Jack the Ripper reincarnated. We haven't seen any taunting letters in the papers. Lots of complaints about the lack of arrests, however. That we have seen."

"No postcards claiming to be the killer?" I asked.

"None that have been published to date."

"What about those that haven't been published? Were they turned over to you?"

"We've asked for them, but I don't know that we've received them all. That's another avenue to pursue." Freddie took out his pad and made a notation on it.

We heard voices down the hall and moments later, Veronica Macdonald walked into the room, followed by Jack Gilliam and George.

Gilliam greeted me warmly; Macdonald simply nodded. George came over and took my hands, his eyes full of concern. "Are you all right? I'm terribly sorry to have caught you up in this mess. I should have been more sensitive to how my visit would be perceived."

"No harm done, George," I said. "I'm a big girl. I can protect myself, although I was very grateful for the assistance of one of the constables today." I gave him a crooked smile.

He sighed. "I'm sorry."

"Don't be," I said. "I can't say that I appreciate the attention from the press, but it comes with the territory. I only hope that all of our combined efforts will result in something that gives the press a real story to cover instead of the one they're making up."

There was an awkward silence and Freddie jumped in, holding up an envelope. "While you gents and this lady were enjoying your luncheon," he said, waving the envelope at George, Gilliam, and Macdonald, "I went to the post office general delivery to retrieve our post." He sniffed the envelope. "I believe this is a *billet-doux* for you, Ronnie. Didn't know you had a beau."

"Oh, don't be daft," she said, reddening. She swiped the letter from his hand and put it in her handbag.

"Something from the home office for you, Jack," he said to Gilliam. Freddie continued passing out the items he'd picked up at the post office and opened the package addressed to him. "Here's my new mini-motherboard," he said. "And look!" He held up what looked like a fountain pen.

"Is that your nineteenth-century writing implement?" Gilliam asked. "Are you going to carry around an inkwell now?"

"So you assume," Freddie said, grinning. "This is a camera, my friend, the latest twenty-first century technological achievement, capable of capturing an image from five hundred meters." He tucked it in his breast pocket.

"Don't lose that," George said. "It took a big chunk of my budget."

"I will guard it with my life."

George turned to me. "Jessica? Something wrong, lass? You appear upset."

"The opposite, George. I just thought of something. Freddie, I can't thank you enough."

"Well, I always hope my contributions will be helpful," he said, "but I must admit, I'm a bit at sea about what I've done."

"I'll let you know later if I'm right." I turned to George. "Can you give me a lift into town?"

"Right now?"

"Yes, please. I'm not sure what time it closes."

"What time what closes?"

"The post office, of course."

Chapter Twenty-two

George circled the block several times but was unable to find a legal parking space and refused to take a spot designated for the handicapped.

"You go in and I'll wait out here," he said. "If something opens up, I'll meet you inside."

Unlike the quaint Perot Post Office, Hamilton's General Post Office was an imposing white building, its cool air a contrast to the warmth outside. I pulled Alicia's book from my bag and checked her message again. "Fairy Fay, GD, 2, Tuesday."

GD hadn't been Gardner's Deli. That had been a good guess, but not the right one. I was still trusting that GD was a location, however. Crossing my fingers that I was right this time, I looked around for a sign saying "general delivery." There wasn't one.

A little less sure of myself, I reread Alicia's note. If the figure "2" didn't refer to a time of day, what could it mean? My eyes roamed the open space and noticed that clerks were stationed behind numbered windows. I found window number two and joined the others in line waiting to pick up their mail. "Excuse me," I said to the woman in front of me. "Is this the window for general delivery?"

"Yes, ma'am," she said. "And there's always a wait." She sighed.

And so did I, but mine was a sigh of relief, not impatience. It was Wednesday, not Tuesday, but if my luck held, no one else would have picked up Alicia's mail, assuming that this time I'd interpreted her note correctly.

When it was my turn to approach the window, I asked the postal employee behind the cage, "Do you have anything for Fairy Fay?"

He looked me up and down and said, "Wondered who had such a strange name. You don't look like a fairy to me."

"Fairies come in all shapes and sizes," I told him.

He picked through a bin of packages and boxes and retrieved a large, padded manila envelope, which he passed through a barcode reader.

"When did it come in?" I asked.

"Was on yesterday morning's plane, I believe. Sign here." He pushed a form through the slot at the bottom of the window. "I need to see some identification."

I hesitated, wondering if after finally discovering the meaning of Alicia's note to herself, I wouldn't be able to see what she had been sent. I signed the name of "Fairy Fay" on the form, put my own name next to it, and slid the form and my passport under the window to the postal clerk.

"Not your real name, huh?"

"I shook my head. A friend is fond of playing jokes on me," I said.

"Well, tell her to cut it out. This is an official government department. If you hadn't given me your passport, I could have decided your ID was not sufficient."

"I'm happy you didn't," I said. "Thank you very much."

"Enjoy your day," he said, shoving the padded envelope under the window. "Who's next?"

I clutched the envelope to my breast, excited to see its contents, but nervous at the same time. *Thank you, Freddie Moore*, I thought. *If you hadn't talked about general delivery when you brought in your mail, I might never have learned the meaning of Alicia's message.*

George was behind the wheel of the car, sitting in an open parking space with the engine running. I walked into the street, opened the passenger door, and climbed inside. I couldn't keep from smiling. Every now and then, the things you work hard for actually come to fruition, and this was one of them. The "GD" in Alicia's note had temporarily led me astray. Gardner's Deli had been the only establishment to fit those initials, but it was merely a misstep along the way. Freddie's visit to the post office had put everything in focus and pointed me in the right direction.

I had a feeling Alicia would have enjoyed hearing about my interpretation of her note. After all, she loved a mystery. What would she have thought of my investigation into her death? Did she have a premonition that her life was in danger? Had she left the note at the back of the book for someone to discover? If so, who had she hoped would find it? Stephen? Madeline? Tom? Certainly not me. However, I was the one to find her puzzle—and pursue it. And now that the case of the mysterious message had been solved, and the prize for solving it was in my hands, would the work have been worth it? Would the contents of this envelope somehow lead me to her killer?

"What's so special about this package?" George asked, breaking into my musings.

"I don't know," I said, turning it over. "I don't know what's in it."

The envelope was hand addressed, and there were initials written on the top left corner where the sender's address would be. But there was no address, just the letters *B* and *L*.

"Why don't you open it?" George said.

"I'm not sure if I should," I said, suddenly overcome with doubt.

"Why not?"

"It's not mine. Is it even legal for me to have it? I'm not a member of Alicia's family. It may be something very private."

"What do you want to do with it, then?"

"Perhaps I should just give it to Tom. She was his niece, after all. He'll know what to do with it."

"Jessica, are your scruples making you hesitate to open this mail because it wasn't addressed to you?"

I nodded.

George took the envelope from my hands. "As a duly appointed member of the Criminal Investigation Division of the Metropolitan Police Service in Great Britain, I believe this package is a piece of evidence in an unsolved murder." He pulled the tab on the back of the envelope and ripped it open.

I leaned over to see a sheaf of papers, protected by a plastic sleeve. A sticky note on top of the sleeve read: "A, Here's what you asked for. Be careful." It was signed "B."

"Do you know who 'B' is?" George asked.

"I have a pretty good idea," I replied.

"Then let's take this to headquarters and have these papers copied. I don't want to contaminate them with our fingerprints. We can put the documents back into the sleeve and into another envelope. I'd like to hold on to the copies in the event it turns out this envelope actually contains evidence, but you may examine them whenever you like. That agreeable to you?"

"Yes, of course," I said.

"If you decide the proper owner of this envelope is the judge, I have a favor to ask."

"What's that?"

"I'd like to be there when you deliver it to him, not in any official capacity, but as your friend. Would that be all right? Can you think of an excuse to have me there?"

"After today's article, they would assume you and I are a couple. I'd say that's excuse enough."

George smiled. "If only it were so," he said.

Chapter Twenty-three

I t took an hour for the copies to be made and returned to us. In the meantime, Veronica Macdonald scoured headquarters for a padded envelope similar to the one the papers had been sent in and brought it to us. Freddie Moore peeled off the bar code on the original envelope and affixed it to the new one. Jack Gilliam carefully copied the handwriting in the address and the initials of the sender, and we passed around the new envelope, trying to make it appear as if it had been wrinkled in its transit through the mail.

When the documents and the photocopies of them were returned, we slipped the originals into the plastic sleeve, made sure the note to "A" from "B" was still affixed, and slid it all into the new envelope, sealing it so it would appear as if it had never been opened.

Then we took the time to see what we had. George gave his team the photocopies, directing them to spread the pages out on the long table.

"Try to arrange them in sections of a similar nature," he instructed.

The five of us circled the table, examining the papers that Alicia had taken such extreme measures to keep hidden—having them sent to her via general delivery so that they wouldn't arrive at the house, and using a false name to disguise who the actual recipient was.

"So, what do you think we have here?" George asked.

"Most of it looks like personal correspondence," I said, lifting a printout of an e-mail and showing it to him. The message had been addressed to a Barry Lovick, instructing him to pick up a package on a particular date and deliver it to "your boss."

"Who's Barry Lovick?" George asked. "Is he the B.L. who sent these papers to Alicia Betterton?"

"I believe so," I said. "He was Tom Betterton's law clerk until about six months ago when he was fired."

"Why was he fired?"

"Tom told his personal assistant, Adam, that he let his law clerk go because he liked doing his own legal research."

"And does he?"

"Do his own research? I highly doubt it," I replied. "Tom, himself, told me that he's in the process of hiring another clerk, one of two he normally maintains. He bragged about how many wanted the job and said a judge needs his clerks not only to research case law, but also to write bench memos, among other duties."

"So he lied to Adam about the reason for the firing. Why would he do that?"

"Perhaps to cover up the real reason," I said. "Adam heard that Lovick had been copying papers and taking them home from the office. I don't know who he heard that from, but he assumed they were legal papers—'party-of-the-first-part stuff,' he said—but maybe they were more personal than professional."

"Money *is* personal, isn't it?" Freddie said, waving a sheet in the air.

"What did you find?" George asked.

"Deposit slips for a bank here in Bermuda. There are three, each in the amount of forty thousand dollars."

"Did you find a copy of the checks, too?" I asked.

"No. Looks like these were cash deposits," Freddie said. "And look here, the dates of the deposits have been circled with a marker."

"What does that mean?" Gilliam asked.

"If the man who sent Miss Betterton the papers made those marks, he could be making a point," Macdonald said, pushing a lock of her dark hair behind her ear. "Perhaps he's tying the dates of the deposits to something else."

"Like what?" Freddie asked.

"I don't know," she said. "He's a judge. Perhaps they're dates of legal decisions."

"In other words, you think these are bribes," I said.

"I'm just speculating," Macdonald said in a defensive tone. "But your American jurists don't normally get paid in forty-thousand-dollar increments, do they? And in cash?"

"I can't think of why they would," I said, sighing. "I'm not challenging your interpretation; I'm just sorry if it's the correct one."

"It's always difficult when someone doesn't live up to one's expectations," she said, lowering her head to peer at some of the other papers.

I wondered if she was talking about Tom, or about George. I couldn't help but ponder whether she had expectations of him of a more personal nature. It wouldn't surprise me if Veronica Macdonald had a crush on George Sutherland. If so, it didn't appear that George returned her feelings. While he was personable with everyone with whom he came in contact, his staff included, I noticed that he maintained a certain professional reserve around his team, as if emphasizing his role as their leader.

"Someone else must have raised that issue," Gilliam said, "but it appears that your host was exonerated."

"What do you have there?" George asked, holding out his hand.

Gilliam gave him the paper.

George scanned the document and showed it to me. "It's a transmittal concerning a ruling from the New Jersey Bar Association in which charges against Judge Thomas L. Betterton have been found to be unsupported."

"Here's another one saying the same thing," Gilliam said, "but it's a different date."

"So, he was suspected of misconduct," I said, "but there wasn't sufficient proof."

"He received congratulations from several people," Gilliam said, looking through other sheets, "and here's one that thanks him for his quote 'attention to their needs.' Kind of an odd wording, don't you think?"

"We're looking for facts, Jack," George said, "not the existence of odd wording. If you can put together a genuine quid pro quo, then we may have something. Let's not read into these papers what's not there. We know that appearance is not necessarily truth."

His team kept their eyes cast downward on the documents on the table, but I knew what they were thinking. Their Chief Inspector George Sutherland himself had been the victim of "appearance" in this morning's newspaper, and they were all acutely aware of the potential harm to his career.

Irrational as it was, I felt guilty that this had happened to George. The damage to his reputation was far worse than to mine. I had no higher-ups to whom I had to report, no organization to shield from false accusations. I'd had no hand in George's decision to come to Bermuda. He'd said his visit was occasioned by the death of the fourth victim, a circumstance for which neither of us was responsible. And yet. And yet. If we were looking for facts, it was that his name was linked with mine, and even though we had never allowed the relationship to advance, the sparks were there. And someone had seen them and photographed them and published them in the Bermuda newspaper.

"I think I've found the facts you're looking for," said Freddie, plucking several pages from one of the piles and passing it to George. "Those first records are deposit slips, but from a Canadian bank. And here are confirmations of wire transfers from the Canadian bank to a Swiss bank, and then to the Bermuda institution. It looks like he's been laundering his bribe money, filtering it through several banks before it reached the island."

We spent another half hour perusing the papers Barry Lovick had sent to Alicia Betterton before gathering them up and sealing them in the new envelope. I stuffed the package in my shoulder bag and thanked George's team for their assistance.

"I know investigating Alicia's death is not in your sphere of responsibility," I said. "Furthermore, I have no idea whether or not these papers have anything to do with it to begin with. But I am very grateful you volunteered your time and expertise in reviewing them."

"No worries," Freddie said. "Always good to get your mind moving on someone else's puzzles. Kind of clears the thinking logjams."

"Glad to have given you some help in return for yours," Gilliam said.

"I hope they turn out to be what you want them to be," Macdonald said to me.

"Thank you," I said, taking her hand. I felt as if we had achieved a measure of peace between us.

George and I left by the rear door, hopefully avoiding the press, and climbed into Freddie's little yellow car for the trip back to Tucker's Town, all the while pondering the meaning of the package that I was now in possession of.

Why had Barry taken those papers? And why had Alicia asked for them?

Was she trying to protect Tom, using her well-known wiles to charm his former clerk into releasing evidence that would be damaging to her uncle should it land in the wrong hands?

Or had she been planning to use them *against* Tom? If so, for what purpose? She'd been the favorite child in a wealthy family, spoiled, cosseted, living a life of travel and luxury. What more could she have wanted?

Chapter Twenty-four

I had asked George to let me off at the Jamisons' house to avoid running the gauntlet of press next door, and suggested that he return later. I was hoping to secure a dinner invitation for him, but I didn't know how I would be received, much less whether the family would welcome another stranger, in particular one from Scotland Yard.

I walked up to my cottage from the beach, feeling a little like a trespasser for not having come through the front door and alerting the Bettertons to my return. I excused myself by rationalizing that I was not about to give the press photographers another opportunity to shoot George and me together. If there were paparazzi floating out there on the water, and if they aimed a telephoto lens in my direction, they would only see a lady inappropriately dressed for sunbathing or strolling along the shore. At worst, it would be a boring shot. At best, it would be one that they wouldn't want to use.

Once back in the cabin, I took the padded envelope from

my bag and stashed it behind the small refrigerator where I hoped no one would think to look. Not that I expected anyone to search my quarters. No one except Alicia had been expecting to receive the papers, and to my knowledge, no one else even knew that she had asked Barry Lovick to send them to her. Still, I reasoned, better to be extra careful with information that could most certainly keep Tom from gaining the seat on the appellate court he so clearly coveted, and that might even land him behind bars.

It was now clear why Barry Lovick had been fired. He'd been carrying home papers that could incriminate his boss. The question was: Had he come upon them himself or had someone guided him to them? And if it was the latter, was that someone from Tom's household. If so, who?

I'd been deeply disappointed to learn that my host was a dishonest man. But I couldn't say that I hadn't been forewarned, or that all the proof hadn't been right there in front of me all along. Apart from Daniel Jamison's bald accusations that Judge Thomas Betterton was less than he purported to be, Tom's lifestyle was far beyond the capabilities of the vast majority of his colleagues. That federal judges were not highly compensated, certainly not to the degree that allowed a champagne and caviar existence, was common knowledge. The chief justice of the Supreme Court himself had complained publicly that federal judges were poorly paid for the critical service they provided. How could Tom have afforded a home in an exclusive area of Bermuda that—even if it couldn't be described as palatial—had to have cost millions of dollars to buy and maintain, not to mention the price of transportation getting to and from his vacation getaway.

Agnes had said that she'd heard that Tom had inherited money from his first wife, and I had no idea how much that might have been. But Stephen had complained that each subsequent wife had walked away with half of Tom's assets. And Tom had defended himself against his fourth wife, Claudia, taking his house and boat on Bermuda by arguing before the judge in his divorce case that it was "all he had left." I would leave it to forensic accountants to expose the cases over which he had presided that were linked to his cash deposits in banks in Canada, Switzerland, and Bermuda. It was enough for me to know that his generosity—of which I'd been a beneficiary all week—had been supported by illegal activities.

I hung up the jacket and skirt I'd worn into town, changed into a lightweight shirtwaist dress, and pulled the envelope out from behind the fridge, feeling a little foolish at my paranoid behavior. No one knew about it except me, George, and his Scotland Yard colleagues; there was no reason to hide it. I tucked the envelope back in my shoulder bag and walked up to the main house, greeting Jock the security guard who was once again at his post.

"Good afternoon, Mrs. Fletcher. Hope you enjoyed the lovely weather we've been having today."

"I have indeed, Jock."

"I'm glad because it's about to change."

"Why do you say that?"

"Look out to sea," he said, pointing. "There's a big storm

brewing, and my aching shoulder tells me it's coming our way."

"I see it," I said. A dark line stretched along the horizon, with a band of lighter gray advancing before it. Yet the sky above me was still blue, and the sun, which was starting to sink westward, was unencumbered by clouds.

"You don't have to do anything just yet," he said, "but if I were you, I'd make sure to take along an umbrella if you go out for dinner tonight."

"I'll keep it in mind," I said and thanked him for the tip.

Margo was alone in the sitting room when I entered through the French doors on the patio. She was sitting on one of the sofas, leafing through a magazine and sipping a cocktail. I assumed it was a sidecar, since that's what she'd wanted Adam to make her the night of the party.

"Oh, hello, Jessica," she said, putting aside the magazine. "I'm so glad you've come. I was longing for some company. Sometimes it's very lonely here."

"I'm happy to keep you company," I said, sitting down opposite her, "but where is Tom?"

"He was behind a locked door in his office all morning, and was very grumpy when I tried to talk to him. Then, this afternoon, he came out and yelled for Madeline."

"Was she here?"

"No. I told him that she went into Hamilton with Daisy Reynolds to do some shopping. Instead he shanghaied Stephen and they went out on his boat. I don't think Stephen was too happy leaving his studio, but Tom pays the bills so Stephen must pay the piper."

"What about Adam?" I asked. "Did he go on the boat, also?"

"Oh, yeah. Adam, too. I forgot about him. He's more like the crew. He's the one who cleans the fish and stuff."

"Why didn't you join them?"

She made a face. "I went out the last time," she said, taking a sip of her drink. "I'm not too great on boats. I get seasick. Tom called me a poor sailor, and I told him he can take his boat and you know what."

"So he left you here?"

"Oh, please, I don't mind at all, except it's a little boring. You know what I mean? With everyone gone, I can't even get into town to shop."

"Couldn't you take a bus or a taxi?"

"I guess, but I don't really know my way around." She shrugged. "It's pretty here and all, but I have to tell you, I hate getting sand in my bathing suit. I don't know why anyone would want to swim in the ocean. You can't see what's under there. I don't even like to walk on the beach. Just as well because Tom said he doesn't want the paparazzi to take my picture like they did yours. Wasn't that just awful?"

"Yes. It certainly was."

"I'm so sorry. I'm being rude. Do you want a drink? Norlene is in the kitchen. I can ask her to get you something if you like. Or I can make you a Dark and Stormy. That seems to be the island specialty."

I waved a hand in front of me. "No, thanks. That drink once gave me a powerful headache."

"Then I can make you a sidecar myself. They're delicious. You can try mine to see if you like it."

"I think I'll skip a drink just now, if you don't mind."

"I don't mind. Of course, it's always more pleasant if you don't have to drink alone, but I'm used to it." She smiled at me over the rim of her glass.

"I'm sorry I missed Tom," I said. "I was hoping to ask if it's all right for me to bring someone to dinner tonight."

"Of course it is. I can speak for him on that. Tom loves company, and especially now that he's so sad, you know, about his niece. It cheers him up to have people around. He's very social."

"It was terribly sad what happened to her."

"He's just been the most awful mess ever since. Not that you can tell."

"He hides it well," I said.

"It's true. He's a rock. But on the night she died, he cried in my arms like a baby."

"He did?"

"You wouldn't know it to look at him—would you?—but he's very sensitive. He was shaking like a leaf, moaning, and crying out, 'Oh, Margo, my baby, my baby is gone.' I didn't know what he was talking about, so I just patted him on the back and stroked his hair while he cried about 'How could she do this to me?' He was so confused. The whole thing gave me the creeps, I'll tell you. I wasn't crazy about her, I have to admit, but she was just a dumb kid. She would have straightened up in time if her former stepmother stayed away from her. Claudia was awful to her, and Alicia hated her."

"Was this before or after the police came?" I asked.

"Let me see," she said, putting down her drink. "I'm not real sure. I'd been sound asleep when Tom came into my room and woke me up, so I was a little foggy. But the next thing I know, the police are asking me all these questions and I don't know the answers to any of them. Eventually, I just started to cry and they left me alone. Tears almost always work, you know, especially if you're dealing with a man. Besides, what did I know? I'd been asleep when she was killed."

"Had Tom been asleep, too?"

"You mean with me?"

I nodded.

"Uh-uh. We don't share a room when his kids are around. He thinks it gives them the wrong impression. I told him that none of them are babies anymore, but he still insists. Frankly, that's why I'd just as soon not come to Bermuda so much. But I can't take the chance of Claudia getting her claws in him again."

"Do you think she really wants him back?" I asked.

"I think she liked the life she had here. Really, who can blame her? But he's not hers anymore, and I'd like to keep it that way."

"I understand."

"I almost forgot," she said, popping up from her seat on the sofa. "Let me tell Norlene you're bringing a guest for dinner. That's what a good hostess should do. Right?"

"Yes. I can tell her if you'd like."

"No. No. I like being the hostess. I'll tell her."

When Margo went into the kitchen to talk with Norlene,

I called George on my cell phone and left a message for him to return at six and to meet me at my cottage. Dinner would likely be later, but with a storm coming in, I wanted to be certain he was able to make it to the Betterton property from Hamilton before it broke. He had said he wanted to be present when I gave Tom the papers in the envelope. I only hoped his arrival wouldn't set off another barrage from the paparazzi, but apparently it was a risk he was willing to take. The press didn't know that Scotland Yard wasn't pursuing Alicia's killer. Perhaps he could claim the need to speak with Judge Betterton if a reporter cornered him.

Restless, I stood and gazed at my surroundings. I remembered the first time I'd walked into the room to see a pretty girl curled up in a chair next to the telescope reading her book on Jack the Ripper. I recalled how she'd slid that book onto the dining room table to show me, and quickly hid it in her pocket again. I pictured her at the party, dressed up and carefree, concealing her plans, yet teasing those around her with hints that she was up to something. She had joked with Agnes's nephew Charles about her plans to "blow them all out of the water." She must have provoked the one person who took her gay spirits seriously, who saw her actions as a threat and not merely another one of her girlish pranks. And now that girl was dead.

"Do you see what's going on out there?" Margo said, coming into the room and interrupting my reverie. "Tom had better get back here soon or they'll get stuck in that storm." She shivered. "I'm glad I'm not on that boat, but I wish they weren't either."

I looked out through the picture window at the expanse

of water as far as the eye could see. The clouds that had been a gray strip on the horizon were approaching. Billows of dark gray were climbing high in the sky, forming towers, and winds menaced the ocean, pulling up whitecaps and making the surface of the sea choppy. A dark shadow moved across the water toward the island. It was as if the uneasy weather echoed my mood.

Chapter Twenty-five

After talking with Margo, I walked down to my cottage to wait for George and to retrieve the golf umbrella that I'd seen propped up in one corner, hoping it would be large enough to shield both of us from the expected downpour on our way back to the house. But my plans had to be changed. The first drops of rain pelted me just as I reached the porch, and George called while I was drying my hair with a towel to say that he'd be late and that I should go ahead without him; he would arrive as soon as he could.

I waited in my room as long as possible, hoping for a break in the weather, watching rivulets stream down the windows, listening to drum rolls of thunder, and seeing the lightning blaze down to the horizon in zigzagging streaks. By the time I braved the storm, umbrella in hand, and climbed up the gravel path to the house, gullies had formed by the side of the walkway, sending the water in rushing torrents down the hill and into the sea.

I was the last to arrive, aside from George, who I assumed would show up at any moment.

"Ah, Jessica is here," Tom said when I entered the living room from the breezeway where I had left my dripping umbrella. "Where is your boyfriend?"

I detected a note in his tone that I hadn't heard before, and wondered if I had finally outstayed my welcome, or if my request to have George as my dinner partner hadn't sat well with him.

"He sends his apologies for being late," I said. "He should be here any minute."

The living room lights were on to counter the storm-darkened skies and someone had lit the logs in the fireplace for the first time since I'd arrived. It added a welcome coziness to the white room, which tended to look cold when the spectacular ocean view wasn't serving as a distraction. Most of the guests were grouped around the hearth on chairs and sofas in that part of the room.

Margo escorted me to a glass-topped cart where Adam stood ready to fix me a cocktail, but I declined. "Nothing to drink?" he asked.

"Ginger ale would be wonderful," I replied.

Stephen, who'd been standing next to the fireplace in a studied pose, his elbow on the mantle, cleared his throat. "Now that we're all here, I have an announcement to make," he said, stepping forward.

"But we're still missing Jessica's friend," Daisy Reynolds pointed out. "Perhaps you should wait for him to give us your news."

"I don't even know the gentleman," Stephen replied, "so I doubt if he would be interested."

"Go ahead," Tom said. "I'm sure the inspector won't mind. Right, Jessica?"

"Please don't wait for George," I said, taking my ginger ale to the sofa and sitting next to Daisy. "I'll be happy to fill him in when he arrives."

"All right, then," Stephen said, rubbing his hands together.

Everyone looked at him expectantly.

"I sold a painting today, or I should say, Dick Mann sold one of my paintings." He paused for the round of congratulations before adding, "And, even better, I received my first commission."

"Are you going into the army?" Margo asked.

"Gawd, Margo, sometimes you can be so dense," Madeline said.

"Don't talk that way to her," Tom said, frowning at Madeline. "Remember your manners."

"It means that someone wants Stephen to paint a picture for them," Daisy said, coming to Margo's rescue. "And they're willing to pay for it. Isn't that right, Stephen?"

Stephen nodded. "In advance, as a matter of fact."

"Which painting sold?" I asked, wondering if the gallery owner had changed his mind about keeping Alicia's portrait in the show.

"The portrait of Madeline," Stephen said, bowing in his sister's direction.

"Oh, I was hoping you'd keep that one," she said, pouting.

"I'll paint you another," he replied, "but in the meantime,

a portrait commission is a piece of luck I don't take lightly."
He looked at Tom. "It could be the beginning of a profitable
career, something I'm sure that you'll appreciate."

"Then we'd better get that studio built for you when the
Jamisons aren't looking," his stepfather said, eliciting laughter. He stood and clapped Stephen on the back. "Looks as
though we'll have our own Picasso in the family."

There was a knock on the door, and I sighed in relief.
George had finally arrived.

"I'll get it," Margo said to me, smiling as she headed for
the breezeway. "You keep your seat." When she returned, the
expression on her face was distressed. The visitor was not
George.

Claudia walked past Margo and said, "Oh, I see you're
having another party. I've always been known to have good
timing. Sorry to intrude, but I was hoping to pick up the
sweater I left the last time I was here."

"We never found any sweater," Margo said. "You must
have left it somewhere else."

"I'm sure it'll turn up," Claudia said, coming into the
room and handing her raincoat to Adam. "How nice to see
you again, Jessica."

"Thank you, Claudia. How are you?"

"Just fine." She waved at Stephen and Madeline, and introduced herself to the Reynoldses.

"As long as you're here, Claudia, I suppose you'd like to
join us for dinner?" Tom said, sighing.

"I'd be delighted," she answered. "I'd hate to go out in that
storm again. It's a mess out there. The roads are flooded. I
might even have to sleep on your couch."

I glanced at Margo, who was working to hide her misery. "I'll go tell Norlene to set another place for dinner," she said and hurried toward the kitchen.

"Stephen was just telling us that he's sold a painting," Tom said to Claudia.

"And received a commission for a portrait," Stephen added.

"How lucky for you," Claudia said to him.

"It's not luck—it's talent," Madeline said brusquely.

"Of course," Claudia said smoothly. "Who gave you the commission?"

"Charles Davis," Stephen said. "He wants a portrait of his Aunt Agnes before she . . . well, he wants a portrait of her. I'm going over there tomorrow to start making sketches."

"Agnes will be delighted. She loves the attention," Claudia said, crossing to the bar cart and fixing herself a drink.

There was another knock on the door and I hoped that this time it was George. "I'll get it," I said.

But as I stood to go to the door, leaving my soda on the coffee table, Adam walked in with George in tow.

I went to greet him. "I'm so glad you made it," I said in a low voice.

"What's going on?" he whispered back.

"I'll tell you later," I said.

I introduced George around. Tom and Adam had already met him briefly. Godfrey was pleased to meet another British citizen, and said that he'd never met a real, live Scotland Yard inspector before. "You probably have and just didn't know it," George replied pleasantly. Godfrey's wife, Daisy, was delighted and gushed over him. Stephen and

Madeline were appropriately polite, and Claudia gave him her best energetic, bone-crushing handshake. I was proud that George didn't wince.

Margo returned to the living room to announce that dinner was served, and we made our way to the dining room.

We were ten at the table. Judge Thomas Betterton; his girlfriend, Margo Silvestry; his ex-wife, Claudia Betterton; his stepchildren, Madeline and Stephen. Daisy and Godfrey Reynolds. Adam Wyse. Chief Inspector George Sutherland. And me.

Margo had briefly debated where to sit and I could see her thinking it through. Should she be opposite Tom as a wife might, or sit next to him as she'd originally planned? As hostess, she chose to take the seat opposite Tom, but her expression said that she regretted her decision when Claudia neatly slid into the chair next to him.

Norlene had outdone herself, creating a feast with plenty for everyone. We started with corn and fontina-cheese ravioli in brown butter, followed by pan roasted rockfish, garnished with seared scallops, and accompanied by truffled risotto, and spinach with sautéed Bermuda onions.

The conversation was subdued, and mostly about the food, which was exceptional; there were kudos around the table for Norlene. The nasty weather naturally became a topic of discussion, and Tom recounted how his boat had made it back to the safety of the harbor just ahead of the storm. "I frankly wondered whether we'd get there," Tom said. "I don't think I've ever seen a storm quite this bad before on Bermuda. I hear that all flights have been cancelled until further notice."

"The weather reports say it will last at least until tomorrow night," Stephen said.

"Well," Tom said, "we *did* make it back, thanks to Adam's piloting skills, and by the way, we have him to thank for our meal tonight. He caught and cleaned these rockfish before the foul weather hit. Nothing like fresh-caught fish."

"And Norlene cooked them perfectly," I said, hoping that she could hear from the kitchen all the praise being heaped upon her. I also wondered whether Adam's fishing success had caused her to change her menu at the last minute. If so, my admiration for her culinary skills was heightened even further.

"Right. Right," Tom said, raising his glass. "To Norlene, best cook on the island."

We all joined in the toast. I was surprised at the good mood Tom seemed to be in considering the tragedy that had befallen him and the family just days earlier. I'm not sure whether I could have hosted yet another dinner party under those circumstances, or would even try. Margo had said he was "an awful mess" but that he hid it well. Perhaps he was a man capable of compartmentalizing his emotions, which would have stood him in good stead on the bench during a difficult trial.

"We were lucky not to lose the fish," Stephen said. "The boat was rocking so hard in the chop that I was sure we were going to capsize."

"At least the storm has accomplished one thing," Adam said, grinning.

"What's that?" Margo asked.

"It got rid of the press. You should have seen them scurrying for cover when the rains came, like the rats that they are." He laughed.

A clap of thunder made everyone jump and the lights flickered.

"I hope it subsides before midnight," Daisy said nervously. "I don't relish walking back to the cottage in that deluge. My shoes were soaked by the time we arrived up here at the house."

"You brought an extra pair," her husband said. "No real harm."

Over a dessert of banana bread pudding with chocolate sauce and crème anglaise, Tom tapped his wineglass with his knife. "Stephen isn't the only one with good news," he said. "You'll be pleased to know that the Bermuda Police Service has released all of us from its demands that we remain on the island. We are free to go at any time."

"Oh, thank goodness," Daisy said, before realizing that her comment might not be appropriate. "Not that it hasn't been lovely here, Tom. I mean, it's a beautiful island and all but we really must get home to London."

"I'm sorry if your forced vacation was not what you had anticipated," Tom said, "but you are welcome back any time." He raised his glass. "To my family, guests, and good friends, all of whom have helped me bear this dreadful episode. I thank each and every one of you."

We touched the rims of our glasses together around the table, me with my ginger ale, George with a goblet of water, and the others with their wineglasses.

Tom put his glass down and pushed back his chair. "Now, if it suits you all, may I suggest we take our coffees to the sitting room to allow Norlene to clean up and get home before the weather worsens? Adam, please give her a hand and then bring in some cordials."

"When did you learn that we don't have to stay on Bermuda any longer?" I asked Tom as the others had left the dining room. "I guess I'm a little surprised that we weren't notified personally."

"Commissioner Hanover called this morning," Tom replied, ushering me into the living room. "He asked me to pass along the news that you are no longer required to stay, but since I didn't see you before you left this morning, I decided to hold the news for tonight and deliver it in person."

I found it odd that the commissioner, whom I had seen earlier in the day, hadn't bothered to give me that information when he'd had the opportunity, but I didn't mention it to avoid having to explain why I had visited the commissioner in the first place.

When we joined the others in the sitting room, Godfrey, who'd taken a chair near the fireplace as his wife settled on one of the sofas, said, "I take this as a sign that the police service are closing in on solving their cases."

"I certainly hope so," Tom said, "but the inspector here would know more about that than I." He turned to George.

"So far as I know, there have been no arrests to date," George said tactfully. "Beyond that, I'm not at liberty to speculate."

"Oh, come now, sir, you must know something more about the Jack the Ripper killer who's been terrorizing this island," Godfrey said. "After all, the niece of our host here was a victim of the monster herself."

"That's right," Stephen said. "The local police may not be the most sophisticated investigators but we'd like to know that the world-famous Scotland Yard is making progress."

The note of sarcasm in Stephen's voice did not escape me, and I was certain George had caught it as well.

"Too bad," Tom said. "I was hoping that you would entertain us with some inside information, the sort of scoop that the media vultures would sell their souls for."

"There's no inside scoop to provide," George said with a noncommittal smile. "All I can say is that we continue to investigate in conjunction with Bermuda's local authorities, who I must say are quite professional in the way they go about things. The Yard are here only in an advisory capacity; the investigation is very much under local control, or as you Americans are fond of saying, the ball is in their court."

I had to admire George's deft diplomatic hand, although I wondered whether he was being entirely truthful. From what I'd seen, George and his colleagues were very much hands-on in the attempt to identify the murderer who'd been stalking young women on the island.

Adam, who had carried in a tray with three bottles of liqueur and a dozen tiny glasses, chimed in as he set them down on a table, "Maybe the government should have called in the FBI instead."

"I have confidence that Scotland Yard will crack the case before long," I said.

"Nice of you to say, lass," George whispered to me.

"I do, too," Margo chimed in. "The police always save the day." She smiled at me.

"I have to speak up for the Yard, as well," Godfrey said. "Every bit as good as your FBI."

"I'd just like to see them solve Alicia's murder," Tom said, "and catch this Jack the Ripper before he slaughters any more of us."

"If I remember correctly, Tom, you said that the Scotland Yard team told you that Alicia was not a victim of the Jack the Ripper killer," I said.

"You don't remember correctly, Jessica," he replied with annoyance. "I'm a little surprised at you."

"But I heard you say it the other day when the inspectors were here."

"What you say is not precisely accurate, Jessica," Tom said, "and accuracy is key in such cases. What the Scotland Yard inspectors said was that they didn't *believe* that she was a victim of Jack the Ripper. That's not a presentation of proof in any court I've ever had jurisdiction over." He sounded as if he were lecturing a law student. "I frankly think they're wrong."

"She was killed by the Bermuda Jack, no doubt about it," Adam said.

"What makes you say that?" George asked.

"The MO, modus operandi," Adam replied. "I read the papers. I read the crime reports. As sickening as it might be, Alicia was killed just like the others."

"Do we have to discuss this?" Madeline wailed. "We will have to continue living with Alicia's murder every day. I don't want to talk about it tonight."

"Very well," Tom said. "What *would* you like to talk about?"

She cocked her head and raised a shoulder. "I don't know."

"I know," Daisy said. "We were in Hamilton shopping today. Would you like to hear about the—?"

Her husband interrupted her. "The last thing we want to talk about is shopping, Daisy," her husband said. "Pick another topic."

"Your loss," she told her husband. "We found this great little place near the post office I was going to take you to, but now I won't. Which reminds me." She turned to me. "Madeline and I saw you coming out of the post office, Jessica. What were you doing in Hamilton today? Maybe your errands are more interesting than mine." She threw her husband a sardonic look.

"You didn't need to go to the post office in Hamilton," Tom said. "We have plenty of stamps here, and Adam makes a post office run every day."

"I was picking up a package in general delivery," I explained.

"I wouldn't think that you've been here long enough to get mail," Claudia said.

"I haven't been," I said. "The package was not for me."

I hadn't been certain how to raise the topic of the envelope addressed to Fairy Fay and wasn't sure if it should be brought up in front of Tom's family and guests. I hesitated. He deserved to learn about it privately, rather than in front of so many witnesses.

"It was sent to Alicia, Tom," I said, "but I think it's something we should discuss privately. It can wait for another time when you're not entertaining."

"For Alicia?" Tom said. "Can't imagine what she sent away for. Probably another mystery book. Now you've piqued my curiosity." He slapped his knees and rose from his chair. "There's no time like the present. I'm sure our guests won't mind if we desert them for a few minutes. Shall we go in the library?"

"Are you sure?"

"Absolutely. These grown-ups can entertain themselves for a few minutes. Can't you?" he said, looking around.

"Go ahead," Godfrey said. "I've got some questions for the inspector."

I glanced at George. "You'll excuse us, won't you?"

"Of course," he said.

As Tom led me across the breezeway toward the library, I heard Claudia say, "So, Daisy, tell us what bargains you found in Hamilton today."

"Yes, Daisy," Margo jumped in. "I was sorry not to be able to join you and Madeline, but we can go together another time."

"I would rather hear about your case, Inspector," Godfrey's voice said.

Tom opened the door to his library and flipped on the lights. "So what's this big secret you have for me, Jessica?" he said heartily.

"I picked up this package today, Tom." I pulled the padded envelope out of my shoulder bag and handed it to him.

He squinted at it. "It's not even addressed to Alicia," he said as he sank into one of the couches flanking the fireplace. "Sit down." He waved me into the sofa across from his and pulled a pair of reading glasses from his shirt pocket.

"How do you know it's for Alicia? Who's this Fairy Fay? I never heard of anyone by that name."

I groped around my bag for Alicia's book. "Alicia left a note in her book," I said, finally putting my hand on the slim volume.

"She did?"

"Yes." I leaned over to show him what she'd written inside the back cover.

He let the envelope fall into his lap and took the book from me, frowning down at the message. "Looks like her handwriting," he said. "You mean you figured out that she sent herself a package from this scribble?"

"Yes."

"How did you come up with that?"

"That's what I do, Tom. Mysteries are how I make a living."

"I thought you wrote mystery novels," he said. "I didn't realize you actually worked real mysteries out in your head." I sensed that he was becoming uneasy.

"Was she really reading this crap?" He tossed Alicia's book on the table between us and leaned back to look at the envelope again. I picked it up and returned it to my bag.

"So what's this?" he said, tapping a finger on the padded envelope.

"Why don't you open it up and see?" I suggested.

"Do you know what's in it?"

"Alicia didn't leave me that information," I said evasively. "Do you know who sent it to her?"

He looked at the return address and grunted, then turned the envelope over and pulled the tab to open it. I watched as he removed the plastic sleeve and fingered through the papers inside. His brows went up and he glanced at me. "These are the papers that I've been looking for."

"You must be happy to have them back, Tom."

"I am," he said, "very happy."

He didn't look happy, however, and I wondered what the evidence of his wrongdoing would prompt him to say and do next.

He stood and tucked the envelope under his arm. "Unless you have anything more to show me, I think we should rejoin the others."

"Why do you think Alicia would send those papers to herself?" I asked. "She went out of her way to make certain no one would know the package was coming in, even to the extent of using a fictitious name."

"I think she wanted to give them to me as a gift," he replied, as if the idea had just occurred to him. "My birthday is coming up. Yes! Alicia must have known I was looking for these and asked someone to send them to her. She said she had a surprise for me. What a loving, wonderful girl to arrange to get these papers for me. You didn't know her, of course, but she was a real pixie, full of pranks, but she could be sweet as well. I'll always remember her that way."

"Who do you think sent them to her?"

"I have no idea."

"I think I do, Tom."

His face turned hard.

"You once had a law clerk you fired, as I understand it."

"Where did you hear that?"

"From Adam. Don't you remember? We talked about it the day after Alicia was killed."

"Adam should know better than to discuss my private business." He glared at me.

"Nevertheless, the clerk's name was Barry Lovick, wasn't it?"

"What the hell are you driving at, Jessica?"

"Look at the return address on the envelope, Tom. It says B.L. Barry Lovick."

"So what?"

"Isn't Barry Lovick Lillian Jamison's son by her first marriage?"

"I don't see what that has to do—"

"There's obviously more to your ongoing battle with your neighbors than the architecture and positioning of Stephen's studio."

"I've heard enough from you, Jessica," he said. "You have a vivid imagination. You're coloring the truth here. I should have known better than to invite a writer of murder mysteries as a guest."

"I appreciated the invitation, Tom, and I'm sorry if what I'm saying is upsetting you. The truth is—and as a judge you should respect the truth—the truth is that Barry Lovick had been bringing the papers in that envelope home with him, important papers, papers you didn't want anyone else to see—and that's why you fired him. That *is* the truth, isn't it, Tom?"

He said nothing.

"And he sent those same papers to Alicia here in Bermuda. The question is, Tom, why did he do that? What did Alicia intend to do with them? It would seem to me to be a strange birthday gift, as you suggested."

"I don't intend to discuss this any further. You have no idea what's in this envelope and I don't plan on sharing these papers with you." He abruptly turned, opened the door, and stormed from the room.

I followed.

"Well, that didn't take long," Claudia said when Tom and I returned to the sitting room.

Margo studied Tom's face. "Are you all right?" she asked him.

"Perfectly fine," he said, striding to the fireplace where Stephen had stationed himself again.

"What was that all about?" Stephen asked.

"Nothing," Tom said. "Nothing at all. Jessica thought she had something really special, perhaps something that I would be upset about, but of course, I'm not. Have a drink, Jessica, and we'll celebrate your soaring imagination. Adam, pour Jessica a cordial."

Adam jumped up to follow Tom's direction.

"No, thanks," I said. "I don't want anything. I'm fine as I am." I sat next to George.

Tom pulled some papers from the envelope and held them up. "Jessica was worried these may have been important. But you see, they're really not. Not important at all," he said as he started dropping them into the fireplace. The fire had burned down to embers, but the papers caught immediately and the flames flared up, lighting the room. "See how important they are, Jessica?" Tom said, feeding more of the papers into the fire.

"But, Tom, maybe you'll need them later," Margo said. "Are you sure you want to burn them?"

TROUBLE AT HIGH TIDE

"I don't need them. I don't want them," Tom said, continuing to add more fuel to the fire.

I purposely avoided looking at George, certain he was thinking the same thing I was. It was fortunate that we'd photocopied all of Tom's documents. Tom thought he was destroying the evidence that could not only end his career, but very possibly send him to jail. He may not have even considered the broader implication that his fortune, however it was accumulated, would be taken away not just from him, but from his family as well.

I knew that Bermuda was sensitive about being used as an off-shore repository of illegal funds. Its reputation as a leading international finance and business center relies on the transparency and honesty of transactions that take place here. When the Bermudian authorities examined the papers, they were likely to share them with the FBI. But it was also probable that they would act on them first, confiscating not just Tom's bank accounts, but his property as well. I wondered how that would sit with the two women vying for his attention, Margo and Claudia.

"As long as you've got the flames up, we should throw another log on there," Stephen said, pulling a piece of wood from a basket next to the hearth.

"Put it in," Tom directed. "I want to burn the rest of these."

George found my hand on the sofa and gave it a squeeze.

"I'm sorry you feel it necessary to burn those papers," I said to Tom, "considering that Alicia was killed because of them."

"What are you talking about?" he said. "She was killed by

the Jack the Ripper killer. Everyone knows that," he said, looking around the room, which had gotten very quiet. "Isn't that right?"

"No, that isn't right," I said.

"Are you accusing me, Jessica?" Tom roared. "How dare you? To even think that I would be capable of brutally murdering a beloved member of my family is—it's—it's outrageous. That poor innocent girl was slashed to death by a madman with a knife. I don't own any knives, and if I did, I wouldn't even know how to use one."

"I find that difficult to believe," I said. "I've heard you say that you're an admirer of Teddy Roosevelt, and Madeline has said that your New Jersey home is filled with hunting trophies. It's a rare hunter who doesn't know how to use a knife."

"Claudia was the one who walked out of here with knives that night," Stephen said, pointing at his former stepmother. "And you hated Alicia. You always hated her," he said coldly.

"She was not the most lovable child," Claudia replied calmly. "But I didn't kill her. I wouldn't waste my time."

"Don't talk about Alicia that way," Tom yelled.

"That's right. Defend her again," Claudia snapped. "She was the one who broke our marriage apart. You know that, don't you?"

"No, you did when you sent her away," Madeline cried out. "You convinced Tom to send her to that terrible school. It broke her spirit. She was miserable there."

"She would have been miserable anywhere," Claudia bit back. "She had to have her way all the time, and all of you kowtowed to her like she was Queen of the May. Well, she wasn't my queen and I wasn't about to let her rule the roost. I got rid of her and all of you loved it. Admit it. It was so quiet without her, so peaceful, no fights, no screaming."

"You drove her insane by sending her to that school," Stephen said. "She said it was like being in prison. She showed me the bruises."

"She just tried her bullying tactics on someone who wasn't about to cave in," Claudia said. "If she'd given it half a chance, she could have done well there. But no, not Queen Alicia. She needed her freedom, freedom to drive everyone else crazy."

"She tried to kill herself," Madeline shouted. "That's how much she hated it. And it was your fault."

"It was not my fault. It was hers," Claudia replied. "She was manipulating you and you were all taken in by her theatrics."

"She spent two years in a hospital," Tom said, "treatment that I paid for. I'd hardly call that caving."

"Clearly it wasn't enough."

"What did Alicia say to you on the night she was killed, Tom?" I asked, hoping to focus the discussion on her death, not on her life.

"What do you mean? I didn't talk to her that night."

"You just told me in the library that she'd said she had a surprise for you. Did she tease you about it? Did she hint at what it was, threaten you?"

"She did that to all of us," Madeline said. "She said that she was going to get us in trouble; we'd be living on skid row, begging her for mercy. She said she had proof that was going to blow us all out of the water. Yes, that's the way she put it.

I was so mad that I told her if she tried it, I would kill her." Madeline looked at Tom. "I did. I said that. But I didn't. I didn't kill her." She started to cry. "She just made me so mad."

"We know you didn't kill her," Stephen put in. "I told her to shut up, too. I told her any pain she inflicted on us was going to come back to bite her. She said she didn't care. She was just ranting." He shook his head. "I don't think the hospital helped. If anything, it made her worse. Or maybe we weren't used to it anymore. It was probably typical Alicia. She always had some grandiose plan."

"But, Tom, you knew it was different this time, didn't you?" I said. "You knew what she was talking about and that it wasn't an idle threat. The papers you just burned would have burned *you* if they'd been seen by the wrong people. Isn't that so? Alicia was trying to blackmail you."

"And just why would she do that, Miss Mystery Writer?" Tom said with a curl of his lip.

"You would know better than I, but revenge sounds like a good motive," I said. "She was angry at you for letting Claudia send her away, for putting her in a strict, regimented school, an unyielding, unsympathetic environment where she wasn't free to do as she pleased. And when she fought back in every way she knew how, even to the point of attempting suicide, she succeeded in breaking up the marriage, didn't she?"

"She certainly did," Claudia put in. "I always thought it was a sham, that pretend suicide attempt."

"The doctors at the mental hospital thought it was real enough," Madeline said.

"She should have gotten an Academy Award for that performance," Claudia replied.

"You never loved her," Tom said to Claudia.

"She never even liked her," Stephen added.

Claudia sighed, but didn't respond.

"At least she got you out of her life," Madeline said.

"Not quite," I said, drawing their attention again. "Even when Claudia was no longer Alicia's stepmother, she still was able to thwart Alicia's plans, convincing you, Tom, to renege on your promise of an apartment in New York. She was still after that apartment, wasn't she? And she knew what she needed to get it from you."

"Her throat was slashed," Tom ground out. "Good God, does anybody here think I'd be capable of slashing anyone's throat, especially my own flesh and blood? It's barbaric."

"I didn't say you slashed Alicia's throat, Tom."

There was an especially violent crack of thunder that punctuated my last statement. It was as if the weather was providing commentary on this sad family scene, reminding them of the price an arrogant young woman had paid for her obstinacy and selfishness. A brilliant, jagged flash of lightning illuminated the room like a giant strobe.

Then everything went black.

Chapter Twenty-six

Margo screamed.

"Get a flashlight," someone yelled.

The only light in the room came from the flickering flame in the fireplace.

I took out a small flashlight the size of a pen, which I always carry, and turned it on.

"Call the power company," Claudia said.

And then, as abruptly as the lights had gone out, they came to life again.

Stephen laughed nervously. "That didn't last long," he said.

Norlene came from the kitchen carrying a large flashlight. "I thought you might need this. But thank goodness, the lights are back on," she said.

I looked around the room. "Where's Adam?" I asked.

"He just left," Norlene said.

"Did you see where he went?" I asked.

"He ran into the kitchen and grabbed the keys to the boat," the cook replied.

"He has to be stopped," I said to George.

"He can't take the boat out in this weather," Stephen said.

George pulled out his cell phone and went to a corner of the room to place a call. I heard him say, "His name is Adam Wyse. He works for Judge Thomas Betterton here in Tucker's Town. Notify the Marine Unit. Try the dock area here. He might be attempting to leave using a boat that belongs to the judge."

I gazed around at those gathered by the fireplace, their faces somber. The dinner party had turned out not to be a festive occasion after all. I counted heads. Someone else was missing.

"Where's Tom?" I asked.

There were shrugs all around.

A flurry of conversation ensued.

"He said he didn't feel well," Madeline said.

"I think he went upstairs. I'll go find him," Stephen said and left the room.

"I hope Tom's all right," Margo said, a worried expression on her face.

"I'm sure he'll be fine, dear," Daisy said and patted Margo's hand.

"Adam's a fool if he thinks he can take a boat out on a night like this," Claudia commented. "And just where does he think he can go?"

"Hope this bloody storm doesn't knock out the lights again," Godfrey said as he poured himself a cordial from the tray. "Anyone else?" he asked.

Stephen returned a few minutes later. "Tom said he's feeling a little queasy," he said. "He's lying down. He told me to tell everyone to continue enjoying themselves."

"Not that we were exactly enjoying ourselves," Claudia said.

"This has been such a strain on him," Margo said. "Maybe I should go see how he is."

"Leave him alone, Margo," Stephen said.

"I'll have a cordial, Godfrey," Daisy said, "and pour one for Margo, too."

"Coming right up."

George's cell phone sounded. I followed him to the corner where he took the call. "Yes, that's good news, good news indeed. Fast work. Well done. What? Yes, hold until I arrive. Many thanks."

"They found Adam?" I said.

"Yes. He was at the dock trying to start the boat. Good thing it wouldn't kick over. They're bringing him to police headquarters in Hamilton." He lowered his voice and asked, "Why is it important that he be retained, Jessica?"

"I'll fill you in on the way. You have your car outside?"

"Yes, I do." I turned to the others and said, "The inspector and I are leaving."

"I would suggest that you all remain here on the property for the interim," George said.

"Why?" Daisy asked. "Tom said that we were all free to go."

"And I say that everyone must remain here," George said, his voice steely.

"But—"

"Calm down, Daisy," Godfrey said to her. "We're not going anywhere in this storm anyway."

"Kindly inform the judge of my order when he awakens," George said, "and thank him for dinner."

The drive to Hamilton was treacherous, and there were times when I thought we might skid off the road into a ditch. Rain pelted the windshield, lowering visibility to almost zero, and the gale-force wind kept threatening to blow us off the pavement, but George skillfully handled the vehicle and we eventually arrived safely at headquarters.

"Where is he?" George asked the desk officer the moment we were inside and he'd shown his credentials.

"We've brought in more than one fellow tonight, Chief Inspector. Who are you looking for?"

"His name is Adam Wyse," I said.

"That fellow the Marine Unit brought in? He's in a holding cell in the back. What's he done?"

George looked at me. I'd told him during the drive of the conclusion I'd come to, and my reasons for having reached it.

"We'll know more after we question him," George told the desk sergeant. "Lead the way."

Adam was huddled on a bench in a corner of the cell, his soaking wet clothing leaving puddles on the metal seat. He sat up upon seeing us and came to the bars. "Am I glad to see you," he said to me.

"I can't imagine why," I said.

The officer opened the cell door and we joined Adam inside. The door had no sooner closed behind us when Adam said, "I didn't kill her. I swear it."

"Then why did you run?" George asked.

"Because I knew I'd be accused."

"You would be?" George said. "By whom?"

"The judge."

"Why would Judge Betterton accuse you of killing his niece?" George asked.

Adam fell silent, so I answered for him. "Tom Betterton would accuse Adam of the murder because he's the one who killed her."

Adam brightened. "Not me. Not me," he said. "It was the judge who slit her throat."

"That's not true," I said, "but Tom did commit the murder. He strangled her."

"Please remind me how you know this," George said to me.

"When I spoke with Margo this afternoon, she told me how Tom cried in her arms, moaning about Alicia's death, saying, 'How could she do this to me?' Margo didn't remember if the police were already there when Tom woke her. But the police questioned each of the family members separately before letting them come together in the library. They wouldn't have informed Tom of Alicia's death and then allowed him to wake Margo. They kept everyone apart until after the initial interviews."

"So Tom knew Alicia was dead before the police came," George said.

"Yes. And tonight Tom kept denying that he slashed her throat. And he didn't. Alicia was strangled to death. However, that piece of information was never released." I turned my gaze to Adam.

"I had nothing to do with Alicia's murder," he said.

"That isn't true either, Adam," I said. "Oh, I'm not suggesting that you killed her. Tom is responsible for having taken her life. Her throat was slit *after* she'd died to make it appear that she was the victim of the Jack the Ripper killer. Her throat was slit to shift suspicion away from Judge Betterton. And that's where you come in, Adam. Was it your suggestion?"

He sat on the cot and hung his head.

"You're handy with a knife. Everyone knows that," I said. "You recently bought a new knife at the marine store in town. Was it to replace the one you used on Alicia? Did you throw the old one in the ocean to get rid of the evidence?"

He didn't answer.

I continued. "Ever since Alicia was killed, you've been repeating that she was a victim of Jack the Ripper. You've said it over and over, which caused me to wonder why you were so certain—unless it was because you wanted to reinforce the lie in order to protect your boss."

"Is Mrs. Fletcher correct?" George asked.

Adam nodded.

"She was about to blackmail him, wasn't she?"

Adam shrugged. "I guess. I overheard her calling that Barry Lovick guy, the one the judge fired. I figured they had a thing going, but maybe I'm wrong. She would hang up every time she thought I was listening."

"Did you actually see the judge kill her?" George asked. "Or did he tell you what had happened?"

I answered for Adam. "He saw it happen." I looked at George. "Remember when you told me the telescope was locked? It was focused on the scene of the crime because Adam had been watching when Tom killed her."

"I didn't know it was going to happen, though," Adam said. "I was just looking at her through the telescope."

"You were spying on her, you mean," I said.

"I was watching her, but she knew it. I'd watched her before. She liked having me watch her. She knew I was thinking of going down there to talk to her, maybe even get something going between us. I kind of think she wanted it. And I was getting up the nerve to go. But then I saw the judge come up behind her, and I was glad I hadn't gone down there."

"Then what happened?" George asked.

"They argued," Adam said. "That wasn't new, but this time he was really angry and he grabbed her by the neck. I couldn't hear anything, but it was obvious that he was yelling at her. I don't think he meant to kill her, just wanted to shake some sense into her. I didn't know what to do, so I just kept watching until I saw her fall to the ground. The judge, he just stood there for a moment, and then he came back to the house."

"And he was aware that you'd seen it happen," George proffered.

"He was shaking like a leaf when he walked in," Adam said. "He saw me sitting next to the telescope and asked me what I thought I was doing. I could have lied, but he never would have bought it. I told him I was waiting for him. I said I saw him kill her. He started to cry and said he didn't mean to squeeze so hard, asked me to help him. I asked him what I could do. He didn't have an answer, but then I thought of all the Jack the Ripper talk and the fact that the victims had been pretty young girls, so I suggested that we make it look like she was just another victim."

"And?" George said.

"And he agreed."

"So you went down to the beach and slashed her throat," I said.

"I didn't want to, believe me. I almost got sick after I did it. I tossed the knife into the ocean and was leaning against these rocks trying not to throw up. Then I heard you. I waited until you left and ran back up to the house to tell him it was over, but I got delayed."

"Because Godfrey Reynolds was following you," I said.

"You knew about that? Yeah. I had to wait for him to go back to his cottage before I could talk to the judge. By that time, you had already called the cops, and they were knocking on the door."

"Did the judge pay you to help cover up his crime?" I asked.

Adam replied sheepishly, "Thirty thousand dollars. In cash. I told him I wasn't blackmailing him; I just wanted some acknowledgment for taking such good care of him. Believe me, I'd never kill anyone for money, not even a million bucks. But she was already dead. I needed the money to set me up for a while. I'm tired of being a PA. I don't want to have to run errands anymore for some fat cats who treat me like a servant. 'Adam, do this. Adam, do that. Adam, get me a drink of water. Adam, get my slippers.' Even, the judge. It was more of the same. I want a new career."

"I think I'd better have the local chaps grab hold of Judge Betterton before he decides to take off," George said.

"A good idea," I said, "although, with the flights canceled, he won't be able to leave the island, at least not until the storm abates."

"I can go, then?" Adam asked. "I didn't kill her, so—"

"You may not have killed her, young man," George said, "but you're an accessory to murder. I'm sure the local constabulary will decide you've committed some very serious offences, including hindering a police homicide investigation, lying to authorities, defacing a corpse, blackmail, even though you don't want to call it that. I'm sure they'll think of others. You'll not be trying out a new career until you've paid for those crimes."

"I'm sorry it's ended this way, Adam," I said. "It didn't have to."

Chapter Twenty-seven

"I was so sure it was Claudia," Agnes whispered to me. "She was the evil stepmother. I never would have suspected Tom. Margo must be crushed."

"She flew home yesterday," I said. "She took Madeline with her."

"She did?"

"I think Margo's going to help her find a job."

Madeline had been distraught when the police arrested Tom three days earlier. She had taken to her bed and refused to get up. Margo had been the one to comfort and mother her, even though there was less than ten years between them. Margo had surprised everyone by rising to the moment and taking charge of the family's needs. She had given Norlene a glowing recommendation, made sure her salary was up to date, notified Tom's lawyer of his situation and that of Adam, secured permission from the police to leave the island, packed up Madeline's clothes, and accompanied her back to New Jersey.

"Poor Madeline. Now she won't be able to win the laziest girl in the world contest," Agnes said, neatly inserting Claudia's assessment of her former stepdaughter into the conversation, as I'd known she would.

"She's led a very sheltered life," I said. "She has a lot of growing up to do, but I think with Margo's help, she'll make it."

"Did you see the headlines? The island is all abuzz."

"I heard about it," I said. "Do you have the newspaper?"

"Over there on the sideboard."

I picked up the paper and turned it over. The news that Tom had been taken into custody had been reported days earlier. This headline read: "At last! Jack the Ripper Killer Arrested." Beneath the giant letters, the subhead read: "Bermudian Police Service nab culprit hiding out in Pembroke Marsh."

Freddie had been elated. He'd danced me around the team's office when I'd gone there to congratulate them the prior evening. George looked on proudly.

"It was you, Jessica Fletcher," Freddie said, twirling me around. "You gave me the key to the solution."

"How was I responsible?" I asked, laughing.

Freddie stopped dancing and caught his breath, mopping his brow and his red mustache with a handkerchief. "You reminded me that the murderer was following in the footsteps of the real Ripper, who had taunted the public with postcards and letters sent to the newspapers. I went down to the news office. The publisher said they'd just turned over another pile of unprinted letters to the police. The local chaps had gone through them, but couldn't make heads nor tails of what was important and what was simply a sham. They'd bundled them up for us. We collected all the missives they'd received having to do with the case and we combed through them looking for signs."

"And how did that lead you to the killer?" I asked.

"There was a postcard from 'Saucy Jacky,'" Gilliam said. "Freddie knew that name had been used in one of the 1888 communications. In it, the writer mentioned details only the killer would know."

"We never give out all the information to the public," George said. "It's important to hold back particulars pertinent to the investigation."

"But how did you know who wrote the card?" I asked.

"We compared the handwriting to all the other correspondence," Macdonald said, "and found several pieces by the same person."

"These kinds of killers are often proud of their accomplishments," Gilliam said. "They may be a solitary, secretive type, but the impulse is not one they can hide forever. They need to boast about their prowess. It adds to the satisfaction." As the team's profiler, he had put together an assessment of the murderer's personality, which had proven correct.

"The laboratory was able to lift unknown fingerprints—not from the letters themselves but from one of the envelopes," Macdonald added. "He'd gotten sloppy with that one."

"It only takes one," Freddie said gleefully. He hauled his

battered suitcase up onto a desk and opened the leather straps. "Voila!" he said. "My traveling criminal library." He lifted out a laptop computer that was nestled amid a profusion of technical equipment and cradled it in his arms. "This little love contains the latest satellite interface and a complete set of crime-mapping software."

George smiled. "Freddie can track criminal patterns in participating police districts around the globe."

"It creates an actual crime map of antisocial behavior," Gilliam added, "to alert police to criminals who've committed similar crimes elsewhere in the world."

"Our man had been questioned about serial killings in South America in his younger days," George said. "He'd been released for lack of evidence."

"What evidence do you have now?" I asked.

"His record was relatively clean," Freddie said, "making it more difficult, but he'd been pulled in for a civil disturbance several years back, when he'd been protesting the Bermuda Immigration and Protection Amendment Act. Once we identified him, the local men were able to get authorization to search his quarters and found just what we needed."

"One room was decorated with photographs he'd taken of his victims," Gilliam said. "Those were his trophies; now they're our evidence."

"And his fingerprints matched those on the envelope," Macdonald added.

The newspaper article had given most of the credit to the investigative expertise of the Bermuda Police Service, but acknowledged that a suggestion from Scotland Yard had led to the arrest, restoring the Yard's good name.

"Is Stephen living in the house all by himself?" Agnes asked.

"I believe so," I said. "The Reynoldses flew to London yesterday, and I'm staying in town at the Hamilton Fairmont Princess Hotel until my flight home."

"You could have continued on in the cottage."

"Under the circumstances, I thought it more prudent to move to a hotel," I said.

"Stephen was here yesterday, you know," Agnes said. "My nephew, Charles, has commissioned my portrait and Stephen came by to take photographs and make some preliminary sketches." She patted her white hair. "I never thought I'd be immortalized with a portrait," she said, smiling. "I wish my husband, Stubby, could see me now. I'll be famous."

"I'm sure Stephen will do a beautiful job," I said. "He's very talented."

"Claudia said that she's going to make arrangements for Richard Mann to hang the finished painting in his gallery for a while before Charles takes it home. She said that way Stephen will get more commissions on the island, maybe even from some tourists."

"That was nice of her," I said.

"Are you ready now, lass?" George asked. "We don't want to be late." He had been waiting patiently while I said my goodbyes to Agnes.

"Yes, George." I gave Agnes a hug and told her I'd be in touch.

"You make sure to let me know when your next book

comes out," she said. "I just know you're going to write about this case."

George held the door for me and I climbed into Freddie's little yellow car. We'd been invited to a celebratory luncheon with Bermuda's governor and officials of the Bermuda Police Service, after which we would be taken to the airport for our respective flights home.

"It's always good to be with you, Jessica," George said, "however briefly."

"Yes," I said, smiling at him. "It's always good."

I9780451236326
MYSTERY FLE
Fletcher, Jessica.
Trouble at high tide :

MAY 1 2 2012
MAY 2 1 2012

'JUN - 5 2012

PROSPECT FREE LIBRARY

915 Trenton Falls Rd.
Prospect, New York 13435
(315) 896-2736

MEMBER
MID-YORK LIBRARY SYSTEM
Utica, N.Y. 13502

150100

Prospect Free Library

0001500091168

PRA 0 3 16 12